The Innocence of Guilt

Also by Eileen Dewhurst

Death Came Smiling
After the Ball
Curtain Fall
Drink This
Trio in Three Flats
Whoever I Am
The House that Jack Built
There Was A Little Girl
Playing Safe
A Private Prosecution
The Sleeper
A Nice Little Business
Dear Mr. Right

The Innocence of Guilt

Eileen Dewhurst

PIATKUS

Copyright © 1991 by Eileen Dewhurst

First published in Great Britain in 1991 by
Judy Piatkus (Publishers) Ltd of
5 Windmill Street, London W1

The moral rights of the author have been asserted.

British Library Cataloguing in Publication Data
Dewhurst, Eileen
 The Innocence of Guilt.
 I. Title
 823[F]

ISBN 0-7499-0079-2

Phototypeset in Compugraphic Times 11/12pt by
Action Typesetting Limited, Gloucester
Printed and bound in Great Britain by
Billing and Sons Ltd, Worcester

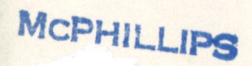

For Gill, with love

Chapter One

'How many is it now?' Jack slurred his words a little, grinning at Bob in the big mirror which showed them straightening their ties.

'How many what?' Bob smiled back into Jack's rosy reflected face.

'How many New Year's Eveses, o' course. Spent together. You and Barbara and Caroline and me. Caroline and I. Must be – '

'Must be six at least. Seven. Eight.'

'We'll have to ask Barbara, she always knows these things.'

'That's with having to be businesslike about the cats.' Bob was surprised to find himself feeling pride in his wife's enterprise rather than his usual slight annoyance. It had to be the mellowing effects of the evening's drinking. 'She's a splen – a splendid businesswoman.'

'So's Caroline. Well, I dunno ... Anyway, the shop – oops, the Flower Bower – seems to do all right. But she wouldn't be able to tell us how many New Year's Eveses the four of us've spent together.'

'Wouldn't think it was important enough,' adjudged Bob. 'We're making it too important now.' He and Jack in the cloakroom mirror were more like straight man and comic than solicitor and accountant, he thought lazily, noting another smile on his lips at the contrast between Jack's thin greying hair, round pink face and heavy body, and his own dark thatch, palely defined features and slim worrier's build. If they weren't both tall and of a height it would have been even funnier ... He had never been able to recognise his own good looks, despite what women other than his wife tended to tell him. 'Better be getting back.'

'All right. No hurry, though.'

As expected, Caroline and Barbara had not yet returned to the table.

'Have another drink,' Jack suggested as they sat down. 'And what about the champagne?'

'Mario promised it faithfully for just short of midnight.'

'I should think so!'

Glasses in hand, Bob and Jack let their conversation lapse, and Bob started vaguely surveying the festive club dining-room. No paper chains, nothing so vulgar, no more than heavily berried holly surmounting the smoke-yellowed portraits of past captains and benefactors, and a huge pair of clever leaf arrangements, poinsettia bracts predominating. Through one of the uncurtained blue-black windows he could see the multicoloured wink of the lighted outdoor Christmas tree which had survived a mild December. Gloom had replaced the lights above the band area while the musicians were refreshing themselves in the bar before their final set, but two of the predominantly younger couples were gyrating to the relayed music that filled the gap of the band's absence and was only slightly less loud.

As usual Bob and Barbara and Caroline and Jack had secured their corner table across the small temporary dance floor from the band, where they weren't deafened by the amplification and where they could have seen most of what was going on around them if the lighting hadn't been so ridiculously low – not much more than the shaded pink points on each of the tables and the diffused glow above the band when it was there. They were getting old, forty-four-year-old Bob decided gloomily, at odds with the current enthusiasm for soft lights and loud music. On their first New Year's Eve as members there had been a vocalist holding the only microphone, and lights overhead to show them what they were eating ...

'Better put your hat back on,' Jack suggested. 'Or Caroline ...'

Bob picked up the papier-maché bowler and shoved it

roughly on to his head, rendering it satisfactorily unwearable as the elastic gave. Caroline had forced him to wear it, and forced Jack to put on the absurd cardboard forage cap which made his face look so big. She herself was wearing a tall, pointed medieval creation with a floating veil — he had seen some rapid hand movements through the gloom when they first arrived at their table, and suspected the becoming head gear might have started life on Barbara's side plate. Caroline hadn't, of course, been able to persuade Barbara to wear the colourful peaked jockey cap which, when they sat down, had been waiting at her place.

Barbara would remain in a fit state to drive them home, she always did. She and Caroline were approaching the table now, as dramatically contrasted as he and Jack — Barbara with her private face and minimal movements, Caroline outgoing and expressive. As always, Barbara seemed noticeably, even obtrusively, sober. Probably just by contrast with the way he was feeling, Bob reasoned, the way Jack and Caroline were looking and sounding. Not drunk, of course, although it had been a long evening, just — well, just expansive, Jack throwing himself about in his chair, Caroline's gestures a bit larger than usual, her lovely, lively face making a slightly bigger meal of the emotions succeeding one another rapidly across it.

Barbara's face, now he thought of it, never really showed much emotion. It was always calm and pale and a bit sort of intense, so that he — even he — never really knew in advance whether she was going to tell him a cat had died or that she'd be a few minutes late serving dinner. Or offer him something killingly funny she had heard or seen or thought up; Barbara was the original deadpan humorist. Suddenly, and on a queer pang of regret, he remembered how exciting this had been in their early days, remembered sitting opposite her that lunchtime in the college refectory and hearing her tell him — tragic eyes staring through him — about a fearful but funny boob one of her fellow students had made that morning. Then saying just as expressionlessly that yes, she had decided she'd be happy to marry him.

Happy? Twenty-two years on they weren't unhappy, of

course, they certainly weren't unhappy. But Barbara's laugh had grown more and more rare, and he was less and less certain that he was still pleasing her. That was why —

'Ah! Here come the boys from the band!'

Jack's satisfaction at the sight of the instrumentalists regaining their ground somewhat less accurately than they had left it took the form of a companionable blow to Bob's ribs. Suddenly, as suddenly as the sun can be swallowed by a cloud, Bob was dog-tired, anxious for the evening to end so that they could go home. Not that it would end even when they did; on New Year's Eve Jack and Caroline always came home with them, having arrived late in the afternoon and settled into the guest bedroom before joining Bob and Barbara in the entertainment of any neighbours who cared to drop in on their way to their evening festivities. Before they all got into Bob's car and drove to the Oakwood Golf and Country Club, from which Barbara, on the far side of one and a half more intolerably long hours, would drive them away ...

'You all right, darling?'

He had leaned across the table, his hand was on Barbara's thin wrist. She had turned from Caroline's one-woman cabaret and was looking at him in surprise.

'I'm fine, Bob. Don't worry, I'll stay under the limit.'

'I know, it wasn't that. I was just — '

'He was just showing husbandly concern,' Caroline supplied, with a laugh that struck Bob's slightly blunted senses as even harsher than the usual sound she made in public. 'And quite right, too.' Caroline smiled at him, still a bit sharply, he thought, and he smiled back. It was Barbara he had smiled at first, but she hadn't responded.

'Let's dance, darling,' he said firmly, turning back to her.

Her response now was to get to her feet and excuse herself to Caroline. As she turned into his arms he heard Caroline, in an unnecessarily loud voice, ask Jack to let her know when he was ready to make the floor.

'Jack and Caroline are in good form,' he pronounced, considering the remark inane as he made it.

'Oh, yes.' Her serious eyes stared through him. 'They tend to be, don't they?'

'How d'you mean?' It was absurd to feel defensive on behalf of his friends against his wife.

'You know what I mean, Bob. We both adore Jack and Caroline, they're part of our lives, but they do tend to be in rather relentless good form.'

'Good manners.' Was he reproving her?

'Yes, I know. But it can be a bit daunting. We're such old friends I sometimes wish they'd let up. I suppose it must be that they can't.'

'Meaning?' His annoyance highlighted a streak of silver in the hair on her brow. Barbara, who had never been brightly, positively coloured — like Caroline — was fading to pastel. The realisation evoked again that strange mingling of exasperation and concern. And why didn't she just sometimes wear a cheerful colour? The dress she had chosen for tonight's turn of the year was, at least in this rotten light, a sort of dusty brown. But he suffered a slight pang as he realised he hadn't noticed it until now, hadn't registered how it had looked under the lights of home.

'Meaning, I wonder sometimes if they're unhappy, if they daren't let up in case they find out.'

'Find out?' His hand had jerked on her cool back.

'That they're not. Not happy. That there isn't anything to be happy about. Oh, I don't know. Forget it.'

'Do you think there are things to be happy about, Barbara?' It was a nonsensical question, but she was taking it with her usual seriousness and he found himself anxious for her reply.

'Oh, yes. I know there are.'

'Yes. You've got the cats, for instance.' To neutralise his lurking self-pity he made himself smile. 'Just as Caroline's got her flowers. If you're getting tired of the friendship I can always come home at the end of my Guildford day.' He realised he had been wanting to say that as he said it.

'Don't be silly, I'm as fond of them as you are.' She gave his shoulder a little shake. 'It's only that I wonder sometimes ... Caroline's so entertaining so much of the time. Would anyone who was really happy keep it up like that? But I love her Flower Bower stories.'

'Does she love your cat ones?'

She shook her head, smiling at last so that he saw the rare dimples and the twin points of her eye teeth. 'Oh, I don't bother her with them. She isn't ... Well ...'

Caroline wasn't a cat person, for a start, despite her invariable ecstasies over Barbara's feline boarders, but neither was she a great listener to women, that was what he thought Barbara wasn't saying. With men she settled down, leaning towards them in grave concentration and asking them to tell her all about it. Barbara would have spotted that, of course, she was devastatingly observant, but she wasn't bitchy enough to put it into words.

'I know, darling.' He pressed her close to him as he whirled her round. Only partly because of the drink. Perhaps it was the drink, though, that made him feel so sad that she didn't respond.

The dance session ended on a saxophone flourish.

'It's funny, isn't it?' said Caroline as the four of them sat down. 'There isn't anything different in the room. Different from earlier on, different from other times we come here, except for the holly. But you can feel ...'

Feel. Did he, Bob, ever really feel anything any more? Was that what the matter was?

'It's the sense of occasion,' said Jack solemnly. 'The one occasion in the year when the least intro — the least introspective man in this room's being forced to think about himself for a few minutes, and how far he's got. All those streamers that'll be whizzing round before we know, all those squeakers blowing, it's relief that the assessment's over for another year.'

'Very profound,' said Caroline. 'And it applies to women as well.'

'It's probably true,' said Barbara. 'If you're in company where New Year's Eve's being made a thing of, you don't have any choice. If you stayed at home and read or went to bed, or —'

'Or communed with cats,' Bob completed, feeling generous.

'Or communed with cats.' Barbara's eyes widened at him on a flash of gratitude. 'Cats don't care about New Year's Eve.'

'It's a concept,' Jack pronounced even more pompously, 'which is beyond them.'

'Sensible creatures!' cried Caroline. 'Oh, what are we going to make of the year ahead? That's the only way to look, all of you. Forward!'

And she could probably manage not to look back, Bob thought. He couldn't. Seeing Jack's large face turn suddenly sad, he didn't think Jack could. Barbara, his wife, now wearing a half-smile? He didn't know.

'And here for you, *messieurs, mesdames* ...'

Mario was Italian but affected French to match the predominant flavour of the club's menus. The champagne cork popped discreetly beneath his white cloth.

'Hurrah!' said Caroline as the fizzing amber sloped into the first glass. She reached for it.

'Happy New Year!'

'Too soon,' Jack admonished, but put a glass in front of Barbara.

'You must drink *immediately*,' Caroline exhorted, 'before the bubbles die. One sip.' She took it, followed by the other three, as the band offered a fanfare and the saxophonist got to his feet to tell them there were two minutes to go. A small spotlight, after fumbling about a bit and causing some laughter by illuminating a couple enjoying a premature kiss, at last found the face of the club's longcase clock and stayed there.

Jack had eased round the table and taken one of Caroline's beautiful hands between his plump red ones. Caroline's profile was aloof from the contact, but Bob longed to make the same gesture towards Barbara, whose hands were out of sight and reach, no doubt folded in their customary pose on her invisible lap.

The clock's reverberating chime and strike had long since been silenced as too obtrusive upon what was normally the scene of sotto voce eating, and its hands reached midnight to the perfectly synchronised accompaniment of an amplified Big Ben.

'Happy New Year!' bawled Jack, shuffling his chair even nearer to Caroline's so that he could embrace her.

Bob didn't see Caroline's reaction; he was making a

similar movement towards Barbara and burying his face in her delicately scented neck. There was no doubt that for a few seconds she pulled him to her. And brought her mouth round to his for their chaste kiss.

'Happy New Year,' he whispered. 'Darling.'

'Happy New Year, Bob.'

'Happy New Year, Bob!'

Caroline was on her feet and he must get to his and go round behind Barbara to embrace and conventionally kiss her. Then go back to his place in order to try as usual to shake hands with Jack and as usual be drawn into a continental two-sided bear hug while Caroline and Barbara — he saw during the second half of his entanglement with Jack — pursed their lips at each other's cheeks.

'Come on!' said Caroline then to Jack, back on her feet and holding out her hand. Jack tripped on an unreleased roll of streamer, cursed, danced off with an exaggerated limp. Another streamer, well thrown from the nearest table, put a red ribbon round Barbara's neck.

Bob made a thing of gently removing it, and when he had finished she put her thin brown hand on his arm.

'Barbara ...' He mustn't cry, for God's sake. And it would only be the drink. 'Let's dance.'

They danced cheek to cheek, one among a group of slowly turning, chunky units which had replaced the active pairs with space between them of the earlier dance sessions.

He had to dance with Caroline next, of course, by which time some of the couples had drawn slightly apart again. Not Barbara and Jack, he noticed, but in Jack slight inebriation always inclined him towards physical contact with other human beings, male or female. In a million years Barbara wouldn't want to be close to Jack, but the thought of it had actually pierced him with a pang of jealousy.

'You're smiling,' Caroline observed.

'Am I? I do sometimes find people funny. Dancing, for instance.'

'And golf.' Caroline didn't play golf and Jack played whenever he could. 'Walking after a ball and then hitting it away from you and then walking after it —'

'I know.' Bob liked a game at weekends.

8

'When's the next time you'll be coming to stay? How long does all this holiday business affect your routine?'

'It doesn't, from next week on. I'll be going to the Guildford office on my usual Tuesday.'

'Your usual Tuesday. So we'll look forward to seeing you that evening.' Caroline hesitated. 'You said last visit that Barbara thought she might come with you again some time.'

'She hasn't talked about it lately. There always seems to be a cat that can't be left overnight. The trouble is they can't lift the phone to say when they need attention.'

'Does she actually go out to them during the night?'

'Sometimes. Very quietly. If there's one she's really worried about.'

'Yes. She would, of course. She's so wonderful with them.'

'I know,' he said shortly. Not for the first time he sensed condescension, but for the first time it annoyed him. That involuntary New Year self-assessment they had jokily talked about seemed to have upset his equilibrium. Or he was just tired; the four days he had worked between Christmas and tonight had thrown up a dispute between semidetached neighbours as well as a divorce drenched in bitterness. He'd try to persuade Barbara to come away on holiday with him when the days started to lengthen, find someone really reliable to take over the cattery for a couple of weeks ...

He kept hold of his wife's hand during 'The Queen'. She drove them home impeccably, and immediately excused herself to go down the garden, not even changing her shoes. Perhaps that was why she had dressed so dowdily, thought Bob on another disagreeable surge of exasperation.

He, Jack and Caroline were drinking scotch round the kitchen table when Barbara came back in. One of the Collins's own cats was sitting by the bottle, so close to Caroline that she was stiffly aware of him.

'All well.' Caroline said it as a statement rather than a question.

'I think so. There are always more than usual this time of

year and quite a few I don't know, who haven't been away from home before.' She was entirely serious.

'Poor little things.' Caroline too looked and sounded serious, but Bob suspected effort.

'They'll be all right now till early morning.'

'Your shoes ...' Caroline breathed, and Bob noticed for the first time that Barbara's shoes were extremely elegant and set off her perfect legs as well as any footwear could.

'Cats don't mess floors.' said Barbara, sitting down, 'they use the loos provided.'

'I know that, Barbara, but really! Such delicate, pretty shoes.'

'We're tired,' said Bob, without knowing he was going to say it. 'I think we should go to bed, give New Year's Day a chance. You'll stay for lunch at the very least, won't you?'

'Thanks, Bob, we'd love to. If that's all right by Barbara?' Jack's anxious look as he leaned across the table was another part of their New Year ritual. The Lamberts always stayed for New Year's Day lunch.

'Yes, of course. I've some cold duck and I made the fruit salad this morning. Yesterday morning. Caroline'll help me put the salad things together.'

'Of course, darling.'

And he and Jack would potter around the garden and the garden shed and the workbench before going down to the White Lion.

How did Barbara and Caroline get on when they were on their own? All these years of friendship and he still couldn't imagine. And now, of course ...

In bed at last, he waited some minutes without hope for Barbara to speak or move. Then took her hand.

'Please,' he said.

She still didn't speak, but her arms enclosed him.

Chapter Two

'Bob! Darling!'
'Caroline! Darling!'
She drew him into the house and shut the front door, and in her elegant hall he took her in his arms in the usual way. 'Good to be alone again and not have to restrain ourselves. Not to have to be so horribly careful every single second of the time.' Those, give or take a few variations, were his usual words when he arrived at the Lamberts' for his first fortnightly visit following a foursome.

'I know.' She led him by the hand into the sitting-room.

'You enjoy it, though, don't you? The behaving absolutely conventionally? Sometimes I think you see it as an art form.'

She laughed, turning to face him and putting her arms round his neck. Her laugh was very different from the strident sound she made in public. 'Perhaps. By nature I'm a perfectionist.'

'I know you are.' Bob glanced as widely as he could beyond Caroline's encircling arms, taking in the ordered pink harmony of the room and its complement of exquisitely organised precocious spring flowers, trying not to think that he preferred Barbara's twigs and snowdrops and aconites. 'But you do the throwing-off-the-scent thing so well I sometimes wonder if Barbara suspects us of disliking one another.'

She laughed again. 'I don't think I go quite that far, Bob. But there is a certain satisfaction ... You know I was on the stage for a while.'

'I didn't know. I might have realised.' This could be why Caroline had chosen as her lover a man she was forced to see regularly in the company of the wife who knew nothing of the affair. The idea nudged uneasily at his male ego, but another part of him seemed to be welcoming it.

As a relief?

'It is *the* most foolproof way for married people to carry on an affair, though, isn't it, Bob? I mean, with Jack — '

'All OK with Jack?'

'Of course!' Caroline unclasped her hands from behind his neck in order to shake his shoulders. 'He went off as usual this morning looking as if he was about to swallow cream and telling me he'd see me tomorrow; he even rang at teatime to tell me again.'

'Well, good. If it wasn't three against one it would be perfect.'

'I know, darling.' Caroline now was holding him at arm's length by the waist, and he saw the self-satisfaction in her face give way to pity. 'If only poor Barbara ...' The pity passed, replaced by a sort of speculative curiosity. 'You don't think ...?'

'No! Barbara isn't like us.' It pleased him, in some strange, fierce way, to hear himself demeaning them both to Barbara's advantage.

'All right, darling, I only wondered. And she's far more naturally cagey then either of us. You wouldn't have a clue.'

'Barbara would never look at another man,' he said firmly, hoping his hitherto solid belief in what he was saying wouldn't break up under the laser beam of Caroline's knowing blue eyes. 'Anyway, let's not talk about Barbara until the time comes to ring her. Shall I get us a drink?'

'Of course, darling. Bring them out to the kitchen, that's where I ought to be.'

Even now he knew it so well, Caroline's kitchen still made Bob think of an upmarket kitchen craft shop with the price tags off; its colour gradations were so subtly perfect, its layout so domestically architectural. So tidy, too, even when she was in the midst of her invariably elaborate dinner preparations, and no cat on the corner of the pinky-mauve central table or the simulated marble surround to the ceramic hob, no saucers to fall over on the dutch-tiled floor.

Sterile! he had suddenly thought the last time he was in it, to his shocked surprise. Especially as he so often seemed to feel annoyed these days when he was in the old-fashioned kitchen at home, seeing it with approval and affection only when he was away from it. Like now.

Dismissing his thoughts of his own kitchen, with Barbara and a couple of cats moving about in it, Bob kissed the back of Caroline's pale neck as he put their drinks down. Despite her expressed envy of Barbara's shiny bob, Caroline had never compromised on the elaborate arrangement of her long fair hair, still gracefully piled in the Grecian manner, a few wavy tendrils on the neck and beside the ears. She had let it down in front of him, that first time, slowly and dramatically, making him feel like a small boy being ritualistically admitted to an adult secret.

'Later, darling. Just a little bit later. When we've had dinner. You're hungry, aren't you?'

'Of course.' He would have said that even if he wasn't; Caroline got upset about such things. Anyway, she was such a good cook, even if a rather too elaborate one for his and Barbara's taste, that it was impossible not to be hungry as he started to eat, even if he hadn't thought he was beforehand.

'Sit down at the table,' Caroline ordered with a flash of smile. 'You won't be under my feet then but you'll be close. I won't talk for a few minutes, I've got to concentrate.'

When he and Barbara had first fallen in love, baked beans had been enough for them, but even at the start of their affair Caroline had continued to give him the sort of meal she had prepared in the old days when Jack was at home and the two men had examined his latest piece of hi-fi or pottered in the garden until she called them to the table.

He still couldn't remember just how long he and Barbara had known the Lamberts, how long since the morning he and Jack had found each other hanging about the club, both unexpectedly partnerless for a round of golf. They had got on well from the first tee, started playing together regularly. Eventually they discovered that Jack's accountancy firm in Guildford and the Guildford branch of Bob's own firm of solicitors had a couple of clients in common. That was about the time Jack and Caroline had first invited him and Barbara to dinner. When they had been dining at each other's houses for a while the Lamberts had suggested, apparently in unison, that Bob might like to stay the night with them the alternate weeks he spent a working day in Guildford. Barbara always welcome too, of course.

Barbara had joined him a couple of times, when she got round to arranging for her young lieutenant Samantha to stay the night so that she could put the cats to bed and get them up the next morning. Barbara and Caroline had always appeared to get on, but now he thought about it Bob realised it had been the camaraderie between him and Jack that had dominated the foursome. Barbara and Caroline sometimes had lunch in each other's houses or shopped together in Guildford or Dorking, but Barbara had other confidantes. So far as the women were concerned the relationship was a thing for high days and holidays — New Year's Eve and sharing a self-catering villa in Portugal. Had it been there by the pool that he had first become subconsciously aware of Caroline?

The first time he had arrived as usual at the Lamberts' and found her on her own was the first time he had been really alone with her. He hadn't thought anything about it at first, and anyway he had been taken up with the change in her which he hadn't been able to interpret. A sort of disarray that was more mental than physical — her dress was as perfect, her hair as elaborately casual as always — and so different from her usual aura of confident control. She had greeted him with the news that Jack was forced to be elsewhere, and asked Bob to excuse him without offering the detailed explanation that Bob would have expected from Jack. Over dinner she had seemed distrait, and in the sitting-room afterwards, when he said he thought it was time he rang Barbara, Caroline asked him not to tell her about Jack's absence.

She made her usual perky interjection into the conversation, but when he signed off and looked at her she was lying back on the sofa with closed eyes, tears squeezing out from between her unnaturally long lashes.

'Caroline! It's to do with Jack, isn't it? Can't you tell me? Or Barbara, if you'd rather?'

She laughed at that, opened her eyes and patted the place beside her, where he sat down with no more thought than for her evident unhappiness.

'Jack's having an affair,' she said.

'Jack!' It amused him afterwards to remember that he had been shocked. 'I can't believe it.'

'It's true. He's just sprung it on me. But I'd known there was something. When you've lived with someone for twenty-odd years ...'

He had tried unsuccessfully to forget she had said that. He had lived for twenty-two years with Barbara. If one day she asked him what was wrong, what would he answer?

'Yes ... Oh, Caroline, I'm so terribly sorry.' Sorry for himself even, fleetingly, as he realised that this might be his last overnight visit; he couldn't carry on staying if Caroline was going to be on her own. That seemed the extent to which he was going to be affected by Jack's behaviour. 'Is he ... Are you thinking of a divorce?'

'Good heavens, no!' The flash of panic across her eyes was followed by amusement. 'An affair, I said. He doesn't want to marry anyone else.'

'And you want him to stay married to you?' Even then he had been aware of the rise and fall of her beautiful breast only in his old academic way.

'Why not? I don't want to marry anyone else, either. It doesn't mean we suddenly dislike one another. Although perhaps it means that I'm probably going to feel a bit freer, too.'

He knew later, of course, that that had been her first move, but at the time he had failed to recognise it. After he had murmured 'Poor Caroline' in his usual friendly tone, she asked him to pour them brandies.

Putting the glass into her hand, he saw fresh tears on her cheeks.

'I've just got to get used to it,' she said bravely, as he sat down again beside her. 'When you lose the one thing you were sure of ...'

'That's it!' he responded understandingly, patting her shoulder the way he'd have patted Jack's if things had been the other way round. 'Jack, of all people!' Even at that stage of his innocence he didn't think he would have said 'Caroline, of all people!' if it had been Jack he'd been comforting.

Jack! He hadn't been able to see it then, and he still couldn't. Jack so – what was the word? – so uxurious, hanging on to Caroline's every word, ready for her every requirement. Her every public requirement, he'd had to keep reminding himself since that night; private needs were private needs ...

'You never know, you see.' Caroline was saying. 'Oh, Bob, I'm so glad you're here tonight.'

'A pity Barbara isn't with me.' He really had said that.

She smiled. 'Not as far as I'm concerned, Bob. You should know me better by now, that I'm not a woman's woman. It's the thought of *your* sympathy this evening that's kept me going all day.'

'Well, I'm glad.' He had scarcely had time to feel uneasy when Caroline put her head on his shoulder before she turned to face him, drew her lips across his cheek and, when they reached his mouth, kissed him, telling his shocked senses it was something they had already dreamed of.

'I'm sorry, Bob.' When she eventually drew away she was all contrition. 'I hadn't meant ...' He had still been prepared to believe her. 'I told you that now I might feel more free ... I think I must have wanted to do that for a long time.'

'I think I must, too.' He had no idea of it, which was the most shocking thing. That his instincts had already been unfaithful to Barbara. And now?

'I suppose I don't quite know what I'm doing.' Caroline went on shakily. 'I might have been trying to avenge myself on Jack.'

'I suppose you might.' Reluctantly but unavoidably he remembered the surge of disappointment, hurt pride.

'Even if I was, though' – she put her hand on his knee and it jerked a reflex – 'I wanted to kiss you.'

'I ... I ...' He had been like a schoolboy, able to think of nothing but the burning pressure of her hand.

'Have you had other women since you married Barbara, Bob?'

'No.' He hadn't wanted any.

'I didn't think so. Look, dear sweet Bob, would you like to go home? You can tell Barbara I wasn't well, didn't feel like an overnight visitor. I'll cope, no need to worry about me, I'm a survivor.'

That was the high point of his shame, the fact that she had been so confident of him. And that he had justified her confidence. 'I won't go home, Caroline, I'll stay as I always do.'

'But it won't be as you always do, Bob, will it? Be realistic, darling, this is the moment of decision, not later.'

'I know.'

By the time she had let him go his sense of shock was as muffled as his conscience and he lay sprawled on the sofa without a past or a future, awaiting the summons to join her upstairs.

'The avocados are super at the moment.'

Caroline went through to the dining-room with a large half in either hand, each artistically overflowing with prawns Marie Rose. Bob got up and trailed after her. The table was laid as meticulously as it had been when there were three of them. That first time they were on their own he suggested they eat in the kitchen, and it had been the only time all evening that Caroline had shown disapproval. He realised now that keeping up appearances was her yardstick of triumphant morale. Once have dinner in the kitchen, let the silver tarnish, fail to throw out less than perfect flowers, and she would be over the edge of the slippery slope.

How would Barbara cope if she knew her husband regularly visited a mistress? (He had to force his mind to put it into words.) She served dinner in the kitchen already. But the question was academic, nothing more than a self-inflicted punishment for his infidelity. Barbara would never know. As

Caroline had said, the set-up was absolutely foolproof, he and she and Jack were equally dependent on each other.

Which meant the situation had to go on as long as Caroline wanted.

'Cold, darling?'

'Goose on the grave.' He was annoyed with himself for shuddering when there was no need. Barbara couldn't know, he reminded himself again angrily, unless he himself somehow gave it away. That was the one certainty, the one thing he didn't have to worry about. He and Caroline and Jack were in each other's hands. Jack had said 'All hang together, eh?' the first time they played golf after the Tuesday night he hadn't been home. That was all he had said, even when Bob had indicated that he was open for confidences. But as reassurance it had been enough. 'That was delicious.'

'It was, wasn't it? Now don't move, darling, the next course is all ready for me to bring in.'

The next course was an exquisite beef and mushroom casserole, and for dessert Caroline had prepared oranges in kirsch, each slice totally free of its pithy surround.

'A marvellous meal, as always. Please let me help you clean up before we have coffee.'

'Cutlery and crockery's going in the machine, but you can dry the glasses, darling, if you'd really like to.'

That by now was another regular exchange. When he had finished his tiny chore the coffee was ready, and she let him carry the tray into the sitting-room and put it on the low table in front of the fire.

'Brandy?' he suggested, confident in the precedent set that first evening *à deux*. He crossed the room to the antique corner cupboard and poured them while Caroline poured the coffee.

'Hadn't you better ring Barbara?' she suggested, as he drained his second cup.

'I suppose so.' He tried not to think that since Jack's defection Caroline had come to enjoy his good night telephone calls to Barbara, that perhaps they fed her sense of power by underlining the fact that Barbara was being deceived. He would have liked to make them on his own, forgo the Caroline interjection even if it landed him with another small lie, but it had been obvious from the start that she was to share them.

All he could do towards independence, as he did each time, was to get to his feet and walk about the room with the portable telephone as he talked into it.

'Hello, this is the Collins Cattery. I'm afraid both Bob and Barbara Collins are unavailable at the moment but if you'd like to leave your name and number ...'

Barbara's recorded voice held even less animation than her live one. He pulled a face. 'Answerphone. She must be down with the cats, perhaps there's something wrong with one of them, it isn't her usual time.'

'You can try again later.'

'I'll do it now.' The bleep sounded as he read Caroline's dislike of his disobedience in the brief tightening of her mouth. 'Hello, darling, it's me.' He never let Caroline catch his eye while he was talking to Barbara, although he didn't dare turn his back on her. 'Just to say good night. Do hope the fact that you're not there to answer the phone doesn't mean a cat's ill.' It occurred to him for the first time that it didn't even have to mean she was with the cats, it might mean she had gone out. After all, what did he know about her fortnightly Tuesdays? He shuddered again. 'We've just had a delicious dinner, as you can imagine –'

'Following which my dear husband has gone to do something nasty in the woodshed!' Caroline had leaped up and seized the phone from him. 'He sends his love and so do I. Good night, Barbara.'

He took it back. 'Look, Barbara, if there's anything wrong, for heaven's sake ring us when you get in, you're not usually with the cats at this time. Then if we don't hear we won't worry. Good night, darling, see you usual time tomorrow.'

'You resent Barbara monopolising the answerphone, don't you?' Caroline suggested as he rang off.

'We agreed it should be that way, the cattery business is run from home and I'm the other director. My business calls come to the office.' He hadn't really answered her because despite the fairness of it his instincts *did* resent it, and even though he had betrayed Barbara there were still a few small areas where he could elect to be loyal to her.

'I see.' There was disbelief and challenge in her face, which his self-dislike met in a rough embrace.

They collapsed on to the sofa.

'Do you still love Jack, Caroline?'

The question kept them upright, checked what had seemed the inevitable turn of events. Caroline liked making love on the sitting-room floor, starting on the sofa and rolling down. But tonight, now, it might not happen that way. Until tonight he had never gone counter to Caroline's mood, but for the first time since their affair had begun he had let something other than being with her dominate his consciousness, he had started wondering if there was any way other than her getting tired of it that might bring the situation to an end.

She was frowning, and he stroked her face and stared at her tenderly until the frown cleared. 'I worry about you,' he said. Absurdly, it made him feel slightly better to deceive them both than only Barbara.

'You mustn't worry, Bob. Yes, I do love Jack. Don't make me angry by reminding me.'

'Perhaps he'll come to his senses. You've never told me anything about him, about – this other woman. It is just one?'

There was a sparkle of new tears. 'Just one could be worse than several, if you think about it.'

'It could be more serious, I suppose. But several ... *That* would mean he wasn't the man we've always thought him.'

The strident note was back in her laugh. 'No man's the man you've always thought him when he gets the middle-aged itch.'

'I don't believe in it.'

'You're not suffering from it, then?'

'You know I'm not,' he said quickly and glibly, realising for the first time that he probably was. 'I love you, Caroline.' He knew as he spoke that he had been in love with her but was falling out of it. The woman he loved was Barbara. How wonderful to be sure of something! The glow coursed through him, momentarily stronger even than his desire for Caroline.

'At least you look the part, darling.'

'Oh, Caroline ...' Could there be other men? Hope died as it was born. Even if he wasn't important to Caroline as the one and only Bob Collins, she wasn't the sort of woman who could be ditched, she'd have to take her revenge. And if Barbara ever found out ... He had put himself in a cage as surely as those pampered pets his wife looked after. 'Darling.' Fortunately his physical reflexes weren't affected, although he'd prefer to postpone things until he had absorbed his realisation that he loved his wife. That he wanted to bring things back to the way they had once been.

'Poor Barbara,' crooned Caroline. He disguised his leap of shock as a reaction to her nearness. 'She must never know, it would do for her.'

'I doubt it, she has too much strength.' If he came to dislike Caroline life would be even more difficult than it was already. 'Anyway, she won't ever know. You haven't told me anything about Jack, by the way.'

'Because he hasn't told me anything about himself, and I haven't asked.' But the sudden red patches in Caroline's creamy cheeks made Bob wonder if she knew something she was withholding. He wouldn't try to force it.

'Barbara's the loser type, really, isn't she?' Caroline was saying. 'I bet she hated school. But she doesn't give one an inkling of what's going on in her head. I can't imagine ever really getting to know her, darling, but then I'm so open.'

'Barbara's on the introverted side, certainly.' He mustn't show his anger. And anyway, all Caroline had done was to reveal her envy of Barbara's self-sufficiency. 'I thought you were fond of her.'

'Of course I'm fond of her, darling!' Caroline's big blue eyes flashed reproach at his unworthy imputation. 'Very, very fond. That's why I'm so anxious she should never, never know.'

At least he was learning that she wasn't wanting to annex him permanently. But she was making him more sure every moment that he would have to dance to her tune so long as she chose to play it. 'Let's forget Barbara, shall we?' He had just learned that he never would. 'Let's just think of ourselves. Caroline ...'

She lay back languorously, smiling up at him.

They were going into the sofa and floor routine after all.

Chapter Three

'Barbara's upset,' said Barbara's brother Vernon, opening the front door as Bob's key found the lock so that Bob was pulled forward by his arm and tripped up the shallow step into the hall. 'Sorry, Bob, but I thought I'd make sure I got to you before . . .'

The hall was dusky and Vernon, who no longer saw well, reached out and flooded it with the light from above which Bob and Barbara used only when they were looking for something lost in the intricate pattern of the carpet. Bob had to force his free hand to stay at his side, not fly up to protect the exposed face of his panic. 'Goodness, old fellow, you look really done in!'

Surreptitiously he let the hall chest take his weight. 'Busy day. Barbara? Upset? What's happened, Vernon?' His blood drummed so loudly in his ears he wondered if he'd be able to hear his brother-in-law's reply. Which was crazy, there was no way anyone could know that when he visited the Lamberts Jack wasn't there.

'I'm afraid old Domino's gone.'

'Old Domino?' The words were just sounds, signifying nothing. Automatically he switched on the lamp beside his hand, switched off the overhead glare.

'Come on, Bob!' Thank God the gentle face was smiling. 'I know you're the sleeping partner but you know old Domino.'

A large round black and white face with tiny ears banished the horrors before his mind's eye. A very English cat. Plump and neat but, on this latest visit, hollow in the flanks.

'Yes, of course. The most regular of the regulars. He hasn't *escaped*, Vernon? I don't believe you, it'd be against his principles.' Relief was making him feel drunk, talk nonsense.

'He's dead, Bob. Barbara's devastated.'

'Oh, no!' The relief gave him room to feel sorry. Poor Barbara – beloved Barbara, he amended on a thrill of novelty – Domino had been her favourite boarder. That he should die in her care ... 'Where is she?'

'Sitting in the kitchen. She's kept herself busy all day but it's sinking in. Just thought I'd let you strike the right note.'

'I'm grateful, Vernon.' But not surprised. Vernon Tennant always struck the right note himself. From a genuine sense of fitness, not for effect. Barbara had brought him no parents-in-law, just this older brother whom he had come to love and who was looking more and more like the older Alec Guinness being his real unobtrusive self. 'I'll go to her.'

'I'll be off.'

'I'm sure we'd both like you to stay.' He was in a fever to get to his wife, but Vernon was someone to whom he always automatically accorded full courtesy.

'Thanks, Bob, but I've got to get back.' To the antique shop he would have closed more than an hour ago? To the house where he had lived alone since his wife died? Sometimes the sense of fitness had an old-fashioned flavour.

'Of course, Vernon, yes. I hope we'll see you again soon.'

Bob closed the front door as gradually as he could manage, then sped out to the kitchen. Barbara was sitting with her elbows on the scrubbed central table, her face in her hands. She turned towards the door as he went in.

'Darling! Vernon's just told me. I'm awfully sorry.'

'Thanks.' Her eyes looked dead, and her face stayed immobile as he kissed her cheek. 'Domino isn't the sort of cat who dies.'

If this wasn't Barbara – if it was Caroline so inanimate and still – he would have said she was in shock. 'I know what you mean. He was so – well, so cheerful.'

'Yes!' There was a brief leap of life in her face. 'Neat and sturdy, that was Domino. He was real peasant stock.'

'I know what you mean.' He'd already said that. 'I really do, Barbara. I notice more about the cats than either of us realises.' It could be true. 'What happened, darling? Do you feel like telling me?'

'When they brought him this time they said he was getting old. Well, I could see. You could see.' *Even you.* 'Those hollows —'

'I saw them.'

'And all that drinking. Kidneys going. It could have been horribly prolonged, I'm glad for him. The vet said he had a heart attack.'

'Were you there?'

'Yes. I was watching him trying to eat, thrilled he was giving it a go. Then he sort of just wobbled over on to his side. I knew, I didn't try and disturb him, I just put my hand under his head and he looked at me before — before sighing and dying.'

'Oh, Barbara!'

'Don't *cry*, Bob.'

Had she cried? It was years since he had seen what in Barbara was a phenomenon. 'I'm sorry, I know it's ridiculous.' And impertinent in the face of her control. 'But I also know how you must be feeling.'

He wasn't crying for the cheery little cat who had died so neatly, he was crying for all the things that made people unhappy and of which its death was a symbol. And for Barbara, in her sorrow. And perhaps for the relief of knowing there was time and the chance in front of them for him to see to it that they got back as they once had been.

Except that there was still Caroline.

'I'm all right. Just — getting used to it.'

'I'm sorry I didn't pay the poor old thing a bit of attention.'

She continued to stare at him. 'There are lots more where he came from. Just a few steps down the garden. Missing their parents.'

'I know.'

Mickey, one of their own cats, appeared from nowhere and jumped on to his knee, richly purring as Bob's hand went busy between the ears. 'You like cats,' said Barbara. 'They like you.'

'Yes.' He was absurdly glad she was bothering, even in that dead tone of voice. 'I'll try and spend more time with the boarders.'

'I used to think it would be nice to share them. Not the work, I've got that organised. Just the concern.'

He couldn't remember when she had last told him anything important about what she thought. Could Barbara, as well, have ideas of a renaissance? 'I will be more concerned,' he said eagerly. 'I'd like to be, really. It's crazy, darling, but I think I've been jealous.'

Her head, which had drooped towards the table, jerked up.

'Jealous!' To his surprise she was smiling.

'Yes. A nasty little macho reaction. I've felt your boarders were getting attention which if they hadn't been there you might have been giving to me.'

'That was absurd.' The smile had gone, but her eyes were no longer totally lifeless.

'I suppose so. I've just realised I don't feel it any more, I'm glad you've got the cattery.'

'Are you, Bob?'

Her gaze was so searching he dropped his eyes to the striped fur warming his lap. 'Yes. I suppose that was why you weren't in the house when I rang last night.'

'He didn't die till this morning but I was concerned as he hadn't eaten his supper, and I went out to him twice. You rang during the second time. At least he seemed comfortable.'

He looked up at her again. Still not a trace of tears in the wide brown eyes or on the beige-brown cheeks. 'You've told his owners?'

'Yes. They didn't want to see his body, or have a physical memorial. The vet's taken him for cremation.'

'They don't blame you, Barbara?'

A smile again, just. 'I think they were thankful. They'd known it was coming, and they'd been spared it. Poor old Domino won't lose me any custom.'

'I'm glad. Shall we go out for dinner?'

'No need. I've had a casserole in the Aga all afternoon. I've been glad of things to do.'

'Of course.' No sitting around and brooding for Barbara. Although she could just as well have chosen to take her mind off Domino by settling into a book and not feeling guilty about it.

'I read Plato for an hour when I'd done the casserole. He helped. Then I read a William story.'

'Oh, Barbara!' Oh, but she was the spice of his life! What on earth had he been doing? 'When did Vernon arrive?'

'In time for a late cup of tea.' She got to her feet as if painfully, but moved in her habitual quiet, quick way to the kitchen's heart, the huge ever-warm Aga that ran the length of one of the shorter walls. 'How were Caroline and Jack?'

The question was inevitable at some stage of the evening after his fortnightly visit, but as usual it set a pulse beating jaggedly in his chest. Barbara had spoken casually, her back to him. 'Their usual selves.' But whatever he said would be a lie.

'Caroline sounded pretty sprightly. Jack seems to spend a lot of time these days in the woodshed.'

He had to sit down. 'Jack likes to show off his new hobby.' It was Caroline who had shown it off, so that he could be up to date with one part of Jack's life. The competence of their deceit made him feel physically nauseated.

'He's making a table now. The trouble's going to be that Caroline won't have it in the house.'

'Caroline won't have anything in the house that doesn't accord with her own precise scheme of things.'

'That's precisely what I mean.'

Listening in amazement to his equally casual voice, clear of the breathlessness which was half choking him, Bob found himself almost believing his night at the Lamberts' had been the way he was telling it. Well, that was the way to make it sound convincing . . .

His self-disgust was suddenly so strong it brought him back to his feet. 'I'll get us some drinks. Wine, darling?'

'I'll have whisky tonight.'

'Good idea.' He wanted to go up to her and put his arms round her, but he'd have to work through the self-loathing first, part of which was the memory of how easy it had been eventually last night to forget that he'd had enough of Caroline.

At least he and Barbara had never had to talk, there was nothing abnormal about the near silence in which they had dinner. In their early days it had been a positive thing, a sign of understanding and of a relaxed ability to live effortlessly together, and as they drifted apart it had continued as a habit, might even be the reason they had never discussed the gradual change in their relationship. It meant now, Bob realised as he watched Barbara toying with her food, that a mutual knowledge too deep for words had become a mutual ignorance unrelieved by them.

When she went out of the back door afterwards he went with her, trying and failing to remember the last time he had done that. The cattery followed the shape of the garden, three sides built against the sandstone wall and the front double-glazed with plants inside and out. Until he got close and saw the furry bodies it always made him think of a conservatory. There were double and single apartments, and a recreational area for the young and gregarious near the double glazing, whose occupants could be observed from the lawn. At present it contained four variously coloured kittens, two sleeping and two half-heartedly fighting across the prone bodies.

'Ferals,' said Barbara as she unlocked the door and led the way in. As always, it was comfortably warm and airily sweet-smelling. 'They were rescued from a colony outside Guildford sentenced to destruction. Their owners — for want of a better term — had to go away unexpectedly. Yes, they really did, they'll be back. I managed to pick one up yesterday without getting too badly scratched.'

But hadn't had the heart to try since. As they passed the empty single which must have housed Domino — he was ashamed not to be sure — he took her hand.

She didn't withdraw it, but it was too inert to sustain the contact. Not touching, they walked down the line. 'Dizzy's enjoying his supper as usual.' The bowl on the first shelf under the black and white cat acrobating about its wire was gleaming clean. But only one had more than smears left in it.

'This fellow's pining.' Barbara put her face to the wire behind which an enormous gold and white puffball drooped inert over its top ledge.

'He's going to fall off.'

'Not him. You know how Mick and Charlie relax on six inches of fencetop. Come and meet him. He's called Lionel.'

'Lionel!'

Barbara opened the door and as they joined the puffball in its private space it slowly extruded a wide, heavily whiskered head with baleful yellow eyes. To Bob's instinctive pleasure the head flattened and the eyes narrowed in instant bliss as Barbara found the chin and scratched underneath it.

'What a disgustingly dirty eater we are!' she accused benevolently.

'Perhaps he's more used to chicken,' Bob suggested, looking away from the lumps of food trailed unattractively through pools of spilt milk.

'I'm sure he is. He's terribly spoiled but he's survived intact three times already, I'm not really worried.'

Bob didn't remember seeing Lionel before. 'You do keep this place nice, Barbara. It even smells good.'

'Samantha's wonderful.'

'You'd keep it like this if she didn't come.'

'I'd try to.'

She'd certainly give it priority over the house, Bob thought, not for the first time, but for the first time with amusement rather than irritation. And it wasn't as if Barbara didn't keep the house basically clean, it was only that it tended to be untidy, with a bit of surface dust here and there, whereas down in her feline kingdom everything was in its place and glowing with cleanliness. Well, it was her business as the office was his, he'd had a young clerk up on his carpet only the day before to tell him his corner looked unacceptably seedy.

Barbara! Watching the little girl figure stretching to the top shelf he though of Alice in the Tenniel picture reaching to the Cheshire Cat and was aware again of Barbara as a person in her own right, as more than his wife who for so long now had been part of his sense of dissatisfaction. His interest in who or what she was hadn't died, it had only been dormant.

Too late? The sudden question stabbed him like a knife.

'What is it, Bob?'

He had thought she was entirely absorbed with Lionel, and his heart leaped. 'Just one of those sudden pains. It's gone.'

'They're odd, aren't they?' With a final pat to the passively approving cat she turned away from it. 'Absolutely excruciating for a few minutes, then as if you'd never had them.'

'Yes. Do you have a word with each of them when you come down, Barbara?'

'Of course. Night and morning as part of my duties, other times if I feel like it. Aren't I lucky my duties are my pleasure?'

'Yes. Anyone who can feel that about their work is lucky. I can myself, most of the time. Let me help you do what's to be done.'

With continuing self-disgust he saw his behaviour as the traditional gift of the guilty husband to the wronged and unsuspecting wife. The gift he knew Barbara would so much prefer to a bunch of red roses or even a diamond bracelet. Only it wasn't, this was the first time in the year since he had been sleeping with Caroline that he wanted to please Barbara. The first time since long before that, otherwise he'd have left when Caroline gave him the opportunity.

He had to believe that. And believe that gradually, as he began to share Barbara's absorption in her business, they might bridge the gap.

While he was still going to bed every other week with Caroline?'

'Are you going to try the wild ones again?'

'Not tonight, Bob. I'm too tired.'

'I know. I know how I'd feel if we lost Mick or Charlie. There's Mick now.'

Their own tabby face loomed furious against the glass. Barbara never let him or ginger Charlie into the cat enclosure, just to be on the safe side, she always said, but Bob suspected her main reason was deference to the feelings of the disadvantaged caged ones.

He helped her collect the bowls and wash them in the sink, then put small measures of milk and munchies back on the centre shelves. When they came out, butting Mickey's head gently away so that they could lock the door, all the feral kittens were asleep.

It was so long since they had walked up the dark garden hand in hand that he didn't risk a rebuff, but he held her arm as they negotiated the dim steps. It was as unresponsive as her hand. Back in the kitchen he took her shoulders, shook them slightly.

'Barbara! I enjoyed that!'

'Well, good!' To his intense disappointment, the brief smile failed to reach her eyes. 'Forgive me, I should have told you as soon as you got home. Jo rang at lunchtime. Pinning herself down to that weekend she promised between now and Easter.'

'That's wonderful!' Looking his daughter in the eye over Christmas had been so shaming he had to simulate what once would have been his delight. He hoped ara wouldn't notice more then his mouth, determinedly smiling.

'Yes, isn't it?' Barbara's eyes were still cold. But although she and Jo seemed to get on well enough, Jo had always been Daddy's girl.

'When are we to be privileged?' Since their daughter had left London drama school for repertory and a flat in Brighton, they had tended to talk sarcastically of her regular but infrequent visits. Jokily on Bob's part, but he had never been sure how seriously or unseriously on Barbara's.

'Mid-February. Have you got that pain again?'

'It's gone now.' If only it had. 'Bedtime, would you say?'

Lying in the dark he longed to turn to her and tell her he loved her. No more than that, but sexual contact was in better case between them than affection, and she would misinterpret his longing. He lay motionless half the night staring into the cage of his head, aware almost nostalgically of her faint breathing.

31

'Hello, Jack.'

Caroline kept moving across the hall as her husband closed the front door behind him. He followed her into the kitchen.

'Hello, darling.' He went up to her in a rush, then paused before diving at her suddenly visible cheek as she turned in search of a seasoning bottle. 'All right?'

'Fine, Jack. Just fine.'

'You and Bob have a good evening?'

'Of course. You and ...? At last she turned to him, and was smiling ferociously.

'Yes, yes,' said Jack hurriedly. 'But I'm home now. You know we agreed ... Whatever — whatever we do, we belong together, Caroline.'

'I'm glad you remember we agreed that, Jack.' The smile softened. 'Now, I've made some watercress soup.'

'My favourite!' He was like a schoolboy after a statutory ticking-off. 'I'll get us a drink, then I'll just go down to the shed.'

'You do that, darling. By the way, Simon rang.'

'Yes?' Jack turned and stood in the kitchen doorway. 'Any special reason?'

'Does there have to be a special reason for a son to telephone his mother?'

Jack shifted from foot to foot, sustaining the schoolboy image. 'Of course not, darling. It was only that —'

'Simon doesn't ring very often, I know. He happens to be a very busy man.'

'I know, darling.'

'And a very clever one. How else d'you think he survived the City crash?'

'I don't think he survived it any other way, I'm not disputing he's clever.' Jack, suddenly exasperated, stood foursquare. 'So he was just saying hello?'

'Yes.'

'Not suggesting paying us a visit?'

'Not at the moment. He's just back from Switzerland, if you remember.'

'And has to settle down again before he can make

arrangements to see his parents. Yes, of course. He's all right?'

'He seems fine. Or perhaps you were meaning is he all right as far as you and I are concerned. He still appears to see us as a happily married couple.'

'That's how everyone sees us, darling.'

'And that's how we are, isn't it? Married to each other, and happy with other people. Well, you happy with – other people.'

'You're not happy with Bob?'

'Every other week for an hour or two?'

'Caroline, I'm so sorry. It's a mess, isn't it?'

'Yes.'

'It isn't that I don't love you any more –'

'Don't go through it all again, Jack, I know it by heart already. Go and get us our drinks.'

Later, lying alone in the wide marriage bed, her isolation defined by the occasional snore from Jack in the small bedroom next door, Caroline wondered if Bob was getting tired of their arrnagement. On his most recent visit she had sensed for the first time that she didn't have all his attention. He had grown into a regular reassurance that she was still desirable, and she didn't want to lose him. Not that she would, with their mutually dependent set-up, unless it got to a point where he brought her more pain than pleasure and she chose to let him go ... It was comforting to remind herself that there was Paul as well. And more than Paul if she wanted; she could still exert a powerful pull. She could even engineer herself a proper marriage again, if she wanted to.

Which she didn't. When Caroline eventually turned on her side, her face was wet with tears that slid down on to the pillow.

Chapter Four

'Nice and quiet in here.' Bob couldn't remember when he had last paid for petrol without the backing of Radio One. But the boy who had just served him wasn't the usual petrol-station attendant. 'You doing a vac job?' Their neighbour's son had been in to see Barbara the night before, saying his Easter vac had begun and was there any way he could help with the cats?

'That's right.'

Bob's credit card and receipt were handed over with a grin. As he stowed them away he noticed the old station clock on the wall behind the boy's head, surrounded by the usual curled yellow forest of outdated notices. Half past six, he ought to be there. He was going to find it sticky enough without giving Caroline cause for annoyance. Until the talking stopped.

'Thanks. Good luck.'

Running back to the car, he was aware of the warm stillness of the air. Spring had arrived, and Caroline would take him in the dusk round her perfect garden, holding his hand. He had taken Barbara's hand last night on their way up from the cats, and for a moment so brief he wondered afterwards if it was wishful thinking, her fingertips had responded.

Jo would be there tomorrow, her hands taking his without reserve, her smile searching his eyes while she tried as always to read his state of heart. Deceiving her would be as horrible as it had been when she was home in February, and as easy — there was no way his wife and daughter could find out what he was doing. Sometimes, now, he could forget that at first his perfidy had been easy for another reason: because he had been infatuated with Caroline, seduced in mind as well as body, everything, even his place in his own family, blotted out by her. Already that past self was someone else, someone he disapproved of. As he got back into the car it hit him with a sense of shock to remember that nothing outside his head had changed.

The expensive chocolates were on the seat beside him, as innocent as the apparent content of his visit. Barbara had even commented at breakfast that she hoped he would remember to take Caroline something for her pains in the kitchen. The choice of words had threatened him with hysterical laughter, harder for a moment to suppress than his longing to shout, 'Forgive me!'

The Lamberts' garage gates were open, the garage doors closed to hide the space beside Caroline's car. When he had parked neatly on the variegated stone paving — everything about the Lamberts encouraged a compatible neatness in Bob, made Barbara want to do things awry — he closed the white wrought-iron gates and followed the careful path as it wound slightly between the front lawn and the rustic brick of the lower front wall of the house. A bland house, he thought idly as the bell chimes died away inside, but not an unattractive one, with its symmetrical double front and small-paned wooden windows. Between the wars ...

Caroline should be on her way by now, he should be seeing the narrow blonde-topped refraction of her approach to the figured glass. But all there was, still, was the featureless blur of her pale hall carpet. Bob rang the bell again while deciding she must be in the garden, gathering some fashionable herb for the finishing touch to tonight's culinary creation. If she didn't come this time he'd walk back along the path and through the white garden door, which she would have left unlocked, sharing his unnecessary instinct to attract as little attention as possible.

But he rang a third time, after laughing at himself for being so absurd as to look round and see if anyone was watching. Even his wife was expecting him to visit Caroline tonight.

Still no one there.

Bob retraced his steps with self-conscious casualness and

pressed the white latch of the garden door. Of course the door opened, and the sharp-edged green lawn curved before him between its neat borders, immaculate from its first cutting of the year.

'Caroline?' Why whisper, for God's sake? He was supposed to be here. And in the old, safe days he had sometimes arrived before Jack. 'Caroline!'

Her herb garden was near the patio doors, she must have gone back into the house while he was walking round it. The only alternative was for her to be down among the vegetables, but that was unlikely at this stage of her dinner preparations — Caroline left her flower shop on Tuesdays at lunchtime, and was always way ahead.

Calling her name again, Bob advanced to the patio doors, but they were locked and there was no one in the sitting-room beyond them. Continuing his circuit of the house he came to the back door, which was ajar.

'Caroline!' Not 'darling' yet, although habit brought the endearment to his lips. There just might be another visitor.

The kitchen too was empty, and as perfectly tidy as every other area of house and garden he had observed on his tour. There was a discreetly good smell, and a shining pan on a hob murmuring to itself. Setting his overnight bag down on a chair, he walked on into the hall.

'Caroline!' She must be upstairs, arranging the provocative disorder of those blonde tendrils, but he wouldn't follow her until he was certain they were alone in the house. 'Jack! I've come in the back way and I'm going into the sitting-room to pour myself a drink.'

No response, but her private bathroom lay the far side of her bedroom and dressing-room. The thought of them together in her big corner bath brought him a mingling of exitement and revulsion.

Trying to subdue both sensations, Bob strolled towards the sitting-room.

Perhaps, he thought later, mental shock as well as a physical blow to the skull can cause concussion, because he couldn't remember entering the room or first seeing her. It just seemed he had been staring down at her for a very long time, learning for the rest of his life the backward sprawl of her body on the eau-de-nil carpet, the arms that had failed to defend her raised to each side of her incredulously staring white face above the shattered throat. And all across the throat, long enough to reach the carpet on both sides, a thick red necklace carelessly spread.

He didn't know how much time went by before he took his eyes off her — he had to lift them away as if they were heavy — and looked round the room. Nothing out of order, just red splashes down the pale marble fireplace and her little desk, and over two of the gold sofa cushions. They brought his gorge up where Caroline herself had simply stunned him, and he was choking into his handkerchief as he noticed Jack's gun, an army relic of his father's that had once shot a sniper, lying beyond the door from the hall he must have opened to get into the room, in front of the Queen Anne chest where it was kept.

Unloaded.

At first he was unable to move, but eventually — again, he didn't know how much later — he walked with stiff painful steps over to the gun (trying not to notice more blood splashes, and failing), and bent towards it. He almost picked it up, but his brain was beginning to function again and he checked himself in time. Then made nonsense of his caution by turning to the drawer where it ought to have been and pulling it open.

There was no gun in the drawer, there was only the box of ammunition. The gun on the floor really was Jack's, but the information could have been too dearly won. Hands shaking, Bob used the handkerchief to close the drawer and wipe the handle. Then stumbled out into the hall.

Better get away before he did himself any more damage.

He was at the front door before he stopped, hearing his harsh laugh echo through the empty house. (It seemed now he had known he was alone even before finding Caroline's body; unoccupied houses announced their emptiness.) What was he doing, thinking of escape? He was at Green Lawns by invitation, that was where he was expected to be. Running off was the one action that would bring suspicion on him, a panic gesture for which there could be no innocent explanation.

He didn't seem to be able to focus his eyes on his watch,

and went back into the kitchen to get some idea from the big round face of the kitchen clock how long he had been standing in the sitting-room.

It was a quarter to seven, and when the police started asking questions they'd probably discover from that intelligent lad at the petrol station round the corner that he had left there at half-past six.

But he couldn't ring the police yet, he had to try and get Jack home. Without Jack, the issue of a warrant to arrest both of them on a charge of conspiracy to murder would probably be a formality. There wouldn't be a pan simmering on Caroline's ceramic hob if she had been dead long enough to provide them both with watertight alibis.

Perhaps she had his girlfriend's telephone number, she was for ever saying how amicable she and Jack were about their new arrangement. (He was still thinking of her in the present.)

It took him a few more precious minutes to manage the necessary move back into the sitting-room. While he was riffling frantically about in the Lambert telephone and address book, his back for once to Caroline, the telephone warbled in his ear. The shock of it sent the book across the carpet, mercifully away from her, and Bob stood trembling and listening for another aeon before remembering his legitimate presence in the Lambert house and seizing the receiver.

'Yes?'

'Mr Lambert? Is that Mr Lambert?'

A man's voice, full of the ingratiating deference of the double-glazing salesman. 'Mr Lambert isn't here, I'm afraid.'

'Oh. I though *you* ...' This double-glazing salesman was an actor *manqué*, the way he was making himself sound so disconcerted. 'Could you tell me when he'll be back?'

'I'm afraid I don't know.' Everything he did now would come under ultimate scrutiny, but he could explain this truthful response by saying he had recognised the breed of caller. 'Can I take a message?'

'No.' The voice was suddenly guarded, increasing Bob's

suspicion that it had hoped to sell something. 'I'll ring again later.'

'Fine.' Bob replaced the receiver and returned to the Lamberts' private telephone directory. It appeared to be no more than the open book Jack's and Caroline's lives superficially presented, and his only hope lay in the entry *Jack – Office*, which at this stage of the evening was unlikely to find him. He recognised the number as Jack's private line which he had used several times himself over the years, but couldn't have remembered without prompting. He dialled it.

Almost at once the ringing tone cut out. 'Jack Lambert here.'

'Jack. Oh, Jack! It's Bob! Don't ring off!'

'I'm hardly likely to ring off, you having just rung on.' Jack sounded even more booming and hearty than usual. Embarrassment, probably, in view of the circumstances in which they were talking. The circumstances as Jack saw them, not knowing the half. Unless . . . 'Bob? What was all that about? You sound a bit strange.'

'Jack. Caroline's dead.' Oh, but he shouldn't have said it like that. In a tumble of words he tried to make amends. 'I arrived a few minutes ago, she didn't answer the front door. The back door was open and I came in and found her on the sitting-room floor. Someone's shot her with your gun. In – in the throat.' He realised he might be sick. 'She's dead. I just looked through your address book, wondering how on earth I could get hold of you, it's a miracle you're still in the office . . . Jack, you've got to come home as if you were coming home anyway. I'll have to ring the police. You can say you were kept at the office. Jack? I'm so sorry . . .'

'Not with my gun, Bob.' Jack's voice now was very quiet. 'It wasn't loaded.'

'I know, but it's lying on the floor. Of course I haven't touched it.'

'It's a joke, isn't it? Not one I like.'

'It isn't a joke, Jack.'

He counted twenty into the silence. 'You're sure she's dead?'

'Yes.'

'Oh, God, Bob . . .'
'I'll be here. Please come as soon as you can.'
'I'll come now.'

Bob's relief was so great there was no room for anything else, not even sorrow for Jack and Caroline, but his brain had recovered before his feelings. It sent him into the kitchen, where he put on Caroline's rubber gloves and then ran into the dining-room and rummaged in the sideboard for a third dinner-place setting. He found crockery and cutlery to match the two places already laid, and a napkin with the blessedly plain and readable initials JML engraved on its silver ring, which he set at the third place.

The two fluffy sweet concoctions in the fridge reminded him that he had left the chocolates in the car. He was relieved to remember from the old, safe days that Jack preferred cheese to pudding, and went back into the dining-room to remove the spoon.

Then he returned the gloves to their drawer, went into the sitting-room and dialled three nines.

'Fire, police or ambulance?'
'Police.' Too late for an ambulance.
'Police here.'

He gave his name and his own address. Open, nothing to hide. Then Jack and Caroline's, as he told them he was ringing from their house. 'I'd arrived to stay the night with them, something I do every other Tuesday.' Would he have said so much at this stage if he was entirely what he seemed? 'Mrs Lambert didn't answer the door and I went round the house and found the back door open. Then found Mrs Lambert on the floor in the sitting-room. Someone's shot her in the throat. She's dead.'

'You're sure of that, sir?'
'Yes.'
'You didn't find out by touching the body, did you, sir?'
'I didn't need to. I haven't touched anything.' The murderer would have wiped the gun drawer clean, too.

'That's right, sir. Now if you'll just wait calmly someone will be with you very shortly. You're on your own? Mr Lambert?'

'Mr Lambert's due home from Guildford any moment.

I – I'm afraid I rang him at his office before I made this call, I just caught him as he was leaving. I suppose I should have rung you first but I felt the most important thing was to prepare her husband.' Portrait of a man with humane priorities.

'That's understandable, sir. Now, just sit down quietly in another room until someone gets there. And try not to touch anything, anything at all. You'll tell that to Mr Lambert if he gets home before we arrive, won't you, sir?'

'Yes, Yes, of course.'

'Even the drinks cupboard, I'm afraid, Mr Collins. But we shan't be long.'

Bob went into the dining-room, and was about to sit down on a chair without arms and possibly vital fingerprints when he remembered the arrangements upstairs.

There might not be time to be sick, and swallowing savagely he took the stairs two at a time. His mind now, independent of his heaving stomach, was functioning brilliantly. It told him to ignore the overnight bag he had put down in the kitchen, to open the guest-room door through his handkerchief because his fingerprints wouldn't last one morning in a house like this, let alone a fortnight. When he was inside he stood panting, staring towards the bed.

Yes, it was as usual. Turned down, with the minimal silk nightdress draped across the angle of the sheet. Bob grabbed the nightdress, used it to close the door behind him, open Jack and Caroline's door – in their house all doors were kept shut – systematically open drawers until he saw other nightdresses, and put this one in among them. Then he got his handkerchief out again to close the drawer. After standing for a moment hesitant, he crossed to the bed and lifted the pillow on the side where a fat best-seller lay splayed by an alarm clock and a pill bottle. Lying beneath it was an elderly-looking cotton garment with sleeves. It took a few more seconds to subdue his hysterical laughter.

He used his handkerchief to cover his retreat and leave upstairs as if he had never been there. He had another look at his overnight bag but didn't touch it; its neat placing on the chair was a true statement of his ignorance when he entered the house.

Then he went back into the dining-room and stood by the window, staring out at the trees along the low wall bounding the front garden, wondering if the people across the road, behind a similar partial screen, had seen the murderer come or go. Despite the new warmth, the sun had spent the day behind cloud, but a sparkle of red gold on the upper windows of the houses opposite told Bob it was setting openly above the Lamberts' southwest-facing back garden. By the time the police car braked audibly beyond the boundary trees, the flush of the sun's public departure was all over the sky.

He had the front door open before they reached it.

'Mr Collins?' It was a couple of uniformed men.

'Yes.' He led them across the hall, stood aside. 'In there.' He didn't follow them further than the threshold.

'Jesus,' the junior breathed.

'All right, Constable.' The senior man dropped to his knees by Caroline's body and stayed there a few seconds. 'Dead all right.' As if Bob had made a brilliant deduction, he glanced towards the doorway approvingly as he got to his feet. 'You came right into the room, sir?'

'As far as the telephone. If my brain had been working I'd have called you from the kitchen. Then I had a look at the gun. I didn't touch it.' He hadn't lied yet.

'Thank you, sir. Where have you been waiting?'

'In the dining-room. And I can watch out for Jack Lambert from there. He knows, but it won't help all that much.' He was managing to keep his eyes off Caroline.

'Maybe not, sir. But perhaps you'll go back in there. We'll get in touch now with CID and the scene-of-crimes officer and things will soon be under way. We're just here to get the picture, see nothing's disturbed.'

See that there really was a crime. Now he had occasion to think about it, it occurred to Bob that hoaxers wouldn't invariably select the fire services. That was why the sergeant had been pleased with him. 'I've had plenty of time to disturb things, Sergeant.' He hadn't known he was going to make a joke. 'But I haven't.' He had a thought. 'Shall I just move my car out of the carport so that Mr Lambert can reach his garage? Then I can drive it back —'

'I think we'll just leave everything as it is, sir.'

The sergeant turned away, dismissive. But of course the uniformed men, the crime preventers, weren't there to ask questions. The questions would come from the crime solvers, the detectives. Having discovered he had told the truth once at least, this sergeant and constable were staying only to ensure that there wasn't any more foul play.

He went slowly back into the dining-room and stood by the window while the sun stains flamed to their apotheosis. Fading, they left him dazzled, so that it took him a few moments to see that what was moving on the other side of the road was a man with a dog, looking back at the police car as he walked, then over at Green Lawns.

The man quickened his pace, jerking the dog away from a lamppost, as the two unmarked cars drew up behind the police car and Jack's car, with ludicrously good timing, passed the other three uncertainly and came to a protracted halt across its own garage entrance.

What seemed like a lot of men with various pieces of equipment got out of the third official car and made for the house. The two men from the other car met Jack as he walked back from his; Bob could see bits of them between the trees as they stood still, talking.

Then, when the first party had been let in by the uniformed men and had gone into the sitting-room, Jack was escorted up his front path by two men in plain clothes, one middle-aged and one young, whom Bob didn't at that stage really notice because of his surprise at seeing how pale Jack's face could go.

He moved out into the hall.

'Robert Collins?' asked the older of the two men with Jack.

'Yes. Jack ...'

'Bob.' Jack shuffled up to him, dropped hands like weights on to his shoulders.

'I'm Detective Inspector Hewitt and this is Detective Sergeant Tabley.' The older man's deep-set blue eyes were moving between Bob and the closed sitting-room door. He had a full head of sandy-coloured hair, and the pale freckled face which so often accompanies it. The expression in his rather sharp features was calm and potentially friendly, but

Bob was not reassured. 'Perhaps you and Mr Lambert would care to wait in − *Not yet*, Mr Lambert!'

But Jack had the sitting-room door open, was staggering through it, was roaring a terrible mixture of incredulity, grief and fury, drowning the sounds of the detective work already begun. Bob wanted to put his hands over his ears. He hadn't seen the detective sergeant follow Jack, but he was in the doorway supporting him, trying to draw him out of the room.

'We wanted to spare you at this stage, Mr Lambert,' said the chief inspector softly. The sergeant sagged momentarily under the big man's weight as Jack's resistance suddenly gave way. They stumbled backwards into the hall. 'But as you went in ... That is your wife?' Jack gulped and nodded. 'Formal identification,' the detective chief inspector murmured, receiving half of Jack's weight in an admirable piece of teamwork. 'I'm sorry you went in, sir, but there'll be no need now to take you to the mortuary. Are there seats in the kitchen?' he asked Bob.

'Several.'

The inspector relinquished his share in Jack. 'Perhaps you and Mr Collins will wait in there, Mr Lambert. The sergeant'll make you some tea or coffee, won't you, Sergeant?'

And make sure they didn't say anything collusive that might help them conceal their guilt.

'Of course, sir.' But the detective sergeant's eyes were rebellious as they lingered on the closed sitting-room door. With a sharp movement he renewed his hold on Jack's arm, motioning Bob in front of them.

'Tea, is it?' he asked in the kitchen, putting Jack on to a chair. Bob sat down too.

'The whisky's in the sitting-room,' said Jack, back to that expressionless quiet voice Bob had first heard on the telephone.

'I should have tea, Mr Lambert, tea's best. Where d'you keep it?'

The detective sergeant already had the kettle on. Jack told him in a murmur where things were, watched him through half-closed eyes as he moved about the kitchen. Moved well, Bob noticed, as if seeing the sergeant in a film; he was slim and lithe with narrow hips, a smooth dark head and darting eyes. Bob hoped he was right to feel glad the man would have the subordinate role in the questioning soon to come.

'Know anything about this bag?' The sergeant was trying to speak conversationally, as his chief had done in the hall, but wasn't managing it so well. His face was sharp as he looked from Jack to Bob.

'It's mine, my overnight bag. I put it down when I came in through the back door. Then forgot it. Well ...'

'Of course, sir.' The kettle was boiling and Detective Sergeant Tabley turned away from them to make the tea.

'Have one yourself, Sergeant,' said Jack, as if the tea were a tip for services rendered.

'Thank you, sir, I'm all right.' It was the ambiguous working-class refusal, but there was little trace of London in the voice. Bob judged the detective sergeant to be ambitious. 'Sugar? Good for shock.'

'I take it anyway,' said Jack.

'Not for me,' said Bob. 'Don't see it as a sign of guilt, Sergeant, I'm shocked enough.'

'Of course, sir.' The sergeant gave him another sharp glance, and it had been a stupid, unnecessary thing to say, in the overconfident, too-clever-by-half category which in films and TV series made the police suspicious. And he hadn't killed Caroline, for heaven's sake, he had only slept with her.

Which, if they ever got to know, would seem to them a whole lot more significant than it was.

The dreadful irony of the situation was that it wasn't significant at all. Barbara! Sitting uneasily at Caroline's kitchen table, sipping tea under the watchful eye of Detective Sergeant Tabley, Bob realised he wanted his wife as years ago when unpleasant things happened he had wanted his mother.

Chapter Five

The front-door bell rang as Bob and Jack sipped tea at the kitchen table, watched unremittingly by Detective Sergeant Tabley leaning in apparent relaxation against a section of Caroline's pinky-mauve colour scheme. Jack leaped on a reflex to his feet, sinking back with a feebly defiant shrug as the detective sergeant made a downward gesture of his hand – a gesture he had made already when the householder had shown signs of responding to the feet and voices overhead and the first of the telephone warbles. The silence in the kitchen was still unbroken when the sounds of downstairs activity came nearer, and there was the shuffling of feet. Tabley crept pantherlike towards the door, but Jack's head by now was down on the table, cradled in his arms, and Bob to his relief saw no reaction to what the new noises might mean.

When the front door had closed again, Detective Chief Inspector Hewitt joined them, followed by a young man wearing a neat grey suit and an expression of enormous earnestness.

'This is Detective Constable Reid,' said the detective chief inspector bracingly, taking in the superficially tranquil scene. 'Sorry about my men being all over the house, Mr Lambert, but you'll appreciate . . .' Jack raised a blank, wet face, and the inspector turned to Bob. 'Better start with you, Mr Collins, seeing you were the first here.' The comparative friendliness didn't reconcile Bob to the choice of phrase. 'If you're ready.'

'Yes. Of course.' The detective sergeant had made the tea

too strong and it had given him indigestion. Unless it was the pumping of his heart, suddenly so loud he wondered if he'd be able to hear the questions. How could he – how could Jack – conceal from these clear-eyed representatives of law and order the fact that they had something to hide? And having recognised that they were being less than honest, how could the police be prepared even to consider that what was being hidden had nothing to do with Caroline's death?

Detective Chief Inspector Hewitt had known what he was doing when he put them straight into the care of his detective sergeant. Bob wished he had used his telephone chance to rally Jack to try and keep up appearances. Even when he wasn't in a state of near collapse, Jack was never a cool customer, he was too vulnerable to the pressures of the moment. And his instinct of self-preservation, anyway, was unlikely to be as strong as Bob's – Jack had an alibi. Whereas Bob ... Reluctant to set out for Green Lawns, he had sat in the car in the Guildford car park for at least a precious quarter of an hour, staring into space. And the car park attendant had gone off duty.

'If you'll stay in here with Mr Lambert,' the detective chief inspector was saying to the hovering constable, 'the rest of us will go through to the dining-room. It seems the best place.'

With heavy curtains to draw against the remains of the day, and Caroline's sewing lamp to turn on the prisoner's chair.

How could he be so stupid? He was merely a friend of the family who had arrived on a routine visit to find that someone had murdered his hostess. All he – all Jack – had to do was to act as if things were precisely as they seemed. As for years they had been.

Despite the feverish internal pep talk Bob could hardly propel himself across the hall, but as he entered the dining-room, one policeman in front of him and one behind, his heart leaped. By expanding the dinner place settings from two to three he had, after all, been able to give Jack a message. Jack would see them, as he had done, the moment he came into the room, and before saying a word he'd draw courage from the realisation that Bob had provided the evidence of an evening *à trois*. He had to be grateful for the lack of time which had made him lay the third place at the side of the table close to the sideboard rather than the end by the window where Jack always sat when he was at home. This had left the police almost half the shining surface on which to spread their papers, so that after having made their own note of his signal they hadn't needed to disturb it.

'Please sit down, Mr Lambert.' The detective chief inspector indicated Jack's carver chair, watched Bob take it, sat down on his left. The detective sergeant took the seat to his right, a notebook already out. 'Was Mrs Lambert a well-organised woman?'

The question came before Hewitt was settled, while he was still fishing in the briefcase he had put down beside him. Bob knew his jerk of alarm had been visible, but it promoted the adrenalin that could help him keep his comparatively innocent secret.

.'I should say very much so.'

'I see. So she might have laid the dinner table early?'

'Again, I should say so, but of course I don't know.' That was good. 'I do know, though, that she only works — worked — a half-day on Tuesdays so unless she had some engagement she would have had the afternoon free.'

'Worked a half-day?'

'Mrs Lambert owns — owned — a shop called Flower Bower in Guildford.'

'I see.' Hewitt was looking at some papers he had taken out of the briefcase. 'Perhaps you'd just repeat and expand what you said on the telephone, Mr Lambert. Starting with your full name and address, and your occupation.' The sergeant wrote something down. 'Thank you. You said when you called the police that your visit tonight was one of a regular series. Business or pleasure?'

'Pleasure, Chief Inspector.' He was proud of himself, managing to answer a question like that in so relaxed a way, even with a brief, sad smile. 'Although you could say that business comes into it. As I've just told you, I'm a solicitor, a partner in Mainwaring and Collins. The main office is in London, but I spend every other Tuesday at our

Guildford branch, and come on here to stay the night with the Lamberts.'

'You're married, Mr Collins?'

'Yes.'

'But your wife doesn't join you here?'

'My wife boards cats.' He could hardly hear himself, the blood had started to drum so loudly in his ears.

The detective chief inspector took Barbara's excuse with one raised eyebrow, an accomplishment striking Bob as an unwelcome pointer to other unexpected skills. 'Which precludes nights away from home?'

'Unless she makes arrangements. She never leaves the cats alone.'

'And she never makes arrangements to enable her to spend a Tuesday night with you and Mr and Mrs Lambert?'

'She has done, but usually I come on my own, straight from the office.'

'Does – did – your wife see Mrs Lambert at other times?'

'Of course.' It was incredible, but Barbara was going to be asked to account for her movements, too. 'And they always stay with us for New Year. We have holidays together. We're old friends.'

'I see, Mr Collins, yes. What time did you and Mr and Mrs Lambert usually have your evening meal?' To think there had been a particular emphasis on *Mr and Mrs* was to show signs of paranoia.

'Round about half past seven.' When had Caroline died? All those people in the sitting-room, all that activity, they knew by now. He wanted to ask, but he didn't think he could get it out.

'What time did you arrive here this evening, Mr Lambert?'

'It must have been soon after half past six. I stopped for petrol at the garage round the corner in Seel Road – I don't know the name – and noticed the clock because I was afraid I was late.'

'Did it matter being late?'

Another warning lurch of the heart, but helping to save him from overconfidence. 'Well, no, of course not, I didn't mean I was afraid, I just meant ...'

'A sense of social obligation. I understand, Mr Lambert. If one's expected at half past six, that's the time one prefers to arrive. And tonight, despite your anxieties, you got here before Mr Lambert. Did that often happen?'

'Sometimes. I suppose on balance he got here first.' The thing was to wipe the last year out of his mind, answer the questions with the truthfulness of twelve months ago. For the first time in his professional life Bob wished his law experience had been criminal instead of civil and matrimonial. 'I remember we once met at the gate.'

'You always put your car in Mr Lambert's carport?'

'Yes. Better off the road, you'll agree, Chief Inspector.'

'Certainly, sir. Only tonight you would have to have backed it out again so that Mr Lambert could get his into the garage.'

A statement rather than a question, but no question had ever been more insistent on an answer. 'Seeing the garage closed I assumed Mr Lambert was already home and had put his car away. When I've got here first other times, the garage has usually been open and I've seen the space. Caroline used to keep it shut during the day and open it just before Jack was due home.' Which tonight he wasn't. 'I suppose ... When did she die, Chief Inspector?'

In the end he'd asked the question quite easily.

'Very shortly before you arrived.' The detective chief inspector's expression was still almost friendly. 'If you'd touched her, which wisely you didn't' — how far could disingenuity go? — 'you would have found her warm. I'm sorry, Mr Collins.'

He had gagged. 'It's all right. It was just the thought ...' Appallingly, he had suddenly remembered Caroline lithe underneath him. He hoped the man wouldn't speak quite so callously to Jack.

'Take your time.' Under Hewitt's not unpitying gaze Bob blew his nose and wiped his streaming eyes. The detective sergeant shifted his impatience around his chair. 'All right? Perhaps you'll tell us now how long it takes you to drive here from your Guildford office.'

Very shortly before you arrived ... They'd be asking the intelligent garage lad what sort of state he was in as well as what time he had called in for petrol. 'About twenty minutes. It depends on the traffic.'

'Of course, Mr Collins. Now, you telephoned the police at 6.53 p.m., having bought petrol at six-thirty.' Hewitt hadn't referred to the papers in front of him. 'So allowing for this and that I suppose you left your office soon after six.'

'Earlier than that.' He had to moisten his lips. 'I came out with an escort of secretaries.' Who'd tell the police the time if he didn't. 'So it must have been just after half past five. I walked round the shops for a while, there were lots of them still open. Bought some chocolates for my hostess — they're still in the car — and looked for birthday ideas for my wife.' He stared at the inspector. 'That's what I did, Chief Inspector. And took my time about it.'

'That all sounds understandable, Mr Collins,' Hewitt commented amiably. 'See anyone you knew between saying good night to the secretaries and paying the garage?'

'No. I've bought things before at the shop where I got the chocolates, but I don't expect they'd remember me. The office car park attendant goes off duty at half past five, and he wasn't there when I collected my car.' So he would have had plenty of time to kill Caroline before filling up with petrol, as well as a short time afterwards.

'I see, sir. Tell me now if you will. Did you notice anything unusual when you arrived at Green Lawns?'

'Nothing at all, Chief Inspector. Until I found ...'

'Quite, sir. Can you tell us precisely what you did after you drove up?'

'Of course.' He must train himself to offer the police the same honest gaze when he was telling the truth as when he wasn't. 'When I saw the garage was closed I assumed Mr Lambert was at home and I drove into the carport. Then I went round to the front door via the path and rang the bell. Usually one or other of them was there after one ring but tonight nobody came so I rang again.'

'What did you think, Mr Collins, when the bell wasn't answered?'

'I thought maybe Caroline was picking herbs for dinner. And that Jack might be working in his tool shed on the table he's making. All sorts of ideas can run through your mind in a very short time — '

'That's quite true, Mr Collins. What did you do when your second ring wasn't answered?'

'I convinced myself one or both of them were in the garden, and I went back along the path and through the door that leads to it.'

'Expecting it to be unlocked?'

If he could just keep in mind that every question was a potential pitfall, there would be fewer shocks. 'I suppose I thought that if either or both of them were in the garden they would have unlocked it.' He was doing wonderfully well, which could mean that he was sounding too thorough and careful in explaining himself. That, though, was how solicitors tended to sound.

'I see, sir,' said Hewitt yet again. There was nothing in his face to suggest how much he saw. 'But when you went through the garden door there was no one in the garden.'

'No one in the part you can see from the doorway. Which included Caroline's herb garden on the patio. I didn't think she'd have gone down to the vegetables at that stage of her dinner preparations, she was always so well ahead. I told you. I called their names' — he was reassured to hear lies and truth so fluently mingling — 'and when there was no reply I decided Caroline must have gone back into the house while I was walking round it.'

'And Mr Lambert?'

'I went down to the tool shed.' Too quick to accept Hewitt's prompt? 'I looked through the shed window' — eyes didn't leave prints — 'but of course he wasn't there. Then I came back up the garden and tried the patio doors but they were locked. I didn't see — Caroline. I wasn't looking at the floor, of course, but I think the sofa probably hid her from the garden.'

'It did, Mr Collins.'

He hoped the latest noises across the hall meant that Caroline's body on her sitting-room carpet really was in the past tense. 'I walked on round the back of the house as far as the back door.' He couldn't get away from this dreadful precision. 'I was calling them again. I went through the kitchen into the hall — Oh, wait a minute.' At last he had forgotten something. 'I put my overnight bag down on a kitchen chair on my way past. I called out in the hall and when there was still no reply I became pretty sure Jack couldn't be home despite the closed garage door' — too clever again, remembering that? — 'and I shouted that I was going to pour myself a drink — I know them that well, Chief Inspector — and went into the sitting-room, and ...'

'Yes, Mr Collins?'

All at once his mind was a swirling emptiness, and the contrast would show. 'I — I must have stood taking it in for a few minutes.' Not long enought to have done it, for God's sake. *Unless he'd had a brainstorm*. 'I ... The shock was terrible. I mean, things like that don't happen in one's own life ...' He was looking from one impassive face to the other in fear and uncertainty, but surely he had reached a stage where he could let them see that that was what he felt. 'Eventually I looked round the room and saw Jack's gun.' And the blood. Would they clean the blood off for Jack?

'You knew about it? Where it was kept?'

'Yes.' All Jack's friends knew about it, he was so fond of his sniper story. 'It lives in the second drawer of the little chest near where it was lying.'

'Go on, Mr Collins.'

'I found myself going over to it.' If he was guilty he'd be doing better than this. 'I was going to pick it up when I realised I shouldn't touch anything —'

'Quite right, Mr Collins. Was it then that you rang Mr Lambert?'

'It was then that some sort of would-be telephone salesman rang. As soon as I'd hung up on him I rang Jack.'

'When you were expecting to hear his key in the lock at any moment?'

Here was the heart of it, the crux of their vulnerability. Detective Sergeant Tabley's head jerked up from his notebook, his face seeming to sharpen as he leaned over the table.

'I know, but I felt the remotest chance of preparing him ... And sparing myself telling him face to face.' He was horrified by his growing ingenuity as a liar. 'The point, though, is that it worked, didn't it, Chief Inspector?'

'It did, sir.' For the first time his opponent registered a setback. 'Have there been other times when Mr Lambert stayed so late at his office?' *And you've had so long alone with his wife*? But it was the only thing Hewitt could have said to regain the upper hand.

'One or two, I suppose, but not many. As I said, on balance he was home when I arrived, and if he wasn't he was only a few minutes behind me. But of course it did happen. As it does with any professional man.' He mustn't protest too much.

'I know that from experience, Mr Collins.' The detective chief inspector permitted himself a brief reminiscent smile.

'How did Mr Lambert react when you told him his wife was dead?' The sudden intervention of Detective Sergeant Tabley, harsh against his superior's soft persistence, made Bob jump again.

The chief inspector had noticed. 'I'm sorry, Mr Lambert, but you'll appreciate certain uncomfortable questions have to be asked.'

'I do, Chief Inspector.' But Jack had an alibi. 'If I can remember. He was his normal cheerful self when he answered the telephone. Then when I'd told him ... he was very quiet. I told him straight out and regretted not doing it more gently. I think then I had the idea of trying to make it better by telling him about — about how it was, which was pretty crazy. Then ... Oh, yes, he said the gun wasn't loaded.'

'Which you knew?'

'Oh, yes. He had a licence for it, of course, but he always kept it unloaded. I suppose he should have kept the ammunition in another place ...'

'That would have been advisable, Mr Collins. Did Mr Lambert say anything else?'

'He asked me if I was sure Caroline was dead. When I said yes we agreed that I'd call the police and he'd come home right away. He'd been about to leave anyway.'

'And so then you dialled nine nine nine?'

'Of course, Chief Inspector.' Laying the table had taken five minutes at the most. And he'd done the business with the nightdress after he had made the emergency call. But it was hard not to start looking particularly honest and truthful.

He blinked and got to work again with his handkerchief.

'And then?'

'Then I went into the dining-room.' Bob blew his nose and put the handkerchief away. 'I sat down, I remember I chose a chair without arms so as not to disturb any possible fingerprints, although I don't suppose the murderer went into the dining-room.' Unlike the adulterer. 'Then I got restless and went and stood by the window, and then the uniformed men arrived.'

'And you're certain that is a complete account of what happened following your arrival at the house, Mr Collins? That there's nothing you've forgotten?'

The supplementary question made it a lot easier. 'I'm certain I've remembered everything, Chief Inspector.' And would do for the rest of his life. Except for his first view of Caroline's body. 'But I suspect I'm still a bit shocked, and if I think of anything else of course I'll get in touch with you.'

'Thank you, Mr Collins. Perhaps you'll have thought of something by the morning, that's when you'll be seeing us again. The sergeant will prepare a statement from what you've just told us, and we'll be glad if you'll come in to the station tomorrow to read it over and then sign it if you're satisfied it's a correct record of what you've said. Forgive me, sir, I know you're professionally aware of the procedure but I have to —'

'I haven't specialised in criminal law, Chief Inspector.'

'No? I must say it's a comparative pleasure to take evidence from a solicitor, whatever his specialisation.' Bob suspected irony. 'Shall we say on your way to work, sir? Eight-thirty to nine o'clock?' Hewitt pushed his chair back from the table, indicating the end of the first encounter.

'Yes. Of course.' And the questions over again, more insistently. At least by then he'd have talked to Jack.

'May I ring my wife, Chief Inspector? I'll stay here overnight as planned if Mr Lambert wants me to, but I'd like to let my wife know what's happened. Particularly as I suppose there's a chance of Mrs Lambert's — death — being mentioned tonight on local TV and radio.'

'National TV or radio, if I know my media.' The detective

chief inspector got up with a sigh. 'Of course, Mr Collins. Detective Sergeant Tabley will take you back to the kitchen and you can ring from there. Bring Mr Lambert back with you, will you, Jago.'

'Right, sir. Let's go, Mr Collins.'

Bob felt that for two pins Detective Sergeant Jago Tabley would have helped him physically on his way.

The detective constable as well as Jack was sitting at the kitchen table. With yet another lurch of his acrobatic heart, Bob saw that Jack had been crying.

'The detective chief inspector wants to see you,' said Tabley disdainfully to Jack's sharply raised, colour-drained face.

'Nothing to worry about,' said Bob as jokily as he could manage, trying to catch Jack's eye. Tabley was behind him and couldn't see, and the other man was looking in a concerned way at Jack.

'Of course not,' Jack muttered, stumbling to his feet, the picture of guilt.

The picture of the tragically bereaved. Jack had an alibi.

'It's OK for Mr Collins to ring his wife,' said Tabley to Detective Constable Reid. 'No other call you want to make, Mr Collins?' *Such as to another solicitor, for instance*? There was no doubt about the irony this time.

'No other call, Sergeant, thank you.' To ask for his solicitor at this stage would be to admit he was in a spot; better to wait for the police to tell him he was.

'If you're ready, Mr Lambert.'

Bob saw Tabley take Jack's arm as they left the kitchen, perhaps only because Jack looked as if otherwise he might fall.

'It's a terrible thing,' said Detective Constable Reid the instant they were alone. 'Would it help at all to talk about it?'

'I've just done so. Once is enough.' He was even wondering if this youth with the concerned brown eyes might be seconded from somewhere like Serious Crimes to encourage him and Jack to talk. Within a couple of hours of Caroline's death? The shock was regressing him to boyhood, *Boy's Own* stuff. 'Thanks, though, for the thought. I'd like to ring my wife.'

'Yes. Of course.' So quickly forgetting his superior's oblique order had made the boy blush. 'Please go ahead.'

He made a mess of his first attempt at button-pushing, but the detective constable wasn't looking for trouble. Barbara's 'Hello?' came quickly, the usual neutral query initially suitable for both friends and cat clients.

'It's Bob, darling. I'm all right but I've some terrible news.' He didn't pause, he didn't want to give her time to imagine. 'Caroline's been shot. When I arrived at Green Lawns Jack wasn't home and she didn't answer the door. I found the back door open and went in and she was on the sitting-room floor —'

'Is she badly hurt?' The soft urgent question forced its way into his narrative, making him realise how wretchedly he was doing it for the second time.

'She's dead. The police are here. They've questioned me and now they're questioning Jack.' He stopped, but she didn't fill the silence. 'Barbara?'

'Jack got back before they arrived?'

'At the same time ... Actually I rang him at the office in the wild hope he wouldn't have left, and just managed to catch him, I wanted him to know before he saw ...' It was awful, having to be as careful with Barbara as with the police. 'So I was at least able to prepare him.'

'That must have helped. If anything can. He mustn't be alone tonight, Bob.'

'I know. I'll stay with him.' If it had been Barbara who was dead — the thought savaged him like a knife — and Caroline he was telephoning, she'd have made herself the centre of a drama by now, and he'd be the audience. But Barbara's admirable view was always outward from herself. 'I love you, Barbara.'

'What about Simon?' she asked, after a pause. But even the early Barbara, he tried to console himself, hadn't felt bound to return his regular declarations.

'I don't know. I don't suppose —'

'No. Bob, Jack might prefer to be out of that house. Suggest to him, will you, that you both come here. There's plenty of food. And Vernon's here for supper. He's such a help always when things are bad, smoothing and soothing.'

'That's much the best idea. Thanks, darling. Jack's with the police now. I'll ask him when they've finished and ring you back —'

'If you're coming, just come. If you're staying where you are, ring me when the police have left.'

'I'll do that.' She had always managed with the minimum of fuss, not seeking explanations or offering them. 'Goodbye, Barbara.'

'All right?' asked Detective Constable Reid, before he had replaced the phone on the wall.

'Yes. My wife suggests I take Mr Lambert home with me tonight, instead of our both staying here.'

'Good idea!' said the detective constable. 'I mean, the bloodstains for a start ...'

'Mind if I read?' asked Bob. 'There's an *Evening Standard* at the top of my bag, you can get it out for me.'

'I should think that will be all right, sir.' Looking disappointed, the young man put his hand out to the bag, then withdrew it, blushing scarlet. 'Just routine, sir.' He took a handkerchief out of his pocket and, following an apologetic glance at Bob, used it to open the bag. The paper was visible. Blushing even more spectacularly, Detective Constable Reid looked quickly through it before handing it across the table.

'I'm sorry, sir.'

'For doing your duty?'

He had asked for the paper as an alternative to talk, but an escapist ability he felt ashamed of turned it into a respite from the nightmare which lasted until Jack came shuffling back.

He looked terrible. The face designed to be cheerful drooped against its prevailing upward lines, the rosy jowls were pale and somehow shrivelled.

'Barbara's asked us for the night.'

'Has she? That's good of her.' The face hadn't lightened. 'I think I'd prefer that, Bob. I don't want to stay here. I don't ever want to stay here again.'

'Tonight at least be with us. Unless Simon ...'

'I don't expect to get hold of him until late. Thanks, Bob, I'll go back with you to Dorking. Try Simon from your place.'

The other two detectives came into the kitchen as the telephone rang.

'I'll get it,' said the detective sergeant. 'For you,' he said to Jack after a few seconds. 'Bloke about some double glazing for a tool shed.'

'Thanks.' Like several heavy men Bob knew, Jack moved quickly.

'Hello,' he said into the receiver, 'it's not really convenient now. And I'm not going to be at this number, you'd better ring me at my office.' He paused, listening. 'All right. Yes. I'll expect to hear from you at the office in due course. You have the number. Thanks for putting the order under way. Good night.' There were isolated rosy spots in Jack's cheeks as he stumbled back to his chair.

'That must be the chap who rang earlier, the one I told you about,' said Bob, turning to Hewitt with a brief but agreeable sensation of honesty and righteousness. 'I wouldn't have been so rude to him if I'd known he wasn't unsolicited. Perhaps you'll apologise some time, Jack.'

'It doesn't matter.' Bob was glad to see the bit of colour back in Jack's face, but he was breathing like an asthmatic.

'We're off now, Mr Lambert.' said Detective Chief Inspector Hewitt. 'The men should have finished in an hour or so. I don't know what your plans are, sir, but if you could hang on – '

'I'm taking Mr Lambert home with me,' said Bob. 'All right?'

'A very good idea, sir. But I'd appreciate it if you could wait until all our people have left. If you're ready, Constable.'

With a last anxious glance at Jack, Detective Constable Reid followed his seniors to the front door. As he closed it on them, Bob saw a man kneeling on the turn of the stairs, his back to him. He went across to the now open sitting-room door and cautiously craned round. Caroline's body had been replaced by a drawn outline of her death shape, the head blurred by partially obliterated bloodstains. The marble fire surround was almost clean, and the rosewood desk seemed to have lost some of its own colour as well as the blood that had spattered it. He went quickly across to the drinks cupboard, found a bottle of whisky and two glasses, and sped back to the kitchen.

Jack was still slumped over the table. The Jack whom for the last twelve months he hadn't known. And hadn't been alone with except on the golf course, where they only talked trivialities and shop.

'I'm so terribly sorry, Jack.' He poured them drinks, feeling embarrassed. They couldn't talk seriously yet, and anything else was impossible.

'Thanks, Bob. It's unbelievable. I can't believe it. Who can have – '

'The police must be considering me. At least you have an alibi.'

Jack drank deeply, then raised his tear-stained face. 'I don't, Bob, I don't. I'd expected to be – elsewhere – but my plans were changed and so I hung on at the office. Everyone else had gone home.'

'Well?' Detective Sergeant Tabley fastened his seat belt.

'There's something,' said his superior, mouth tight. 'Something to do with Collins, at least. I don't know yet what it is, but I'll find out.'

Chapter Six

'It's a bad business, Bob,' said Vernon gently, when Jack had groped his way out from the supper table to the downstairs cloakroom.

'Yes. It is.'

Vernon smiled, advancing a pale hand across the table in Bob's direction. 'Someone will have seen something,' he murmured consolingly. 'The police are so thorough, and I fancy the area is affluent enough for there to be a number of ladies at home during the daytime to look out of the window or up from their gardening.'

'Yes. Thanks, Vernon. Anyway, at the moment I can't think about much more than finding her. Seeing ... There was blood all over the place. The police did their best – took the polish off her desk as well.' Dear God, could there have been anything in that desk? Caroline had a reckless streak. 'But Jack can't possibly go back in there. He pushed his way in, you know, saw it all ...'

'Caroline's daily's a treasure,' said Barbara. For the first time in years she had looked at him during a meal. Could she be wondering ... 'And no shrinking violet. She'll put things to rights. But as you say, Bob, of course he can't go back. Well, he can stay here as long as he wants.'

'Of course.' Bob didn't feel the enthusiasm he forced into his voice. When he and Jack were together in company their secret would hang on the air with double weight. And when they were on their own ...

If Jack hadn't answered his office telephone he could probably have fixed himself an alibi. So answering it meant innocence. Unless, of course, he had answered because he had been expecting a call to help him fix one ...

When they were all leaving Green Lawns, the police had had to help him get Jack past the closed sitting-room door, he had suddenly wanted to go back in. Suddenly remembered something he was afraid of? Jack's office wasn't much more than ten minutes from his home by car ...

He really was getting paranoiac. Jack had been the first member of their quartet − trio, he amended painfully − to defect, and Caroline had accepted his defection.

Apparently.

'I suppose we ought to be saying that naturally Jack will want to be with Simon,' Barbara observed. 'But father and son don't seem all that natural a combination.'

'They hardly meet −'

'Come and sit down, old man.' Vernon's voice cut with gentle warning across Bob's.

'All right, Jack?' asked Barbara, as Jack stumbled back into his chair. Bob realised for the first time that his wife didn't need to look or sound consoling in order to be so.

'Better than I'd be anywhere else.' Jack's expressive face was registering profound, even abject, gratitude. All the time he was there Bob would be terrified it might register something else, that his quavering voice might splash their secret out like water. When Jack went on to say that he had decided all the same to move in the morning to the club and he hoped Barbara would understand, relief flowed over Bob in a warm wave.

'You don't need to do that, you know,' he said.

'I know I don't.' Their eyes met, and he fancied agreement between them on the wisdom of avoiding long-term proximity under Barbara's eyes. 'But I think − I'm so grateful, Barbara − I think I'll be better where I can see that for most people life goes on as usual.'

'I'm afraid you'll still get sympathy.'

Her half-smile was fleetingly returned. 'Not if I say please don't. And not for long, anyway; people get pretty quickly used to things that don't affect them. I'd like to have gone to a hotel, been anonymous, but the press will knock that possibility on the head.'

'There's Simon,' Bob suggested. Someone had to. 'And you haven't spoken to him yet, have you?'

'Simon?' Jack passed his hand tiredly across his face. 'God, no. Perhaps I might try again. His mother ... God ... I don't think I'll stay with Simon, though.' *Won't give him the chance to say it isn't actually convenient*, Bob continued reluctantly in his head. 'Then there's my sister in Bristol, but the police said they hoped I'd be available ...' Jack's eyes swivelled anxiously round to Bob's.

'They said they hoped I would be, too. Better go and ring Simon then, Jack.' He got to his feet. 'I'll come down to the cats with you, darling. Vernon?'

Stiffly Vernon rose. 'Thanks, Bob, but I'll be on my way.' For years, now, when Vernon came to supper, it had been he and Barbara who went down to the cats. Bob couldn't remember the last time they had bothered asking him if he wanted to join them, and to his surprise felt a pang which temporarily eclipsed his last view of Caroline in her sitting-room. Vernon, who had strong beliefs in feline therapeutic power, must tonight have decided in his usual self-effacing way that it would work better if husband and wife were on their own.

Vernon put his hand on Bob's shoulder, the other on Jack's as Jack got up. 'Keep your courage up,' he said impartially, then turned exclusively to Jack. 'And remember I have a spare room. If you really don't intend going to your son.' Bob fancied a moment's severity in Vernon's eyes. 'I can offer tea with or without sympathy. Or something stronger.' It was his sister's turn. 'Forgive me, Barbara, but I suspect Jack's making it a one-night stand because over the years you've drawn so close, and now –'

'Now for Jack it's claustrophobic?' Barbara suggested. 'You're probably right, Vernon.' Bob's agonising hypersensitivity made him think himself aware of a sudden uneasiness in her, but she turned to Jack with another brief smile. 'Forgive us, Jack, settling your immediate future as if we were your collective nanny. I shan't be in the least put out if you decide to go to Vernon or the club or anywhere else, rather than stay here. I just feel you'll do best not to go home for a while.'

'For a while?' Jack echoed savagely. 'I'll never go back to that house again. I'll put it on the market tomorrow, look round for a smaller place. Probably ask you eventually, Barbara, to go in and look round and tell me what to take with me and what to sell.'

'Of course, if you like. Eventually. Now Nanny will take you up to your room and show you her bedroom telephone on the way. You can ring Simon from there. Good night, Vernon. Thanks for everything, as always.' She kissed his cheek.

'Thanks, Vernon.' Bob and Jack spoke in chorus.

'Bob ...' Jack stopped in the doorway, fidgeting. He could have been playing a small boy to Barbara's nanny in a revue sketch. Grotesquely, he looked very old and tired. 'I shan't sleep yet if at all. Come in on your way to bed?'

'Surely.' He didn't want to be on his own with Jack again that night, but he had to be relieved that Jack was creating the opportunity, realising the need for mutual consultation and encouragement before their imminent next encounters with the police.

Vernon handed Jack a card. 'Here's my number. Home and shop are the same, it switches through. So you can get me any time.'

'Thanks, Vernon, I very well may. Good night.'

Bob walked with Vernon to the front door as Barbara and Jack disappeared upstairs. 'You're very kind,' he told his brother-in-law. 'You've suggested what's probably the best thing Jack could do just now.' If Jack had been merely the stricken husband, it obviously would have been.

'I thought so.' Again Vernon put his hand on Bob's shoulder, looking searchingly now into his face. 'Are you all right?'

Returning that kind, steady gaze was a dummy run for returning his daughter's the next day. He managed not to flinch.

But for God's sake why should he? He was innocent.

Of murder.

Did Vernon believe that? Did Barbara? Did he himself?

'Yes, I'm all right.' But again he had to let the hall chest take his weight. 'Not looking forward to the moments after the light goes out.'

'Barbara will be there.'

'Thank heaven.' He meant it, but his feeling that he didn't deserve her was growing unruly, already strong enough to inhibit expression of his renewed sense of affection. And it was affection he needed tonight, to give and to get, rather than the mutual isolation of sex. But as Vernon had just said, she was there. As he shut the front door Bob realised that his chief spur to successful deception of the police wasn't to avoid suspicion of having killed Caroline, it was not to lose Barbara.

Which came to the same thing.

They met at the foot of the stairs. He didn't have to go quite all the way to take her hand. Gripping it he led the way back into the kitchen.

'You don't really want to come down to the cats, do you, Bob?'

'I've never wanted it more.'

She cast a swift look at him. 'Fine, then.'

Going down the garden they had never been able to hold hands, hers always held milk for the cats' fridge and a few soothers. There was no one in the run, the ferals' protectors had been as good as their word, and for the moment the other cats were the usual range of short-term boarders.

'Come and have a look at this.' Barbara opened a cage and stood aside for him to precede her into it. 'The origin of the phrase They've Got Each Other, wouldn't you say?'

'Oh, yes.' Blinking at them from the top shelf, a lilac and a chocolate Burmese each flexed a paw across the surface of the other's shining flank.

'Inseparable,' said Barbara. 'I never feel as sorry for pairs of cats who come to me in that sort of relationship as I do for the singletons. Aren't they beautiful?'

'Yes.' Delicately he stroked one lazily thrusting forehead, then the other. 'I still feel like that with you, you know.' Until he spoke he hadn't known he was going to say that, but he didn't regret it, although it made the guilt rise even more sourly in his chest.

'What brought that on?' The words were neutralised by the drawling murmur in which she said them.

'Perhaps – what's happened today. Makes you realise how precarious life is.'

'Ah, yes. You never know, do you, what's going to happen.'

He turned away from the richly purring cats, and she was staring at him with her prevailing lack of expression.

'Barbara. Just to get it out of the way. I didn't kill Caroline.'

With a leap of the heart he saw in her face that the idea was hitting her for the first time. 'Of course not, Bob.' She leaned back against the wires of the cage. 'You haven't got it in you to kill anyone. And even if you had, why would you kill Caroline?' Her face was blank again, not even registering her question. Which anyway, please God, was rhetorical.

'Why indeed?' He forced himself to kept his eyes on her. 'I'm sorry I even mentioned it, but the police will.'

'The police ... The police are so thorough, Bob' – she was only quoting Vernon – 'they'll find the killer.'

'And if they don't, they'll suspect me. And perhaps Jack.' He should have said *Or perhaps Jack*, kept away from the suggestion of conspiracy. With luck the police wouldn't think about it – either the true conspiracy to deceive or the false one to murder – so no need for him to offer anyone the idea. 'Jack hasn't got an alibi either, you know.'

'You said he was in the office.' Her face was suddenly alert.

'So he was, all on his own. Everyone else had gone home.'

'Alone long enough to get home and back?'

'I don't know. But I know he didn't.'

'How d'you know?'

He stared his amazement, ashamed of the brief gush of pleasure. 'Because I know Jack. You know Jack.'

'Not really, I don't think I really know – knew – either of them.'

'So you feel Jack *could* be a killer?' He turned back to the cats. The lilac stomach, now, was cradling the chocolate head.

'I don't know, I don't have an instinct one way or the other. I was thinking of his gun being used. No intruder could have known it was in that drawer. And it wasn't loaded.'

'There were cartridges in the drawer too. He showed me once. If anyone prowling about found it they could have loaded it, had it ready. Then when they were disturbed by Caroline and were afraid of being recognised ... ' It didn't sound very likely, nothing unpremeditated sounded likely in the face of that unloaded gun. 'I knew where it was, Barbara, I could have had a brainstorm. I can't remember anything between walking into that room and feeling I'd spent a lifetime gazing down at her – '

'Don't be ridiculous.' But she didn't know. 'Look, Bob, I think we'll do better not to talk about it. Put the water out for me, will you?'

'Yes, of course. Did Lionel depart all right this morning?'

'With his customary panache. Flossy's taken his place over, she's a nice placid old thing. You'll remember – Oh, perhaps not.'

No, he didn't remember Flossy, but he would remember her next time, and the other boarders; he was going to keep up the routine of going down the garden last thing with Barbara.

Flossy, untidy black and white moggy, was comfortably asleep, but opened one orange eye as he replenished her water bowl.

'I've got to call at the police station in the morning,' he said as they walked back to the house. 'Approve and sign my statement. Like Jack. What time's Jo arriving?'

'She mentioned afternoon, she'll probably be here when you get home.'

Having learned that her father was helping the police with their inquiries. But why had he used those words? They belonged to a stage that came later, when the police were confident ... 'If she gets here before I do, I think I'd like you to put her in the picture.'

'Yes, but she's not interested in the Lamberts.'

'She'll be interested in the idea of her father being suspected of Caroline Lambert's death.' Her hand against his went into spasm, and he took hold of it. 'I will be, I am, suspected, Barbara. It's inevitable.'

'I don't see why. You've no motive.'

She had made a statement, not asked a question. Not knowing he had wanted to be rid of Caroline, or why. Squeezing her hand to hide the sudden trembling of his, he turned to her on a reflex he couldn't control and saw that she was looking straight ahead, her impassive profile pale against the dark mass of the boundary trees.

'No motive, no.' he responded, trying to say it in the light way one tossed off an axiom. 'But the police will look for one.' He opened the back door. 'Jack's had time to get into bed. I'd better go up to him.'

'Offer him this,' said Barbara, opening and closing a drawer.'With some water. He may refuse to take it the way he refused to see the doctor, but just to know it's there could help him sleep.'

'Where did these come from?'

She smiled. 'It's only a mild tranquilliser, the minimum dose. I got them ages ago when the cats were being troublesome.'

'I see.' He welcomed the breathtaking pang that she had gone for help to the doctor rather than to him. 'D'you still use them?'

'Hardly ever.'

His mouth was framing the next question, and she touched it lightly with a finger. 'Go in to Jack, I'll see you upstairs.'

Reluctantly, feeling old and heavy although he was normally proud that he hadn't begun to thicken at the waist, Bob climbed the stairs and knocked on the guest-room door.

'Come in, Bob.' Jack was huddled in the twin bed farthest from the window, the bedclothes up to his chin. 'Sit down. What have you got there?'

'Tranquillisers from Barbara. There's a glass on your wash basin.'

Bob cast himself down on the other bed, on Barbara's batik spread, trying not to remember Caroline's dismayed reaction when once he had started to sit on the white lawn cover on her spare double bed. Barbara's spreads didn't crush, but even if they did she wouldn't have minded.

'Thoughtful of her. I'll be glad of them.' Jack's brimming, red-rimmed eyes sought reassurance over the bedclothes, which were now up to his nose. How would he stand up to the days ahead, the police persistence?

'You managed to get hold of Simon? How did he seem to take it?'

'He was very shocked.'

'Well, one would expect that. You'll see him tomorrow?'

'He's coming to the office.'

'You're going to the office?'

'What else can I do, Bob, for Chrissake? I can't go home, and there's nowhere else I want to go. Unless it's miles away, and that's not allowed.' Anxiously Bob watched as Jack gulped and sniffed and restored precarious self-control. 'No, I'll be best in the office. Simon said he'll be over at twelve and take me for a long lunch.' There was the fleeting glimmer of a smile.

'You wouldn't stay with him?'

Jack's forehead creased. 'He's got his own life, Bob.' Was Jack already quoting his son? But he would probably feel better at his club. Or with Vernon. As long as he was strong enough to remain proof against Vernon's kindness and understanding.

'Well, that's up to him and to you.' Bob paused, knowing the time had come to tackle things as far as they could or would be tackled. 'It's a mess, isn't it?'

'It's a mess.' They stared at one another.

'It's crazy, but I keep feeling guilty.' Saying that was to voice the assumption that he wasn't. 'Don't you?'

'God, yes. I feel terrible.' Jack's head had flopped to one side, his eyes now were gazing across the top sheet to the foot of the bed. 'If only. If only. Those are the most awful words in the world.'

'I know. We *are* both guilty. But not of murder.'

Jack's head had slewed round to him, their eyes were locked again. Bob hoped there was no question in his, to reflect the unavoidable question in his mind. He didn't think there was one in Jack's. Which didn't mean Jack knew the truth ...

'Not of murder,' Jack muttered. 'But if we hadn't ...'

'Things as they used to be wouldn't have stopped someone breaking in, finding your gun —'

'Loading it? Could that really have been a burglar, Bob?'

'Someone prowling, taking precautions ...'

'Whoever it was, if I'd come home in the old way I might have saved her.'

'So might I, if I'd got there earlier. But we didn't know.' The constant working on Jack to keep him safe in the hands of the police was going to take strength.

'If I hadn't left the gun and the cartridges together ... Oh, God, Bob!'

'That had nothing to do with — with anything else. If you'd been coming home in your usual way, that wouldn't have put them in different places. Tell me, Jack' — he realised he had been working towards the question — 'if I hadn't rung, were you going to come home tonight?'

'Of course not! I'd have let you know.' Jack actually looked shocked at the idea that he might have bust in on what happened every other Tuesday between his wife and his friend. Although he should have known it would be all right so long as he arrived before dinner. Caroline could never be caught *in flagrante delicto* before dishing up.

'Yes. You really were working late then, were you?'

Surely if he'd had a woman with him in the office he'd be using her for the missing alibi — in the territory where he and Bob found themselves the writ of chivalry didn't run. Unless she had told him she'd deny —

'I was on my own in the office, Bob. Maybe not working, maybe staring into space waiting for the telephone to ring, but on my own.' Jack stopped abruptly, pulling the sheet a fraction higher, knowing perhaps that he had told Bob more than he had said, told him his answering of Bob's telephone call wasn't necessarily a sign of innocence.

'D'you know if Caroline had any enemies?' Any other lovers, Bob added in his mind, reviving his recent faint hope. Having acquired one, having leaped the psychological barrier, it might be easier to acquire a second. A third might be easier again. And why did he assume he was the first? It would be a long time between every other Tuesday for a woman used to admiration. Oh, please God he was an also-ran.'

'Any enemies?' Jack screwed up what Bob could see of his face. 'Of course not, that's a ridiculous idea. She was a bit high-handed sometimes if things weren't just right, but I can't imagine ... Not to get *murdered*, Bob.'

'Her assistants?'

'There's only Mrs Oliphant and a couple of girls. Caroline's got one of them into horticultural college. Oh, God! The place is all right, Bob; whenever I've been in I've felt a good atmosphere. It's crazy even to imagine ...' There was no doubt Jack appeared willing, even anxious, to seal off a direction that might have deflected police interest from himself and Bob. Which could imply honesty as well as innocence ...

'All right. Then it must have been a very cool burglary that went wrong.' Bob forced Jack to meet his eyes, and for another long, unrevealing moment they stared at one another.

'That's right,' said Jack at last. 'A burglary that went wrong. There are obviously people who know I'm not lacking in this world's goods. Someone could have cased the place earlier, even taken a gamble and loaded the gun in preparation, I haven't looked at it for ages. Then got in again while Caroline was in the kitchen or the garden, and picked up the gun for insurance just as she ... God, Bob, that blood!' He began to sob noisily into the pillow.

'I know.' If Jack broke down in the morning at the police station, then said 'That blood!' like that, he might get away with it. If, of course, he hadn't blown it already.

'Jack.' The sudden panic made him breathless. 'You have managed to convince the police so far that things are exactly as they seem?'

'What!' Surprise brought an abrupt recovery. 'Of course I have. There's no alternative. And you'd laid dinner for me.'

'I knew you'd see that.' Now he was light-headed with relief. 'But it means keeping up a superhuman effort. Looking them in the eye, answering all their questions as easily and freely as if they were asking them twelve months ago. Are we going to be able to do it?'

'As if they were asking them twelve months ago.' Jack's wan face sprang to life. 'That's *brilliant*, Bob, that's how we'll do it. Blot out this last year when we're facing the police. Both of us.'

'Both of us. And we'll both keep reminding ourselves that we don't need to feel guilty, because we haven't committed a crime. That we're only concealing our private behaviour from the police because they'd link it to Caroline's death. It sounds ludicrous, it is ludicrous, but that's what they'd do. And to prevent it we've got to keep control of ourselves absolutely every moment we're with them. And with other people, too.' He was all right, nobody he knew was aware of their secret, but Jack's contacts could be as unreliable as Jack himself. 'Jack, I hope — '

'No one I know'll say anything, Bob.'

'That's good. That's *essential*. We mustn't relax our guard for a moment, however sympathetic ...' He thought again, nervously, of Jack vis-à-vis Vernon's gentle sympathy.

'I do realise that,' said Jack with dignity, lowering and straightening the sheet.

Bob welcomed the sudden access of wounded pride. 'I know you do. I've been trying to give myself some needed stiffening, too. And I have the spur of Barbara. I don't want to lose Barbara.' Another goose on his grave. 'The next thing we need is sleep, I'll leave you now.' He hesitated, but it would be inhuman not to risk it. 'I'm so desperately sorry, Jack.' He put his hand on Jack's shoulder.

'Thanks, Bob.' Jack brought a hand from under the bedclothes to acknowledge the gesture, but his face held firm.

'Just remember all the time,' said Bob as he got to his feet, 'that we didn't kill Caroline.'

As he stared down at Jack he was appalled to realise that the purpose of his statement had been to study the effect of it in Jack's face.

But Jack just said, 'Of course we didn't,' and stared back at him as expressionlessly as he had done the other times Bob had skirted the question neither of them could ask.

Chapter Seven

'Bright lad in that garage,' Detective Sergeant Jago Tabley commented, flopping down a little distance from the table across which his superior was preparing to confront Messrs Collins and Lambert. His long denimed legs stretched over the drugget floor as he slumped, until Detective Chief Inspector Hewitt's eyes travelling the length of his body brought him upright on his chair. 'So that when he says Collins seemed in a perfectly normal state when he went in for petrol, Collins probably was.'

'All right. But I'll continue to swear Collins isn't telling us everything. And although he had time enough before the petrol-buying as well as after it, he needn't have been planning murder, Jago.'

'Point taken. Lambert?'

'Oh, Mr Lambert had the time. He also had a private door and what if he was lucky would have been a private staircase. And a secretary who brought his letters in earlier than usual and then went off to the doctor's with his blessing. He had to tell us that, didn't he, the secretary's probably telling it this moment to Inspector Newby. It would be nice if someone else in Lambert's set-up tells him he or she wanted to see Lambert and found his office empty.'

'One hell of a risk.'

'He needn't have been intending murder, either. But if he was, no doubt he'd have locked his door and taken his private phone off the hook while he was away, so that he could tell anyone who tried to make an appointment on the regular phone or the intercom that he'd been in his office but not wanting to interrupt an important call. The phone worked when Collins rang. If Lambert had in fact nipped home and back, he'd have been glad to get that call. I wish there was a bit more help the home end. From the layout of her sitting-room there's no way of knowing if Mrs Lambert knew her killer.'

'Would a burglar have loaded Lambert's gun?'

'Probably not. But we've got to consider the possibility, Jago; the cartridges were in the same drawer. So.' Detective Chief Inspector Hewitt leaned back in his chair and laid splayed fingertips together. 'She could have been in the room with her husband or Mr Collins, or someone else she knew, not worrying about whoever it was walking over to that drawer in the corner where the gun was. Or she could have come into the room where someone she didn't know was waiting behind the door. Pushing it open would hide him or her, and then, when she'd crossed the room thinking she was alone in it and heard a sound, she'd have whirled round and the effect would have been the same. Then, Collins says he came in through the open back door, and if it really was open an intruder could have done the same thing. Plus the patio door to the sitting-room could have been open earlier, giving the intruder the chance to hide.'

'You still feel Collins and Lambert are hiding something, sir?'

'I still feel it, Jago. Don't you?'

'Maybe. Or maybe you've put the idea into my head. Murder, you think?'

'What else? Circumstances are hardly in favour of either of them. And ... Didn't you think Collins at least was a bit — well, a bit pulled together, as things were?'

'He's a solicitor.'

'Who's not usually on the wrong end of the questioning. I'd expect a solicitor to be horribly put out.'

'Shock.'

'Yes. Yes, I know.' said Hewitt irritably.

'The other fellow, the bereaved husband. He's a bit of a jelly baby. I wouldn't have thought — '

'Neither would I, but you never know. However, my beady eye's primarily on Collins.'

'Instinct, then, sir? In the absence of – '

'I've had plenty of time to develop an instinct, Jago. Yes, come in!' Hewitt raised his voice to the tap on the door.

'Mr Robert Collins to see you, sir. By appointment.'

'He's not a member of the royal family, Jenkins. Show him in. Good morning, Mr Collins,' said the detective chief inspector genially. 'Please sit down. I'm sorry about the fingerprint business, but in order to eliminate – '

'I understand why they took them,' said Bob shortly. His unique fingertips were still lightly defined in black.

'Of course you do. I hope you managed some sleep last night.'

'Not much.' In the bathroom mirror Bob's face had looked as if he hadn't slept at all. But somehow to his shame he had been out for five hours, his head against Barbara's shoulder, a cat behind his knees.

'That's understandable, sir. Now, Detective Sergeant Tabley's prepared a statement from what you told us last evening. If you'd just like to read it through, and then sign it if you agree it's a correct record of what you said. If there's anything you'd like to add, now's the time. Anything else you've remembered as the worst of the shock has worn off. Anything – different – in the Lambert house or garden, for instance. That's not a question we feel we can ask Mr Lambert just at the moment' – Hewitt offered the lie without blinking – 'so that your knowledge of the usual arrangements of the household could be helpful.' *To yourself as well as to the police*, Bob continued in his head. If he could pinpoint something different at Green Lawns that was more likely to have been caused by an intruder than a *persona grata*, he'd be doing himself a favour. Only he couldn't.

'I'm sorry, Chief Inspector. I didn't notice anything amiss when I went in, and afterwards ... Well, afterwards, I wasn't noticing.'

'That's understandable, sir.' To judge by the chief inspector's words if not his tone, he was an exceptionally understanding man. 'How is Mr Lambert this morning?'

'Coping. My wife gave him a sleeping tablet last night so he's a bit sluggish. He'll be along here any moment.'

'You didn't take one yourself?'

'No. I'm not a pill person. And I had my wife, Chief Inspector.'

'Of course, sir.' Hewitt blinked noticeably at last, perhaps in acknowledgement of his opponent's tactical victory. 'If you'd just like to read the statement.'

The detective sergeant had been as competent as he had expected; the account read to Bob like his own words, and there were no unfair emphases. When he had read it through a couple of times, he signed it without comment.

'Thank you, Mr Collins. I think you said last night you hadn't any current plans for going away?'

'I said that, Chief Inspector. I'm much too busy. And there's the inquest.'

'I was just coming to that.' He should have known he couldn't spring that sort of unpleasant surprise on a solicitor. 'The inquest is to be at 10 a.m. on Friday. It'll be a formal affair quickly adjourned for further police inquiries. As you know. And you know of course that you are obliged to attend. Is Mr Lambert going to continue staying with you and your wife?'

'He's going to his club. The Oakwood. I think he'd rather be with people who have nothing to do with his tragedy. Although – ' Bob felt the uneasiness that crept over him whenever he thought of Jack and Vernon alone together beside a whisky bottle.

'Yes, sir?'

'He seemed inclined last night to accept my brother-in-law's invitation to put him up for a while. In Dorking, don't worry. Vernon – Vernon Tennant, the antique dealer – doesn't know him and Caroline all that well and he's a widower with a sense of fitness.'

'That sounds a very satisfactory, suitable arrangement, Mr Collins. In so far, of course, as anything can be satisfactory in view of what's happened.' The chief inspector, with a brief, grave smile, got to his feet to show that the current encounter was over. 'We'll probably want another word with you some time,' he said amiably, 'but we know where to find you.'

'Any time.' Bob bowed ironically, not feeling relieved that he was free to go, suspecting Hewitt had scarcely begun.

'Well?' asked Tabley lazily as the door closed.

'All very correct, Jago. But I was thinking ... When we were working out possible scenarios before Collins arrived, one of us said he or Lambert could have helped himself to the gun. How about he *and* Lambert? Not just over the gun, I mean — generally. In which case there might not have been a phone call.'

'It's an intriguing thought, sir.'

'But at the moment, a thought is all it is.' Hewitt sighed. 'By the way, Jago, you'd better get a man over to talk to Mrs Collins before the working day's out.'

Jo threw herself on her father as he got out of his car, a whirl of indignation.

'Daddy! The police have been to see Mummy, they were here when I got home. They've seen you twice!'

'It's all right, Jo. It's all right, darling.'

It was better than all right, this unquestioning furious loyalty which so consolingly contradicted his anticipation, which had her eyes darting with proprietorial affection all over him, not resting on his, not asking him any questions because she could never consider him anything but innocent. Her long red hair was all over the place and there was a crumb in the corner of her wide mouth. 'At least you've had some tea,' he commented, actually laughing as he hugged her, approving as he always did the mingling of strength and delicacy in her face, her tall slim body and elusive scent. Her ribs seemed even more prominent than usual.

'Have I? Yes, I made some for Mummy when the police had gone. She was afraid they'd spoiled her scones but they hadn't. Daddy, it's dreadful.'

'I know. Poor Caroline —'

'Oh, that's dreadful, of course,' she said impatiently. 'But for you to find her!' For the first time, bringing them to an abrupt halt in the open front doorway, she concentrated on his face. 'You look awful, darling. And no wonder! All that upheaval for you both because of Caroline Lambert! Such an unimportant sort of person —'

'Jo!'

'I'm sorry, Daddy, I know she's dead, but that doesn't suddenly make her less trivial —'

'You only met her once or twice.' When Caroline had patronised her. And probably, to be fair, talked about things Jo considered beneath her notice. 'Let's find your mother.'

For a few exhilarating moments he had forgotten that things weren't as they seemed, but the sight of Barbara was enough to remind him as he and Jo went hand in hand into the kitchen.

'Darling, Jo tells me the police came to see you.'

'Yes. Just to ask me a few questions. I don't merit a statement.'

'I should think not!' fumed Jo.

'What did they ask you, Barbara?' He was glad Jo had offered them a hand apiece, perched on the edge of the chair between them.

'They asked me what I'd been doing yesterday afternoon and early evening. When I said I'd been at home they asked me if anyone had been with me. Samantha had, until half past six, so that was the end of that. Then they asked me if I'd had any contact with you, Bob, during that time —'

'That was why they came,' Bob interrupted.

'I told them I hadn't. I couldn't tell them anything else. They didn't stay long'

'Couldn't wait to get to Samantha,' growled Jo.

'They've got to do their job,' said Bob. 'Jo, it's good to see you. Apart from fury, are you all right?'

'Yes, of course, but I *am* furious.'

'They don't know us like you do, darling.' said Barbara drily. 'You haven't been down to the cats yet, you've never left them so long.'

'I'll go down in a minute. I've just got to make a phone call. I'll keep count . . .'

She whirled away, and Bob fancied the silence settling back as if it were a component of the air. He had to force himself not to break it, to remember how natural an element it had once been for him and Barbara to breathe. When she spoke first, he felt he had passed a test.

'Are you all right?'

'Yes. It's been a busy day, which has helped. Did Jack clear his things out?'

'Yes. He decided to accept Vernon's offer.'

'I thought he would.' He hadn't thought it, he had known it, it was a clause of Murphy's Law. If he himself had been playing with the insane thought of making Vernon his one and only confidante – a self-indulgence, he'd never actually do it – how much greater the temptation for Jack the sentimentalist, the man who wasn't married to Vernon's sister. 'But he'd be better with Simon.'

'Simon obviously doesn't think so.'

Upstairs Jo was being lucky enough to catch Simon, just through the front door from work before dashing under the shower and out again.

'It's Jo Collins. Simon, I'm so very sorry.' And ashamed that her pleasure at having an excuse to ring him was stronger than her concern at his loss. He hadn't approved of her as she had approved of him at their only sustained meeting, a partnership at a club dance engineered by their parents, and she hadn't expected to be in touch with him again.

'Jo – Collins? Jo! It's good to hear from you.'

He sounded as though it was. After that frost of an evening and his mother's murder. 'I'm working in Brighton now and just got home for a holiday. My mother told me.' She had to work to keep the elation out of her voice.

'You'd have heard anyway. It was on the news.'

'Oh, Simon.' He had already given her enough to make her glad the warmth had gone, leaving his voice appropriately flat and bitter. 'I suppose your father's with you. How is he?'

'He isn't with me. He's as well as can be expected and he's staying with your Uncle Vernon.'

'Uncle Vernon!' Jo was shocked to find herself more surprised than she had been to hear about the murder. 'Why?'

'Because he invited him, and the prospect must have appealed.'

'I – I see.'

'I'm not close to my father.'

'No.' And it was hard to imagine him being close to a mother like Mrs Lambert. 'Simon, would you like to meet?

Talk, perhaps? I mean — we're involved, too.' Surprisingly, in the end it had been pity for him rather than concern for herself that had prompted her forward move. 'I have to be in town tomorrow,' she lied, recovering her caution. 'Lunchtime.'

'Yes, I'd like to meet you for lunch, Jo. Could you get to the City? My pub's the Grapes of Wrath. Lime Street, EC3. Practically next door to the stockbrokers where I work. If you could manage ...'

'Of course I can manage. What time would suit you?'

'Can you make it twelve-thirty?'

'Surely.'

'Good. Look, I've got to go now.' His voice was suddenly a choke. If Caroline Lambert hadn't inspired love in her son, he was probably feeling remorse. Which might be as devastating. 'Bank's the nearest tube, Central Line,' said Simon hurriedly. 'Goodbye, Jo.'

'Good night, Simon.'

Jo flung herself downstairs and back into the kitchen.

'Everything as you would wish it?' Barbara turned round from the Aga with a half-smile.

'Probably.' Her mother had turned away again. From as far back as Jo could remember, there had never been questions. 'I'm going down to the cats now. Anyone I know?'

'Only Flossy at the moment. I'd better come with you and make a few introductions.'

'I hoped you would. Is Daddy really all right?' Jo matched her mother's easy stride, Mick skitting ahead of them.

'I think so. He's still shocked. And I can't think he enjoyed the police any more than I did. Jo ...' Barbara paused short of the playpen. 'They'll want to talk to him again, you know. He found Caroline.'

'It's absurd —'

'No, it isn't.' Barbara spoke sharply. '*You're* absurd, if you think the police aren't going to investigate a murder. And work with the material they've got.'

'They should knock on doors and ask people what they saw!' said Jo hotly.

'That's what they'll do as well, of course. But at the

moment Daddy's bound to be the one they're most interested in.'

To her renewed rage Jo felt her face crumpling, the heat of tears on her cheek. But her mother's normally undemonstrative arms were round her, her mother's body was shaking, indicating perhaps that she too was crying, although when they drew apart there was no sign of it.

'We're not the only ones.' said Barbara. 'Mr Lambert may not have – found Caroline, but he hasn't got an alibi either, he left his office after the staff had gone and no one saw him. It's as bad for him and Simon as it is for us. Well, much worse, of course.'

'Yes. Poor Simon.' But she was thinking about his father's lack of alibi ... 'No youngsters?' The run was empty.

'Two honeys until yesterday. How long can you stay?'

Her mother would never ask her not to go, tell her it was a comfort to have her there, but Jo hoped the unaccustomed question, the sudden turning away, might be a form of entreaty.

Anyway, she had things to do at home. 'I've a fortnight's holiday and no plans, I can spend it here. Would you like me to?'

'You're being silly again.' Barbara turned round smiling, letting Jo see she had been pleased with her response. 'Daddy and I would both love you to stay with us for as long as you can manage it.'

'Oh, I know Daddy –' Jo stopped abruptly. She had been very young when she realised she found her father easier to get on with than her mother, and had started trying to hide the fact. Being away most of the time, now, meant that she made more gaffes than she had done as a child. 'Daddy said he'd be glad if I didn't have to go straight off again,' she amended lamely.

'That's all right, then,' said Barbara coldly. Being suddenly cold was the only form in which Jo ever saw her mother's displeasure, except for the rare times she was really angry. But why would she care, now, about one more instance of her husband behaving more spontaneously than she did? Perhaps, thought Jo hopefully, her mother's reserve was something she couldn't help, something, even, she felt imprisoned by ...

'Come and introduce me. No, Mick, you can't come in with us. He still doesn't give up, does he? I miss cats like a pain sometimes, but it wouldn't be fair in the flat and I'm out such a lot. Mummy, I'm being head-hunted by Barry Fox!'

'Barry Fox?'

'The resident producer of the new theatre in the round at Highgate. He's a genius, don't tell me you haven't — Aren't they lovely?' She stopped beside the Burmese beauties.

'And so devoted,' said Barbara. Jo wondered if she had really heard irony in her mother's voice. 'Yes, they're gorgeous. They make me feel even more sorry for that lonely tabby next door.'

'First time away?'

'Yes. Name of Mr What. A stray who went from hell to heaven in the course of a day, and isn't sure yet that he isn't dreaming. I suspect his parents almost cancelled their holiday in his interests. But when they've come back for him once, he'll learn they'll come back again.'

'Yes. He's already learned not to be afraid of people he doesn't know.' Expertly Jo substituted her face for her hand against the butting jaw. 'Ouch, he almost broke my nose. I'll adopt him for the duration. And I'll help you generally as much as I can while I'm home, although I expect I'll be out quite a bit — '

'Daddy's been helping lately.'

'Has he?' Jo looked up, pleasure at the news shining in her pale, freckled face. 'You know, I've sometimes thought he was a bit jealous, the one unfair thing about Daddy — he has *his* kingdom, why shouldn't you have yours?'

'Impeccable logic, darling.' For once Jo was sure her mother's smile indicated amusement. 'But life isn't logical. Or fair. I rather hoped you were beginning to learn that.'

'Oh, I am. But I suppose one always wants one's loved ones to be beyond reproach, however cynical one becomes about everyone else.'

'Don't go that far, darling,' said Barbara, more quickly than she usually responded.

'I don't suppose I shall,' said Jo comfortably. 'I go on always expecting the best, I don't seem able to help it. I'm glad Daddy's joining in with the cats, he's just as fond of them as we are.'

'Yes. When Charlie comes on the bed, it's always Daddy's side. I hope you won't get bored at home, Jo, even with the cats.'

'Of course not. And anyway I'm going to try to keep up a regime of swimming and jogging, I feel a bit flabby.'

It was the best cover she could think up on the spur of the moment for whatever she might find herself wanting to do for her father. Jo smiled at her mother, unhappily aware of how useful it was to have the reputation of being somewhat guileless.

Chapter Eight

'Sorry to be a nuisance again so early in the morning.' Detective Chief Inspector Hewitt smiled at Bob apologetically across the interview-room table. The telephone message had come just as Barbara was about to take him to the station. 'But I've had a request which I feel I must carry out. It's contained in this letter.'

The detective chief inspector picked up the unevenly folded sheet, opened it out so that Bob could see irregular blocks of shadow through its thinness, and read aloud.

'"Ask Robert Collins about his relations with Caroline Lambert." That's all it says, Mr Collins. Like to see?'

Hewitt held out the paper and Bob had to grope for it because the cell-like space was swimming and his eyes couldn't tell him precisely where it was. Even the detective sergeant's features were blurred. But he just had the wit to put the paper down on his side of the table before focusing it, to hide the tremor in his hands.

Ask Robert Collins about his relations with Caroline Lambert. Yes, that really was what he had heard the detective chief inspector say. The words were put together in the way he had seen them over the years in films — the letters cut out of newspapers or magazines and stuck waveringly to a bit of cheap paper. *Ask Robert Collins about his relations with Caroline Lambert. Our Father which art in heaven.*

Was he praying? All he was sure of was that he had learned the new words as well and as finally as he had learned those old ones.

'This is absurd, Chief Inspector.'

The adrenalin flowed again, on a gush of hope, as he heard the outraged calm of his voice. All he had to do was what he had advised Jack. Act as if the past year hadn't happened. Jack ... Act as if Jack were as strong as he was.

'It's distasteful, Mr Collins. I can't abide anonymous letters.' Hewitt was speaking calmly, too.

'It's absurd,' Bob repeated. 'Oh, I know you've got to show it to me, that it says something about somebody. But not me, Chief Inspector.' Not too laid back. And anyway, he wasn't. He was terrified. 'My God ...'

'Just try to relax, Mr Collins.'

The shock of Detective Sergeant Tabley's intervention twisted in Bob's guts, but he tried to take the advice. 'How did it reach you?'

'Found among the morning's post,' said Hewitt. 'Addressed to me personally. I'm sorry, Mr Collins, but as you so sensibly say, I had to show it to you. Can you think of anyone you know who might be capable of compiling it?'

'No! But if a friend or acquaintance had that sort of sick mind I hardly think I'd be aware of it.'

'That's a fair point,' said Hewitt carefully. 'But you might think in a general sort of a way that someone you knew was behaving a little oddly.'

'I haven't even thought that, lately.' Apart from himself. Bob handed the paper back across the table, felt like wiping his trembling hands. 'Anyway, isn't the simplest and most likely explanation that whoever killed Caroline is trying to put the blame on me because I found her? And that could be someone I've never met.'

'Of course, Mr Collins, that could well be the case. If whoever killed Mrs Lambert was afraid he — or she — might be suspected of the crime.' *Not Jack*, Bob's subconscious told him consolingly, *an anonymous letter could be as bad for Jack as it could be for you.* 'All the same you'll appreciate that we can't ignore anything in a murder inquiry which presents itself in the guise of evidence. So I'm afraid this — communication — forces me to ask you if there has been anything in your friendship with Mrs Lambert that could possibly give rise to the impulse behind it.'

Detective Sergeant Tabley leaned forward.

'That sentence was worthy of a solicitor, Chief Inspector.' Which was more than he could say for the one he himself had just uttered. No need to celebrate his sang-froid aloud, for God's sake. He managed a sputter of laughter. 'I'm sorry, Chief Inspector, Sergeant, but it's so utterly ludicrous. I'll be angry in a minute, but so far I'm boggling. My wife and I are — were — friends of Jack and Caroline Lambert. I shouldn't think I've so much as been alone with Caroline in seven or eight years for more than a few minutes while waiting for Jack or Babara to join us. She was a fascinating, beautiful woman' — as a bonus for his nerve, his eyes actually filled with tears as he remembered the sense of life she had given him on two or three memorable nights — 'and I admired her. But in the words of the cliché I really am a happily married man.'

Had Jack been summoned too, for his reaction to his that repulsive piece of paper? He mustn't think about Jack until his own interview was over.

Hewitt was thanking him for coming in. 'I wish this hadn't been necessary.' Detective Sergeant Tabley jerked on the chair, which looked too small for him.

'Just about everyone in Britain knows I discovered Caroline's body.' Mustn't warm too passionately to his theme, protest too much. 'I do rather feel, Chief Inspector, that the odds are on my *not* knowing the paster-together of those crazy letters. But as I said, I appreciate that you had to show me. Will you be showing the press?' The possibility presented itself as he spoke, ran like poison through his body. 'I've already had reporters at the door and on the telephone and told them they've already printed or pronounced the whole truth so far as I'm concerned.' He was pleased with that, particularly as he felt so breathless it was a miracle he could speak at all. 'But if this letter's released ... And the inquest ...'

'Oh, I'm not intending to make this piece of paper public, Mr Collins.' Hewitt smiled at him reassuringly, but Bob wondered if the further words 'at the moment' might be trembling in the air between them. 'Although of course it will colour my thinking about Mrs Lambert's death.'

'Of course.' But his relief was still heady. 'I suppose you'll be showing it to Mr Lambert, too. It will upset him.'

'Yes, I shall be showing it to Mr Lambert, Mr Collins, although it's a task I shan't relish.' Detective Sergeant Tabley's chair scraped for a second time on the worn floor. 'I've no choice.' Hewitt leaned back in his own chair, sighing. 'So you can't help me at all? Well, I hardly expected it.'

He was smiling again, but Bob suspected irony in his eyes. Suspected, suddenly, that Hewitt's instincts had told him from the start that there was more to him and Jack than met the eye. All the more of a challenge to frustrate those instincts.

'I'm sorry, of course. And I'm getting angrier by the minute. Do you want me to stay and fume here?'

'I wouldn't dream of keeping you from your working day any longer, Mr Collins.' Hewitt was on his feet.

'I'll be on my way then, Chief Inspector.' Bob rose slowly, as if in no hurry to leave the limelight. And perhaps, anyway, Hewitt under his eye was less unnerving than Hewitt at large. Hewitt receiving another anonymous letter. Such as *Find out where Jack Lambert went to on Tuesday nights*.

For the first time Bob experienced a sense of anger against Jack. If he hadn't strayed from Caroline ... And someone connected with his extramarital affair or affairs had to be responsible for this letter, because there was no other source with the information to paste it together. How would Jack stand up to that realisation? How would he keep the furious activity of his brain, hurled by the shock of Hewitt's revelation into darting about among his hidden contacts, out of the eyes Hewitt would be looking into so keenly? Oh, he should have insisted on Jack staying with him and Barbara whatever the discomfort of it, he needed to encourage him, keep him strong, and now he felt afraid of so much as making a lunch date, it was on the cards that both of them had a tail ...

Golf. After the funeral they'd play golf together. As they did three Sunday mornings out of four. Hewitt could find it as significant for them not to play as for them to keep up their routine. He'd ring Jack and make the date. And try not to think, while awaiting Jack's admission that he had made someone among his exclusive acquaintance aware of his wife's retaliatory behaviour, that he himself, unable to recall the moment of his discovery of Caroline's body, might have been guilty of murder as well as adultery. There was no way he could hide from himself, any more, that the end of the affair had been his dearest wish ...

'All right, then, Mr Collins?'

'Thank you, Chief Inspector.'

How long had it taken for all that to go through his mind? The detective chief inspector's eyes were speculative. In Hewitt's presence he couldn't afford to slacken for a single second. 'Can we assume that the coroner will release the body tomorrow?'

'I think we can, sir. The injury leading to death was – unambiguous.' Briefly Hewitt dropped his gaze. 'So Mr Lambert should be in a position to make funeral arrangements for early next week. I'm afraid he – you too, sir – will have to be prepared for a press presence. These things get out.'

'I suppose so.' And the press would watch them both as keenly as the police.

Jack in the lobby looked unnaturally pale, but in charge of himself. It would have been another significant gesture in the eyes of their respective police escorts not to stop and speak. Not to demonstrate that they'd had no recent contact.

'Jack! How are you? Is Vernon looking after you?'

'Vernon's tremendous, Bob. I'm all right. You? Barbara?'

'All right, yes.' He hesitated. 'The chief inspector tells me you'll be able to arrange the funeral any time after tomorrow. Let me know details.'

'Of course, Bob, I'll ring as soon as I have them.'

The uniformed constable left Bob at the door, but he couldn't assume that a plain-clothes one wasn't going with him.

'You think?' asked Jago when the door had closed.

'Oh, but I do.'

'No smoke without fire, you'd say?'

'I would, Sergeant, and I'm not the cat's father.'

'Sorry, sir. You said you didn't relish it!' Jago jeered, unchastened.

'I relish the truth, Jago. I resent attempts to mislead me.'

'Is that what Robert Collins is doing?'

'I don't know.' Hewitt was walking about the room. 'There isn't a single soul as yet with an alibi for the time of Caroline Lambert's death.' The detective sergeant was still seated. 'Not even her son.'

'That I do know, Jago. Make sure I'm free for the funeral.'

Jo burst into the Grapes, EC3, at twenty minutes to one, and saw a good looking young man ensconced in a corner whom it took her a few seconds to recognise as Simon Lambert, even though she thought she had been cherishing his image.

'Sorry I'm late, Simon.' He was staring at her. 'I've had such a rush, I'm not surprised if there's a smut on my nose.'

The blue eyes blinked. 'There isn't. It's just ... I thought I remembered you.'

'I thought I remembered *you*.'

'That was badly put, I *did* remember you.'

'Me, too.'

The exchange broke down in smiles, during which Jo remembered the situation.

'I'm so sorry, Simon,' she said, grave-faced. 'Which sounds pretty feeble.'

'No. Sit down and keep this table while I go and order. What will you have?'

'Oh ... A cheese and tomato sandwich and apple juice with a sparkle. I'll give you the money when you find out how much —'

'I'd rather you didn't.'

Jo hugged her hands with her knees among the folds of her cotton skirt, watching Simon where she could in the scrum at the bar which had instantly taken him to its heart. It was wonderful the way the most disgusting event could throw up something good. She had been gloomily certain Simon Lambert hadn't given her a thought, and if his mother hadn't been murdered neither of them would ever have discovered that their evening together had left a memory with the other ...

'Here we are.' Simon disposed the lunch about the table and sat down beside her.

'Are you all right?' Suddenly overwhelmed, Jo picked up her glass, sneezing on the bubbles.

'I'm all right. Still in shock, I expect. It's a bit like a local anaesthetic.'

'Perhaps that's a help.'

'Perhaps. I don't know. I'm not fighting it.' He wasn't eating, either, he was just arranging pieces of sandwich different ways on his plate.

'That sounds wise,' said Jo, trying to control the hungry relish her own sandwiches had aroused in her.

'I'm sorry your father had to find —'

'So am I,' she said quickly, 'but it's nothing compared with ...' It might be the best opening she would get. 'Simon, I don't see how either of our fathers will be able to get on with their lives if the police don't discover who killed your mother. That must be why my feet took me to the Flower Bower when I was in Guildford this morning.'

'And walked you inside to buy a bunch of daffodils?'

'Yes, I think they would have done. But Simon, there was a notice in the window asking for an assistant.' Dear God, what was she admitting to? What had seemed logical and inevitable to her could to him seem irredeemably vulgar.

'The girls come and go. So?'

She had to carry it on now. 'So I found myself applying for the job. If it's anyone connected with your mother's work ... It seemed meant, Simon. And I'm an actress.'

It was time to meet his eyes. They stared into hers for an expressionless eternity before joining his mouth in a smile. 'You're a one-off job, Jo. When do you start?'

She took a gulp of apple juice while the giddiness wore off. 'Tomorrow. Mornings only. One of the two girls is about to start taking the mornings off to go to horticultural college and the manageress wants her to overlap with the new part-timer. Actually, I started today, in a way. I told Mrs Oliphant I had a lunch appointment in town, but she said if I wanted I could hang around for as long as I had time without any pay, just seeing how things worked, so of course I did. She had to go out, and you can guess there was no time

after that before one of the girls brought up the subject ...'
Jo faltered, shocked by the fact that she almost hadn't.

'Of the murder of my mother. Of course. Go on.'

'I'm sorry, Simon. Naturally I pretended I hadn't made the connection, and – and I asked a whole lot of naive questions.' She didn't know whether she was reassured or not by his snort of laughter. 'It was ridiculously easy, both girls had been overflowing with the news and made the most of me. I was all geared to ask things like did any sinister-looking character come in more than once but I didn't have to ...'

'More to the point to ask things like did Mrs Lambert tell you which of her male customers she slept with.'

'Simon!'

It wasn't just what he had said, it was the look of him, too. Suddenly red-faced, gasping at his loss of control, his disloyalty, tears starting in his beautiful eyes. Instinctively she reached for his hand, and he let her hold it.

'I'm sorry. Sorry I had to choose this moment.'

'I'm not. You've got to give way at some point, and I'm exceptionally sympathetic.' But trying to consolidate her success she withdrew her hand on a squeeze. 'I'm just shocked you should think ...'

'I used to worship my mother.' He was back in charge of himself, he was choosing now to tell her things. Or maybe he was just thinking aloud. Either way, if she kept quiet ... 'I suppose we were a sort of superior secret society, Mum and I, of which poor Dad wasn't a member. Poor Daddy, she'd say, kind and compassionate, and I'd say, Poor Daddy. She was strong and beautiful and wise. And angelically good, of course.'

Simon paused so long, staring into space, that eventually, reluctantly, Jo said, 'So?'

'Oh, as I grew up I saw gradually that the only qualities I'd got right were the strength and the beauty. But it wasn't until ... I went to see her as a surprise one night when she'd told me on the phone Dad would be away on business. I went quite late because I'd been on business, too. She took a long time to come to the door, and when she did ... she was wearing a dressing-gown and was sort of all to bits.

My mother was never all to bits. And I was aware of her mouth, somehow, it was — noticeable and red although she wasn't wearing lipstick. She took me into the kitchen very quickly and fussily — not like herself at all — but she hadn't quite closed the sitting-room door and I had time to see that although it was dark the curtains weren't drawn over the patio door and there were cushions on the floor. And then I heard a car engine very near, and when I mentioned it she laughed in an inane sort of way — not at all her usual laugh — and said next door needed his exhaust seeing to.'

'Simon, that really wasn't enough to make you believe —'

'She left me after a few moments and when she came back she was — normal, and when I went into the sitting-room it was tidy.'

'Oh, Simon, you couldn't really think —'

'And then I started remembering things. How she'd been sometimes when I'd telephoned in the evenings and Dad wasn't there, and how I'd met her in the Hilton another evening with a man she said was a floral wholesaler, and I remembered from the way she was looking at me that evening how she'd looked at me then ...' Simon winced the length of his body, Jo felt the vibrations through the bench seat. Simon sent temporarily mad by the revelation that he could no longer admire his mother? Men and woman had killed for less.

'I still think you're imagining it all,' she declared untruthfully, wanting to take the pain out of his face. Wanting to go on talking about Caroline Lambert. 'Was this recently?'

'During the winter.'

'Had your father seemed — any different?'

'Dad?' Simon's expression, to her infinite relief, relaxed into a mild contempt. 'Not Dad. He just goes his own sweet selfish way.'

'Selfish?'

'Oh, only by default. He keeps — oh, God, kept — Mum in luxury, felt rather proud and in awe of her if he thought about it, and lived his life his own way.'

'Other women, you mean?'

Her wildest dreams could not have had Jo asking Simon Lambert such a qestion, but he had given her the right, if only because she had happened to be sitting next to him when his nerve gave way.

'Heavens, I shouldn't think so!' Simon looked genuinely amused. 'Not Dad. Unless she'd driven him to it. Womanising, I mean, not murder. Oh, God!'

His face was suddenly terrible, and perhaps she was witnessing the moment in which it occurred to him that his father might be a murderer. Which meant he, Simon, was innocent. Unless it was merely occurring to him that his father might be accused of the crime committed by his son . . .

Jealous husband, disillusioned son, reluctant or overeager lover, burglar by chance or by the design of knowing what the Lamberts were worth in terms of money. A motivated cast of suspects. And the police were interested in her father. 'Simon. Listen. I'd hardly been on my own a moment with the two girls when one of them started telling me about a sales rep they deal with regularly coming in yesterday afternoon and stealing a photograph Mrs Oliphant had pinned up at the back of the shop.'

'Stealing a photograph?' Astonishment distracted him as she had hoped, and might be giving him a chance to push the worst thoughts away.

'She was out of sight round the back but there was a mirror . . . Mrs Oliphant had acquired a new camera a month or so ago and taken this photograph and then pinned a copy up. It had come out rather well and this man — a Mr Gibson — had his arm round your mother, jokily but rather intimately . . .' Again too late, she faltered. 'I'm quoting young Maureen. Apparently your mother hadn't much liked the photo being put on show, but she hadn't actually asked Mrs O to take it down. Well, Maureen saw this Mr Gibson reach up sort of sneakily and take the photo down and crumple it up into his pocket. When she eventually went back into the shop he looked a bit uneasy but of course he didn't say anything. No one else noticed the photo had gone because of being so devastated. They've only kept the shop open because they thought your mother would have wanted them to. Oh, Simon, I'm so sorry, this is a terrible conversation —'

'No more terrible than what's happened. You've been very

enterprising, Jo, learning so much without even getting paid.' He didn't manage to hold his smile. 'I'd hoped it was a burglar,' he said forlornly. 'But Dad's gun wasn't loaded.'

'A burglar could have loaded it, just ... Simon, I've told Maureen she should go to the police about that photograph.' She felt the shudder in the hand she had picked up again. 'I was right, wasn't I?'

'Of course you were. It's too much of a coincidence, Mum doing what she was doing, and then getting shot.'

'I didn't mean that. I just meant for getting at the truth. Anyway, you still don't *know* about your mother, Simon. And if she did have a lover, that doesn't put her beyond the pale. And perhaps you don't really know much about her relationship with your father. Do you?'

'Not much. No.'

'So they might just have been keeping up appearances.'

Simon's face actually brightened. 'Yes. So that if Dad had known about — about another man in Mum's life, he mightn't even have minded.'

'Exactly. These mystery men.' Jo pursued eagerly. 'If they exist they're probably one and the same. I know you said your mother introduced the one in the Hilton as a floral wholesaler, but perhaps she just thought that sounded better than sales representative. Simon, what was the name of the man with your mother?'

'I haven't the faintest idea.'

'Could it have been Paul Gibson?'

'It could have been Joe Soap. Sorry.'

'It doesn't matter. Simon, if you saw Paul Gibson you'd know if he was the same man! I'll find out tomorrow where he lives and we'll track him down and you can ... D'you realise we might be on the way to solving your mother's murder?'

'And plastering her indiscretions all over the tabloid press?'

'Not necessarily. I'm sure the police can be —'

'For God's sake stop being such a bloody little Pangloss. Everything for the best in the best of all possible worlds.'

'I'm sorry. I played him last term in a reading we did of *Candide*, it must have rubbed off.'

'Oh, Jo!' Although it didn't last, for a moment he had been laughing. 'Look, dear, you've done wonders, you've got that girl in the flower shop to tell the police what she saw, that'll take care of your Mr Gibson, the police will have him in for questioning, leave it there.'

'But Simon, if you can tell them that you saw him, too, it'll make them a lot keener to investigate Mr Gibson. And don't you want to find out if it was him your mother was with at the Hilton?'

Simon ran his free hand through his abundant hair. 'Yes on both counts.'

She tried not to be distracted by the gesture, which had left him so attractively untidy. 'Then I'll continue my investigation.'

More widely than she could tell him. It had been easy to discover from her father where Simon tended to hang out at lunchtime.

Chapter Nine

'Are you sure you're all right, Mr Collins?'

'Yes, of course, Gail.'

All day he had jumped each time the telephone rang, expecting it to be the police asking to see him again in the light of Mr Lambert's interesting revelations with reference to the anonymous letter, and really his secretary had been very contained, observing his nervous reactions from across the desk and not making her comment on them until five o'clock.

At first Bob had felt relieved that the onus of making the next contact was on Jack, but by the time Gail said good night, her gaze lingering on him for an unprecedented moment of anxiety, his ignorance of how Jack had fared at his second session with Hewitt and Tabley had become insupportable. And the office was the only place he could risk asking the real questions; at home Barbara and Jo would be within actual or potential earshot. If he hadn't left it too late and Jack was already on his way to a cosy evening with Vernon ...

He had seen his last client of the day, and the instant Gail finally closed his door he rang Jack's private line. The relief of Jack answering reminded him of the last time, and Caroline on her sitting-room floor.

'It's Bob.' He was out of breath. 'How was it this morning?'

'I'm still at large.'

He had to get straight to it. 'Jack, you realise that letter has to have come from your direction? No one my end knows anything.'

'I don't think you're being terribly bright, Bob. Not recognising the third possibility.'

'Which is?'

'Caroline. Someone else she was – seeing. I'm sorry.'

'It's all right.' He had said that on a reflex before properly realising that Jack had just apologised to him for the suggestion that he might not have been his wife's only lover. The situation he had longed for. He had to choke on another paroxysm of that terrible waiting laughter, but it wasn't solely an appreciation of the irony, it was also relief at realising Jack was right, the most likely explanation of Caroline's murder was that he had shared her. The relief made it easy to go through the motions. 'Look, Jack. I knew – we all knew – I mean, the three of us' – it was in the past, but the exclusion of Barbara still hurt – 'that it was just an affair. That Caroline loved you' – he had made Jack wince too, he heard the sharp breath – 'and that I love Barbara. It wasn't male pride that blinded me. Just panic and native pessimism. Did Caroline – did she actually tell you about anyone else?'

'No. I think I only knew about you because you hadn't stopped your visits, and with Barbara –'

'Yes. I see that. Jack, if Caroline was killed by another – another man she knew, a man who wrote that letter, she'd told him my name. And when I paid my regular visits. But she never said a word to me about – anyone else.'

'That doesn't matter, Bob. Don't you see?' The insistent whisper seemed to be inside his head. 'Caroline needn't have said a word to Mr X either, it could have come out in the most innocent way that Bob Collins, family friend, stayed at Green Lawns every other Tuesday night. And if Mr X thought you were innocent – I'm sorry, Bob, but you know what I mean – he would have assumed I was to be there as well. In which case careful timing with his killing could have given him a pair of innocent red-handed suspects.'

'If he'd gone to the house intending to kill.'

'Well, yes. And if he hadn't, he could still capitalise on his luck.'

It was as likely as it was attractive. 'You worked all this

out in the moment of Hewitt showing you that letter?' He remembered his own reactions.

'I suppose so. I couldn't believe it was my end and I knew it wasn't yours. There was nowhere else.'

'You've said all this to the police? Oh, Jack, forgive me!'

'What for?'

'For suggesting you'd tell them you suspected your wife – '

'I'm past that sort of squeamishness, Bob. Yes, I did tell the police it looked as if Caroline must have had a lover. As well as leaving you and me innocent all round, it's the most likely explanation. Far more likely than the burglar theory, with that unloaded gun ... And a breaker and enterer would hardly have written an anonymous letter.'

'You've kept a pretty clear head, Jack.' Far clearer than he had himself, spotting that common sense and their own interests coincided. He felt his apprehension over Jack vis-á-vis the inquest beginning to dissolve. 'I'd better be frank, hadn't I, next time I'm summoned, tell them we've talked it over and both see things the same way? That we're white as white, and Caroline's a dead adulteress?'

'She was an adulteress, Bob.'

And you were her adulterer ...

How ready had Jack been, really, to accept those Tuesday visits?

He pulled his mind back from the path it had suddenly tried to take. 'I'm sorry I leaped at you the way I did, Jack, but knowing the letter couldn't have come from my end I had to look somewhere else and didn't come up with your logical conclusion.' Whatever he thought or didn't think, it was hard to equate the cool customer at the other end of the telephone with jolly Jack Lambert. It had taken him seven-odd years to learn that the soft impression made by Jack was a façade. To be able to stand up so constructively to Hewitt and Tabley while reeling from Caroline's death – discovering a dead lover you were out of love with was nothing to being presented with a dead wife you had been married to for twenty years – indicated exceptional strength of character where Bob, despite his fondness of Jack, had unthinkingly assumed there was exceptionally little. Unless ... 'I've felt churned up all day after sensing this morning that Hewitt suspects me. Must be an instinct, it can't be through anything I've said or done. So far I'll swear I've managed to behave as if it was early last year.'

'I'll swear I have, too. A good idea of yours to put it that way, gives one a guideline. You're probably imagining about Hewitt.'

'No. And I was there, Jack. Moments after she was killed.' Moments before? 'Whatever our theories, we can't get away from that.'

'We can try not to dwell on it.'

'You're right again. I'll try to dwell on the fact that thanks to you we have the formula to explain our innocence. Even if the mystery man is never found, his existence is so likely they'll hardly be able to accuse us – me, I mean' – he didn't mean only himself, of course – 'of killing Caroline. Or even suspect you or me of marital infidelity.' He'd also do his best to keep his mind off the quality of his life following an eventual open verdict. 'Let's play golf as soon as we can. Soon after the funeral.'

'Let's do that, yes. Look, I'll have to go now, Bob, my last client's waiting.'

'A long day.'

'I've arranged it like that.'

'Yes, of course. I'll see you in the coroner's court in the morning, Jack. Thank heaven Hewitt's not producing that letter. He said the inquest is pretty well bound to be adjourned once you and he and I have gone through our paces.'

'Let's hope he's right.'

'I'm almost glad now that he's rehearsed us so well.'

Working out the tactics of his part in Jack's strategy for the next time he found himself up before Hewitt and Tabley, feeling unfamiliarly cheerful in his new confidence that neither he nor Jack would offer a grip on the slippery slope of their proclaimed innocence to coroner or to police, Bob found himself among the usual dense crowd on the Underground platform without any recollection of having got there. Realising only in retrospect, from the throb of his nose and cheeks, that outside the spring evening was cold.

But that had happened on other evenings, when his mind had been wrestling with his clients' business rather than his own; there was no surprise in it.

The surprise was in the sudden sensation of being propelled towards the edge of the platform, of actually being guided through the throng towards the live rail and the crescendoing draught of an approaching train. It was such a surprise he wasn't even struggling, he was observing it happening as if he were outside his body and watching, only if he had been he would have been able to see behind him, identify the steady force which had him on the move, irresistible because he wasn't resisting it ...

On the very edge of the platform the pressure ceased, and as the train swept into the station the momentum went into reverse, drawing him back into the front line of waiting passengers. As the train doors opened the people to each side of him were looking at him strangely; two men exchanged glances, a woman seemed to be going to say something, then smiled, reddening. He smiled back as they squashed on, smiled at the men as well, forcing cheerfulness. If he seemed like a potential suicide having second thoughts, one of them might decide to do something about him ...

Had he been a potential suicide having second thoughts? The question jagged through Bob's brain, rendering him so instantly weak he was glad for the first time in his life of his back against the partition, the press of people against his chest. If he didn't know whether or not he had killed Caroline, couldn't remember what had happened before his conscious self was aware of her lying on the sitting-room floor, how could he be sure that for a few seconds he hadn't intended to take his own life, too? He had moved forward like a zombie, without fear or feeling, and backward as numbly ...

No! The people pressed against him looked at him again as he tried to jerk straight, sloughing off his newest and worst fear. Someone had pushed him. Someone had pressed against him from behind and walked him forward. Then, with perfect timing vis-à-vis the approaching train, had hauled him back and disappeared into the crowd. Hadn't been able to disappear but of course hadn't needed to, had only to cease the pressure to be instantly unconnected with him. The crowd had been so dense no one could have seen anything happening below head level — what about his vague running fantasy of two people having it off standing up on the train without anyone being the wiser ...?

He was holding on to the anonymous letter now, like a drowning man. He hadn't composed it and sent it to Hewitt, of that at least he was sure. So thinking of what that morning had seemed so horrible should help him now not to think of something infinitely worse: that he might be a murderer whose conscious mind had blotted out the killing ...

He was reacting in exactly the way the person who had pushed him was hoping he would react, allowing himself to be rattled, to behave with uncharacteristic nervousness under the eye of the tail Hewitt had probably put on him. The tail wouldn't have seen his assailant in the scrum, but he would have seen the subject of his vigilance lurch forward like a man possessed. And the assailant would have realised that if Bob tried to tell the police what had happened it would do him more harm than good ...

At Waterloo he stood well back from the platform, telling himself it was other people he was afraid of. He had to sit in the car for a few minutes at Dorking before he could get the strength up to drive home.

'You look ill, Bob.' Barbara was arranging spring flowers on the hall chest when he opened the front door. 'Tired out.' She and the space around her both needed redecorating, both were beloved as they were. She let his face linger against her shining hair. 'I'm sorry now I asked Vernon for supper. Bringing Jack if Jack wants to come.'

'I'm not sorry.' Now he had made that telephone call he didn't need to be afraid of Jack.

Didn't need to be afraid of Jack in the old way, that he might break down.

'Good.'

He held her hand on their stroll to the kitchen. Jo was there, and hurled herself forward to bear-hug him.

So long as they never knew, nothing else mattered. But to keep it that way he had to trust himself. Remind himself constantly that all he had done against them was to sleep for a year with Caroline Lambert. Nothing else.

If only he could stop recreating the sensation of being propelled towards the underground live rail. Part of it, of course, must be delayed shock, but the other part was still an attempt to analyse the sensation, discover whether he had been active or passive ...

'How did you get on with the police?' Barbara was at the Aga, her back to them.

'You might know.' He was grinning into Jo's anxious face, he still had his outrageous year-old ability to dissemble. 'They hoped I might have remembered something at Green Lawns that struck me as unusual. I wish to God I could.'

He hadn't known if he was going to tell them about the anonymous letter until he heard himself not doing. He knew at once he had taken the right decision. As things were, he was gratefully convinced that the conduct it obliquely accused him of hadn't so much as entered Barbara's mind. Planted there so obscenely, wouldn't it grow despite the initial attempts she would make to dig it out?

'That's their third go.' Barbara turned round, looking faintly puzzled. Jo was growling.

'Probably my own fault. I put the idea into Hewitt's head that I might remember something as the shock wore off. I told you it was so bad I couldn't remember my first reactions. I still can't. I was just there, looking at her. Hewitt's obviously hoping he can help my memory recover.' All at once he was so weak and tired he had to make himself sit rather than fall into the nearest of the Victorian bentwood chairs around the kitchen table. The half-truth he had just told them, withholding the heart of it, had made him feel even more disloyal than he had felt before. No chance, any more, of moments of forgetfulness. But at least he wouldn't be paying for them when they were over. Smelling the meal Barbara was preparing was like being forced to eat it, it was making him feel physically sick when all he'd had since breakfast was half a beefburger and innumerable cups of coffee. 'I'm afraid I'm not going to be very hungry tonight.'

'Never mind. Would you like me to come to the inquest?'

'I don't think so. I'd like you to come down with me now to the cats.'

'Leave me out, will you? I've a phone call to make.' Jo had changed enough in the past few months to make Bob suspect her of being tactful.

The evening had turned steely, and colour was drained even from the bright young fists of leaves on the horse chestnut which was the pride of their garden. Mick and Charlie joined them along the way, one from each boundary hedge, and froze scornfully outside the run where kittens were tumbling, ears and tails down.

'Don't be so disgustingly superior.' Barbara whipped a hand along Charlie's spine, forcing his tail up as she reached it. His ears followed suit. Mick jumped him while he was still mellowing, and Bob and Barbara got the door open and closed while the pair of them were still wrestling. 'Ben's gone but Dorothy's taken his place.'

'Dorothy!' He didn't have to be told, now, where Ben had been, and when Barbara rejoined him after her inevitably slower progress he was already inside the cage and caressing the small black and white newcomer. 'She looks scared to death. First time away?'

'Yes.' Barbara added a hand, and the purring swelled as the cat dashed her nose against it, her tail rising against Bob's. 'She's yet to learn they'll come back. She's named for a deceased maiden aunt ailurophile who left them a lot of money. Her people are both extroverts, I enjoyed their visit.'

'How long's she with us?'

'Only a couple of days. They've taken their daughter to a new school. Boarding.'

An unearthly wail drowned their voices as well as Dorothy's purrs.

'Jingpaws is back!'

'I'm afraid so. More demanding than ever. I think he's the most unrewarding visitor I've ever had.'

'Doesn't he get love at home?'

'He gets worship, that's probably his trouble. He'll accept caresses if he's in the mood, but if he isn't, or suddenly stops being, he'll draw blood. The largest appetite I've ever coped with, too, but his people know that and pay for it. He's beautiful, isn't he?'

'Yes.'

They admired Jingpaws from outside his terrain. 'I don't go in unless I've something to give him, he prefers it that way. All Siamese have voices, but I've never heard one like his.'

Jingpaws raised it again in illustration, a piercing shriek of bad temper and dissatisfaction. Then, slowly and gracefully, he sank into a circle and closed his huge blue eyes.

'How're you feeling now?' asked Barbara, as they moved on.

'Much better.' It was true, and despite his fears he had managed a few more moments of forgetfulness, which came painfully to an end as he spoke. 'It's good to come down here. Barbara ...'

'Yes?'

'I love you, you know.'

He forced himself to look into her face as he spoke, and saw something flicker across her eyes. She said, 'We'd better go back. You haven't washed or changed yet, and after that you'll feel better still.'

He seized her hand. 'Do you love *me*?' Respecting her nature he hadn't put her on the spot for years. But suddenly he couldn't help it.

'You know I do.' Her eyes hadn't wavered. But he scarcely had time to register his happiness before it was swept away on an agonising wave of anxiety. Barbara's love was all in the world that mattered, but he had put it at risk for nothing and it was only through luck and his own hypocrisy that it was still his. At any moment he could fall off the tightrope and it would be gone.

'Have you and Jack been in touch?' she asked, as they turned away from the kittens. Mick and Charlie had disappeared.

'We had a word on the telephone. I was reassuring him about the inquest mark one.' It was for Jack to tell people, or not, that he too had been summoned back by the police. 'It'll take about ten minutes, a total formality. Which I'm afraid we can't expect of its resumption. Caroline's body should be released by the coroner and then Jack can make arrangements for the funeral. He didn't say anything about coming tonight.'

'He wouldn't know I'd invited him until he got back to Vernon's. And he may decide not to, although I asked Vernon to try and persuade him.'

They ran the last steps of the way as the rain, which had been threatening, came suddenly, soakingly down. Bob had taken his time over a bath, sorted out drinks, and tried to read the front page of the *Evening Standard* by the time Jack followed Vernon into the house, the pair of them shaking water drops off their hair.

'Actually, it's a bit warmer.' Vernon put a hand on Bob's arm. 'How are you, Bob?'

'I'm all right. The police had me back this morning.'

'They had me, too,' said Jack, his eyes on Bob. 'Wanted me to go through it again. Through what? I asked them. Your statement, they said. All two paragraphs of it.'

'It was a burglar,' said Barbara. 'Who had the time and the luck to find Jack's gun and the cartridges. I can't think why the police — Is there a fire upstairs, Jo?'

'Sorry!' Jo tumbled to a halt on the bottom step. 'I was just looking forward rather specially to seeing Uncle Vernon.' She had changed out of her shirt and jeans into a flowing, glowing, green gown, and was transformed, in her father's eyes, into a creature of shimmering, mysterious beauty. He thought he heard Barbara, too, catch her breath.'

'You're lovely, Jo darling.' said Vernon.

Jo moved forward slowly and gracefully to kiss him. 'It's wonderful to see you, Uncle Vernon. Mr Lambert.' She held out a regal hand, making Bob hope she might be offering them a prevision of her presence on the London stage. 'I'm so very sorry. How's Simon?'

'He's all right.' Looking confused, Jack dabbed a kiss at the hand. 'Well ...'

'Come and have a drink,' she suggested consolingly. 'We're drinking in the sitting-room tonight and eating in the dining-room. To match my dress.'

She took their orders and carried the drinks round as Bob dispensed them, then went and sat by Vernon on the sofa. Watching them and the usual evidence of their mutual affection, Bob was assailed afresh by a crazy desire to confide in Vernon, to pour out his disloyalty, his stupidity, his deceit to that gentle smile, ask for the forgiveness he would never accord himself. Even if he didn't get it he would surely get understanding, he had never known Vernon pass a harsh or hasty judgement ...

For God's sake, he was Barbara's brother.

'All right, Bob?'

Vernon was looking at him, his thin face gnomishly puckered in anxiety.

'Yes, I'm all right, Vernon. But you know ...'

'Of course. The police aren't worrying you, though, are they?'

'I don't suppose so. I mean, I don't suppose they intend to. I do get the feeling the chief inspector would like me to have had something to do with Caroline's death.'

'I suppose one can understand that,' said Vernon reflectively, 'if he finds himself at a loss. Seeing you were on the spot. But even chief inspectors can't make something out of nothing. They'll find witnesses. Fingerprints ...'

'I hope so.' At least his fingerprints were expected to be there. To be everywhere but Caroline's bedroom, and thank God that was a place where she had never invited him. The only time he had properly crossed the threshold had been when he put her night dress back, and then he had been wearing her kitchen gloves ...

Vernon and Jo kept dinner going, assisted, when the plates had been cleared, by Mick and Charlie. Mick forced Jack to move back from the table so that he could sprawl upside down across his knees. Charlie on Bob's lap seemed to steady his heartbeat.

'We aren't staying late,' Vernon announced after coffee. 'I'll come down to the cats with you, Barbara, and Bob and Jack can have a few private moments to talk about the inquest.' He smiled round them, his gaze coming to rest fondly on Jo. 'And Jo – '

'Jo'll do some clearing up. Time she stopped treating this house like a hotel.' Jo shot to her feet.

'Cover your dress?' Bob suggested. It had always been he rather than Barbara who thought of things like that.

'Don't fuss, Daddy. And shoo.'

He led Jack to the sitting-room. 'Brandy?'

'All right. Thanks. And Vernon's driving. He treats me as if he was my old nanny, Bob. It's helped.'

'Nannies take the pram handle, not the wheel.' The feeble joke was a reflex attempt to prevent Jack's eyes spilling out the tears sparkling in them, although after the cool-brained, emotionless Jack he'd had on the telephone earlier, Bob found himself relieved to see them.

They were both so awkward that they made a few comments on the change in the weather. Casting about for another subject Bob was tempted to tell Jack what had happened on the Underground platform, but the fear he had been unable as yet to stifle, that no one else had been involved, helped him withstand it. 'I'm not telling Barbara about the letter. You haven't told Vernon?'

'No.'

'You're glad you went to him?'

'Yes.' Jack looked embarrassed. The appearance in his face of a trivial emotion was another reassuring glimpse of the old Jack. 'It wasn't that I didn't want to stay with you and Barbara, Bob, but I just felt ... in the circumstances ...'

'You don't have to spell it out. Does Vernon try to talk about things? He's hardly said anything to us, just been extra-specially nice and consoling, if that's possible for Vernon.'

'That's the nanny-thing I was meaning. No, he doesn't talk about it, apart from saying at intervals that he can understand how I must be feeling.'

'I'm sure he can, I really think he suffers with us.'

'He seems like a happy man, contented, so far as his own life's concerned?'

'I think he is, although he'd never say so, one way or the other. He's been in the antique trade since he was a teenager, and he told me once he was a teenager when he met his wife. He was obviously terribly lonely when she died, although he never said so.'

'No children? I haven't liked to ask —'

'No. That could explain his devotion to Jo. How long d'you think you'll stay with him?'

Jack looked helpless. 'I don't know. I can't take any decisions at the moment. Perhaps after the funeral ...'

'After the funeral. Yes. Of course. Jack, we've been sent in here to talk about the inquest. Hewitt's told you the coroner will release Caroline's body tomorrow? That's why you'll be able to arrange the funeral –'

'He's told me.'

Jack stared bleakly through him. Having discovered that there was more to his friend than he had realised, Bob began to wonder what Jack was thinking.

Whatever I have done, you, my friend, have had my wife?

He only had Caroline's word for it that Jack had been the first one to defect. And reassuring though Jack's assessment of his wife's murder appeared to be, Jack was in a position to punish him.

Chapter Ten

Cold floor under inadequately shod feet. Cold hands which never got properly dry before being plunged back into cold water. Cold body because of the Flower Bower not being the sort of establishment where employees could wear outdoor clothes while serving customers. Door constantly ajar and nowhere to escape the draught.

Yesterday's hour of becoated, dry-handed conversation hadn't given her a clue. Working in a flower shop, Jo had decided by the time she was gratefully cradling her mid-morning mug of coffee, was a real test of stamina, mental as well as physical. It was a constant struggle not to let her powers of observation and deduction be hijacked to swell the energy needed simply to try to keep warm. At least, though, she had none left over for studying her mental picture of her father defending himself in the coroner's court. He and her mother had been too preoccupied to register the uncivilised hour she had left home.

The only pleasant surprise of the job was the layered, pervasive scent.

It might have been easier if she had discovered a hitherto unknown talent for wrapping flowers and leaves attractively, but by her first coffee break Jo realised she had no natural aptitude. At least the daffodils and tulips, the most popular purchases of the moment, were already encased in cellophane tubes, but it could only be a matter of time before Mrs Oliphant suggested she found a job more suited to her abilities. And Jo was, of course, on the outside of the bond currently uniting the manageress and her two assistants in their mutual shock and sorrow at the violent death of their proprietress. Anyway, she had probably made the most of being taken on at the Flower Bower already, and with a bit of luck she should be able to learn that morning how to follow it up.

Luck had been there at the start. Jo and Maureen had arrived together at the shop door so that they'd had a moment of privacy right away in the cubbyhole at the back while reluctantly shedding their coats. But when Jo murmured her question, Maureen snapped back that no, she hadn't got round to it and yes, all right, she would when she had the time, there was no hurry.

'There is a hurry, Maureen, really. You see, trails go cold.' She had to force herself not to sound intense, not to bully, or what she had found out would go for nothing – or for the lesser impact of her rather than Maureen getting in touch with that detective inspector, and then Maureen even perhaps denying that she had seen Paul Gibson take down the snapshot of himself and Simon's mother from the public place where Mrs Oliphant had pinned it.

'Trails go cold! You really saying you think Mr Gibson killed Mrs Lambert?'

'Of course I'm not. I'm only saying the police ought to know everything that could have a bearing –'

'And I'm saying I'll go and tell them when I get round to it.'

'Would you like me to come with you?'

'No, thanks. And do me a favour, will you? Get off my back.'

'Sorry. I just thought you might be scared to go on your own.' Jo had already decided that the round baby face and self-satisfied expression hid a massive egotism which evaluated all courses of action according to their effect on Maureen herself. If she had come to the conclusion overnight that it would be uncomfortable for her to go to the police, she'd simply decide not to go. But to give the impression of being scared might strike her as an even less desirable alternative. At least, by now, with Maureen as a source of information clearly dried up, Jo felt it was a risk worth taking.

'Well, I'm not. Good morning, Mrs Oliphant.'

Mrs Oliphant, her demeanour subtly less wan than it had been the day before, showed no sign this morning of going out, and it was impossible to detach the girls from the counter and from her admonitory gaze — Jo didn't want to be sacked for subversion, any more than for incompetence, before she had done all she could with her chilly job. Joan, in the moments Mrs Oliphant was taken up with the Flower Bower's more lavishly spending customers — she had a nose for them the moment they were over the threshold — showed signs of still being prepared to talk about her boss's death, but Maureen stayed sullen and postponed her coffee break until Joan and Jo were back at the counter. Joan, of course, had been told by Maureen at the time about the incident with the photograph, had in fact herself wondered aloud in Maureen's presence whether the police ought to be told, but hadn't gone so far as to urge Maureen to approach them. Jo, seeing the cornerstone of her research crumbling, begged Joan to try.

'She'll only be telling them a *fact*. Simply that she saw your Mr Gibson take the photograph down when he thought no one was watching him. He might only have wanted to spare himself being asked questions, being drawn into a murder inquiry. I mean, it wasn't as if there was anything between him and Mrs Lambert ...' Jo hesitated, plunged on. 'There wasn't, was there, Joan?'

'Mrs Lambert was married!'

Joan wasn't as dizzy as Maureen, but the comment still seemed uncharacteristically severe. Jo reflected on the puritan reactions of her own generation to any sign of illicit sex among their elders. They were aware of two sets of rules. Well, so was she, when it was a question of the older people she knew, loved and respected. That was why she had found it outrageous that the police were round her father about Simon's mother's death.

'Yes, I know. But they could have had the odd business lunch together.'

Her heart leaped to hear Joan's reminiscent giggle. 'They did. Maureen and I saw them once. In the restaurant part of the Antelope. We'd never been in there, just thought we'd have a change, and there were Mrs Lambert and Mr Gibson, leaning towards one another across a little table. Mrs Lambert looked ever so surprised to see us. Not very pleased for a moment, I thought, but then she was saying hello and he was too, he recommended the moussaka, I remember.'

'Have you been there since?'

'No! You need time for a place like that. No good if you have to keep looking at your watch, wondering if the real price of freshly cooked whatever is going to be a telling-off from Mrs O.'

'Perhaps it's Mr Gibson's local.' Jo had drunk her coffee and her hands were as cold as they had been before she took the mug between them. She curled her thin-soled shoes round the bar of the stool where she was perched.

'Hardly, he lives in London. Only comes out here on a Tuesday ...'

Joan's voice died away, and her shocked eyes stared into Jo's. Jo managed to say, casually, 'Probably only coincidence, but I do think Maureen ought to tell the police what she saw.'

'I know. I'll try —'

'Joan! Jo! Shop!'

'Where in London does he live?' asked Jo quickly, as they came to attention.

'I dunno. It'll be on his card, I suppose. Somewhere in that pile.' Joan pointed vaguely over her shoulder as they ran out front.

'Other people would like a coffee, too,' said Maureen crossly, flouncing past them.

'Maureen's a bit moody?' Jo suggested to Joan when the straightforward sales awaiting them had been successfully completed, and she was wiping her hands on a sheet of the florally decorated kitchen paper hanging behind the counter which she had decided was more effective than her skirt.

'Yeah. Can be. But you'll find her all right. I think she's just worried about what she saw. Wishes she hadn't. You know.'

'Yes. But I can't say anything else to her. You really will, Joan?'

'Yeah.'

'Anything wrong, Jo?'

'Nothing, Mrs Oliphant. I was just asking Joan to explain ...' But the fact that she was a subversive intruder into the small mourning circle of the Flower Bower was now clear to Mrs Oliphant's subconscious, and it wasn't going to take long for her resentment of Jo's presence to erupt to the surface in a suggestion that she didn't quite fit in. Jo managed to start on the pile of business cards stacked on the shelf in the back room while wrestling with half a dozen sprays of unseasonal chrysanthemum she had been asked to combine with a couple of knobbly background stems eager to shed their leaves, and found Paul Gibson's card almost at the bottom of it when she was putting her coat on at twelve noon. Scribbling the details into her diary, she decided it would be easier to tell Mrs Oliphant by telephone than face to face that she wouldn't be in the next or any other morning.

By eleven-thirty Jack was back in his office. The inquest had been the doddle everyone had told him it would be this first time around, although he had felt a bit concerned for Bob, so pale and straight and serious, going through it all again under the eye of the coroner and his officers and the press and of course the sharp-eyed Detective Chief Inspector Hewitt and his disturbing sidekick. The reporters could only have been looking for human interest; they knew as well as everyone else that this first leg of the inquest was merely a formality. When it was resumed things would be different, if the police by then hadn't nailed a culprit.

There was a client waiting, and his worries had to be postponed while he tried to explain the intricacies of double taxation. But when he had seen the client out, Jack could only pace about his room, unable to settle into either his chair or further work. Since Caroline's death he had lunched at his desk on a roll and coffee. Longing but not daring to make a move. Dreading, this Friday morning, the imminent interruption of the weekend before he could start hoping again.

When his private line rang soon after twelve, he fell on it.

'Jack Lambert.'

'Can't give you more than a moment, dear, the big white chief's breathing down my neck. All right your end?'

'Yes! I've been hoping – '

'How are you, dear?'

'I'm all right. Better for hearing you.'

'Give yourself a break this lunchtime, come on out to the Antelope. I imagine your life's a bit sober at the moment. Well, I hope it is!'

'It is, it is. Of course I'll come out, but not the Antelope, not yet. I've had enough sympathy.'

'The Antelope's your stamping ground. And mine. Why would I avoid it?'

'I see your point.'

'The Antelope, then, dear. And you've got to get the sympathy over sooner or later. Between one and half past.'

He could have gone on arguing but he didn't, he was weak with the relief of being back in touch. The disadvantage of staying with Vernon was that there couldn't be safe telephone calls in or out, but even that deprivation wasn't enough to send him back to the house of horrors, which he had come to loathe even when Caroline was alive and which was already on the market. And it would be all right. What had been his handicap before Caroline's death would now be his advantage. If one of Hewitt's minions followed him to the Antelope, all he would see him do – all he would do – was pass the time of day with a fellow regular. He wouldn't even risk taking advantage of the inevitable crush, not knowing which of the men – or women – around him might be that minion. And it was time to get going; his cloistered evenings with Vernon were mourning enough.

It was a quarter past one when he reached the bar, and the crush was easing. Fortunately, though, all the tables were still occupied. Jack bought himself a pint of bitter and ordered a prawn sandwich, enduring the shocked sympathy of landlord, barmaid, and a couple of regulars standing at the counter. Looking round the old-fashioned, comfortable room, he felt the usual reflex thrill of danger. Then, with a nod and a murmur to the people so carefully avoiding his eye, he made his way casually across to Vivian's table.

'All right if I sit here?'

'Of course. No, don't take the stool, they're not exactly comfortable and there's plenty of room on the bench. All right?'

'Fine. Thanks. Cheers.'

Vivian picked up his half-empty glass. 'Cheers.' He set it down. 'Look, the landlord's been talking and I've put two and two together. I'm so terribly sorry.' The wide eyes fixed on Jack didn't match the words, but anyone at the bar was too far away to interpret them.

'Thanks.' For the formality and the quiet, uninflected voice.

'It's – appalling. No, really.' For a moment the eyes were solemn and shocked, as if the speaker had suddenly realised what he was talking about. 'One can't offer any comfort.'

'It's a comfort just having – people – be sorry. Don't feel you've got to say any more. Or not say other things. That's why I came out.'

There was a man leaning against the bar, looking round the room in an apparently lazy way, who could well be a policeman. How long would he have to look out for one? At the table to one side of them was a group of cheerful young people, totally self-absorbed. To the other side a man nearly always in the Antelope at lunchtime, deep in his *Times*. Nothing different, nothing whatsoever to worry about. But he wouldn't ... 'How's the world of retail trading?'

'Booming. The girls sense spring. More and more shorter and shorter shirts. Are you having a sandwich?'

'Yes. You?'

'I've ordered. Prawns.'

'Snap.'

When the sandwiches came, they ate them slowly and in silence; Vivian even filled in a few *Telegraph* crossword clues. It was a consoling half-hour, not long enough to breed frustration, and if the man still lolling at the bar was a policeman he had to be getting bored.

'I'd better be on my way,' said Vivian after the last mouthful of his invariable half-pint. 'My lunch hour's exactly that, and it's just about up.'

'Of course,' said Jack. He had to get to his feet to let Vivian out. Beside them now at the small corner table was a drab-looking woman in an unbecoming pull-on hat, reading a paperback book.

'Cheerio, then,' said Vivian. 'See you around.'

'Now I've broken the ice I'll be in on Monday.'

They were side by side, facing the room. Between and behind them, for a motionless moment before Vivian completed his manoeuvre of passing Jack, their little fingers met and intertwined.

'Was the inquest all right, Daddy?'

'Jo, how lovely! Yes, I suppose so. Darling, how nice of you to ring.'

'Daddy, can I come up and see you?'

'Now, Jo? To the office?'

'Yes. Don't tell me you're tied up all afternoon.'

'No, but I'll be home this evening and it seems – '

'I want to see you on your own, and as soon as possible. What was that noise?'

He'd had to put his head between his knees, and the receiver had caught on the edge of the desk as it fell.

'I knocked the telephone. Carry on.'

'I'll talk when I see you. What would be the best time?'

'I don't – '

'Daddy, it's important.'

The wrench at his heart was the most agonising yet. But at least she was offering him the chance of his punishment soon, and in private.

What punishment, for God's sake? There was nothing Jo could know.

'Daddy?'

'All right, Jo. Just come to suit yourself. Where are you?'

'At home. I've been to Guildford in the car, but I won't attempt the City in it. So I'll be with you as soon as public transport permits. If I arrive during an appointment I can wait – '

'You'll be shown straight in.'

When he had replaced the receiver he sat paralysed, his body rigid to contain his struggle between a dread of witnessing Jo's disgust and a longing to learn the worst and have it over. He was astonished to hear his usual calm response to Gail's tap on the door, to find himself straightening the papers on his desk as she crossed the room.

She offered him another set. 'The Dalby dispute, Mr Collins. And you said you'd have more letters?'

'My daughter's just been on, Gail, she's coming to see me. She should be here in an hour or so.' An hour! Sixty minutes in which to devise scenario after scenario, each one culminating in the loss of everything that made his life worth living. There was no way Jo could know of his affair with Caroline, but that wasn't going to stop him torturing himself for the next hour if he didn't find something else to put in his mind. The strain of the inquest, even though he knew he had done well, seemed to have sapped his willpower. 'Yes, I do have some letters. I'll dictate them and then until Jo arrives we'll go on to some of those non-urgent bits and pieces I keep putting off. Tidying up Mrs MacGregor's file — you'll be glad about that, won't you, Gail? — and telling Gooch & Jones that we really aren't going to get anywhere with our inquiry into the whereabouts of Mr Peter Jory. And the rest, I suspect you know them better than I do. They'll be for you to do any time, but it's a good opportunity to get them out of my hair if not yours, as they're the sort of thing we can easily break off when Jo comes ...'

'That's all right, Mr Collins.'

He was protesting too much. As Gail insinuated her neat self into the chair opposite and her small white hands composed themselves over her notebook, he thought he could see yesterday's speculation back in her eyes, continuing loss of the personal indifference which for four or five years now had combined with her professional understanding to form so orthodox and reassuring a bond between them.

Jo arrived, panting and with her long red hair wind-lashed across her face, when Bob had dealt with the letters and was about halfway through the bits and pieces. She paused at reception for the girl on duty to buzz him, then swept in on his all clear. She and Gail greeted one another with the wary respect of specialists in different fields. On another day Bob could have been amused by the dramatic contrast between them: Gail tidily inside the frame of her smooth short hair, straight-skirted suit and minimal gestures; Jo overshooting her physical outline in all directions — swirling hair and skirt, flying scarf, expressive arms.

'I'll leave you, then, Mr Collins.'

'Thank you, Gail. Just the letters. The rest of it when you can.'

'Thank you. Nice to see you, Jo.' The speculative look moved from him to his daughter as Gail reached the door. Well, she was human, and had restricted herself to one comment only on his unfortunate connection with the Lambert murder ... As the door closed, Bob forced himself to look properly at Jo, and with a lift of the heart so violent it made him giddy again he saw that she was radiating a pure and joyous triumph.

'Darling, you look as if you've found a fortune. What is it? Please sit down.' So that he could collapse back into his chair.

'Daddy, I've just discovered something. Something that could be very important.'

'Important?' Pressing his hands down on the desk prevented them so noticeably trembling.

'Yes. About Simon's mother's ... Mrs Lambert's death. Mr Lambert's gay.'

For a few seconds he couldn't think what she'd said. Then he found himself laughing.

'Old Jack? Don't be absurd, darling. And how would *you* know?'

The radiance dimmed as a pink stain swept over the pearly skin of her face. 'I'm about to tell you.'

What on earth had he found funny? 'Tell me, then.'

She glared defiantly into his eyes, across a desk which seemed much smaller than when Gail sat the other side of it. Where it dwarfed his secretary, his daughter shrank it. 'You told me where Mr Lambert goes for lunch. I went there too.'

'But he knows you. For heaven's sake, Jo!' He was annoyed with himself for so much as taking part in such a ridiculous conversation.

'I'm an actress, Daddy. I'll never be Margaret Leighton, but I *have* played in *Separate Tables*. It wasn't very difficult to become a drab, insignificant woman in a bobbly hat.'

'But why did you want to become one, darling? I don't understand — '

'You do, Daddy. Mr Lambert doesn't have an alibi for his wife's murder. Of course I'm not saying ... I just wanted to observe his demeanour, as the police put it in old movies when they're in the witness box. I didn't really expect him to be there today, so soon after his wife's death, and then the inquest. But he was. He bought a drink at the bar, then went in a casual sort of a way to sit by a young chap on his own. A pretty boy, fair-haired, but not too noticeably — '

'Because there were no free tables!'

'No, there weren't any free tables,' said Jo impatiently, just managing to catch the photograph of herself and her mother which her gesturing arm had swept off the desk, 'but that was his bit of luck. Daddy, while they were sitting eating, I managed to move to the table in the corner next to them, and when the young man got up to go he and Mr Lambert held hands. Behind them, out of sight of everyone but me. Just for a second but I saw it, I saw their little fingers twisting together. D'you think we ought to tell that detective inspector?'

'No! For God's sake, no, Jo!' He was ashamed of the sense of relief mingling with his shock. And of course his mind was tumbling backwards, trying to see Jack in yet another light. Failing. 'I just can't believe ...'

'Daddy, I promise you! You're not intending to do nothing about it, are you?'

'I'm certainly not intending to go to the police. But I'll talk to Jack. You realise I'll have to tell him it was you — '

'If I'd been worried about that I wouldn't have gone to the Antelope.'

'I suppose not,' he said helplessly. 'Jo, you're sure ...?'

'I'm sure. One hundred per cent convinced. I'm sorry, Daddy. It does make one start thinking, doesn't it?'

'Perhaps. But leave it to me, Jo. You must promise.'

'All right,' said Jo reluctantly. 'I promise.' And Jack Lambert was Simon's father, whatever Simon felt about him. 'And I suppose I'd better tell you what else I've been doing. Yesterday morning I found myself outside the Flower Bower and was going to —'

'Jo!'

'Hang on. I was only going to buy a bunch of flowers if it was open. It was, and there was a notice in the window asking for a part-time assistant. How could I pass up on *that*?'

'You really are —' Absurdly, his twenty-one-year-old daughter was a pair of strong hands, holding him up.

'I got the job. Starting officially this morning, as I had a lunch date in London yesterday, but the manageress said I could hang around and start learning the ropes if I wanted. She went out soon after I'd arrived, and the two girls working there couldn't tell me enough.'

'Tell you ...?'

'About Mrs Lambert's death. Oh, they didn't know anything, of course, they just wanted to talk about it. But one of them said there was a sales rep called Paul Gibson who calls regularly – on *Tuesdays*, Daddy! – and who Mrs Oliphant the manageress once photographed with his arm round Mrs Lambert. Just sort of jokey, they'd all thought, only he came in the day after the murder and when Maureen — one of the girls — went into the back for something, she saw him in a mirror take the photograph down from where Mrs O had pinned it up, and crumple it into his pocket. And the other girl said she and Maureen had once seen this Paul Gibson having lunch with Mrs Lambert in the Antelope. Are you all right, Daddy? You look as if you're going to pass out. I'm sorry for so many shocks but I had to tell you —'

'Of course, Jo.' It was relief again that had made him giddy. Glorious relief that the lover of Jack's panic logic might already be accessible flesh and blood. 'She's told the police, of course?'

'She hadn't, but I've persuaded her.' Jo dropped her eyes to the desk.

'I have to give you full marks for enterprise. What else are you planning?'

'Don't be sarcastic, Daddy, it doesn't suit you. And don't worry about the Flower Bower, I'm not going back there.' Jo hesitated, wondering whether to say more, but decided against it.

'I suppose that's something. But I don't want you to go anywhere else, either. Not just because the police don't need your help to make them more suspicious of me than they are already. There's a murderer about and I don't want you getting into trouble.' Try as he would he couldn't keep the severity up, his pride in her, his astonished gratitude for what she had done, was glowing its way into his face. 'You're amazing, Jo.'

'I had to do what I could, Daddy.'

She would like to have reassured him that she wasn't going to do anything more, but she'd been so lucky with the Flower Bower and Mr Lambert that she had to believe fate was beckoning her to go for the hat trick.

Chapter Eleven

Jo left a glow behind to sustain her father through the remains of the afternoon and his frustrated attempts to get hold of Jack and arrange a meeting. At first Bob couldn't psych himself into a state to make the call, his mind dizzy as he looked back over the past few years, trying to reinterpret every remembered incident that had included the Lamberts, trying to see the hitherto ordinary as significant, and hoping, despite his gut belief in Jo's passionate certainty, that he would be unable to.

He *was* unable to, of course, all the way along the Lambert-strewn road behind him, but that didn't mean she wasn't right. And what Jo had seen explained why Jack had found it so comparatively easy to dissemble to Hewitt and company. He had had years — perhaps a lifetime? — of practice.

He'd also had years when he could have 'come out' so far as society was concerned. Not, though, with a wife like Caroline. Even if Caroline had known the truth — and Bob, recalling her face when she told him Jack was straying, felt sickly sure she had known — it would have been impossible for Jack to have revealed his propensities publicly and have remained her husband. A woman who refused on principle to serve dinner in the kitchen, who presented herself at all times as a conventionally contented wife, would have made utter secrecy the price of her agreement to preserve the status quo. Which must mean Jack had wanted to preserve it, too, wanted to appear the straightforward heterosexual he wasn't. Bisexual? At one time, perhaps; there was the boy Simon. But not – Bob was unable to duck a second vivid memory of Caroline's initial assault on him – not during the last year or so of their marriage.

Jack at least was alive, open to question. Still trying to subdue his whirling thoughts, Bob at last reached for his private telephone, just as Gail rang through on his intercom to announce a client calling on the chance of finding him free. As the client left twenty minutes and as many reassurances later, Bob's junior partner passed him in the doorway and sat for a further ten minutes spilling out an anxiety which Bob had to force himself not to adjudge trivial. Tony was still there when the telephone rang.

'Can you talk, Bob?'

Jack.

'Hang on.' He covered the mouthpiece. 'Has that helped, Tony? This is a bit of a complex one, and may take some time. We'll resume tomorrow if you –'

'No, no, you've sorted me out, Bob. I know now what to say to Tompkins. I'll get straight back to him with the precedent and ...' Tony was talking his way to the door, going out with a nod and a smile, closing it behind him.

'All right, Jack, sorry.'

'The funeral's Tuesday, Bob. Eleven o'clock at the crematorium. Vernon's persuaded me there's no need for anything afterwards. In the circumstances ...'

'I'm sure he's right. You'll feel better when it's over. Jack, I must see you before Tuesday. As soon as possible, in fact.'

'Oh?'

Was it simply Jo's visit that had put a world of wariness into a monosyllable? 'Yes. What d'you suggest? No point in my coming over to Vernon's, I have to speak to you on your own.'

'Vernon will be home late tonight,' said Jack. He sounded grudging. 'Some antique dealers' jamboree. If you could get there around six-thirty we could have an hour. Nothing wrong, is there?'

'I hope not. But I've heard something we ought to talk about.' There was no doubt he would have to give Jo's game away, but she had shown herself prepared for that. 'You'll be at Vernon's by half past six?'

'As near as. Everything really is all right?'
'So far as I know.'

So long as Jack was able to persuade him that his theory of Caroline's murder was an interpretation of events rather than a smokescreen.

Jo rang Simon from a callbox at Blackfriars tube station.

'I've something to tell you, but not over the telephone.' Only, for certain, the shape of her rapidly developing plans. 'I'm in the City, I've just been visiting my father. Could we meet for a drink when you've finished work?'

'We certainly could. Not before a quarter to six, though, I'm inundated. Will the Grapes do?'

'Of course.' Jo's eyes flashed triumph at the elderly woman waiting to use the telephone, eliciting an involuntary smile. 'See you then, Simon.'

The rain hd stopped, blown away by the strengthening wind, and there were blue rifts in the ragged sky. Jo filled in the long late afternoon by striding down to the river and inspecting various archaeologically interesting building sites and the burgeoning of the plane trees. Told suddenly by her stomach that she hadn't lunched, she had a sandwich and a coffee at the window of a café looking on to a small square where old men sat solitary at the extreme ends of wooden seats, forcing herself to read the whole of the *Evening Standard* and thus be very slightly late for her appointment with Simon.

As she had hoped, he was in the same remote seat where he had awaited her the first time, his dark head turned towards the bar so that she was looking at his perfect profile.

'Sorry I'm late.'

'You're early by the standards of most of the girls I meet.' He was smiling his obvious pleasure at seeing her — he hadn't said it deliberately, as a macho ploy — but she felt a venomous jet of jealousy which she tried to dilute with her own answering smile. 'What'll you have?'

'Wine tonight, please. White. Dry.'

He came back with identical glasses, which they raised to each other.

'Simon,' said Jo as she set hers down, 'there's a bit of a

snag over Maureen at the Flower Bower. I don't think she'll go to the police about Paul Gibson.'

'But you made her see ...' His dismay told Jo he had been more impressed by the Paul Gibson possibility than he had revealed when she told him about it.

'I know. I just don't think she wants to get mixed up with the police inquiry, she's a total egotist. She fell out with me over it, so I've left her friend Joan to try and persuade her. And I've left the Flower Bower — I wasn't a success and I've got frostbite. As well as all I could out of it. Including Mr Gibson's home address.'

'Which won't be much good to us if the lady doesn't deliver.'

'Oh, I intend going to the police myself about the photograph if I find out from Joan on Monday that Maureen still hasn't done her civic duty. And if I can tell them at the same time that you saw Paul Gibson with your mother ... Oh, Simon, I'm sorry.'

'Don't be. So I'm to stand outside some house in the sticks and look for a man I saw for a moment one night in Park Lane?'

'The house isn't in the sticks, it's in London. Well, Ravenscourt Park. And I'll be the one doing most of the standing. Sitting, that is. I'll take the car early on Monday and try to park as near as I can to the house. I'll also take my Polaroid and try to get a picutre. Even if I manage a reasonable one, though, it'll be no substitute for your seeing the man for yourself — '

'Ah. We're getting to it.'

'Could you possibly take a long lunch hour? As a sales rep Gibson won't be keeping office hours and he just might come home for lunch. It's important, Simon.'

'I know. I'll take a long lunch hour.'

'Good. And if we draw a blank then there'll be another chance in the early evening.'

'A better chance, I should say, than in the afternoon. So I suggest you go and do something else after lunch as well and we'll meet back in Ravenscourt Park about five. I reckon I've a few more days for trading on my tragedy and I'll be able to get off early.'

'Simon!' But she was too excited to be really shocked. 'That'll be marvellous. And even if we don't see Mr Gibson at all and Joan doesn't get anywhere with Maureen, I'll still go to the police on Tuesday about what he did with the snapshot.'

'Tuesday's the funeral.'

'Oh, Simon ... I'll be there with my parents, of course.'

Because of you rather than your mother. It was the moment for telling him about his father, if she was going to, and Jo picked up her glass and held it in front of her face. There was no doubt the revelation would help him understand his mother, perhaps recover some of his old feeling for her. But even though his opinion of his father was already low, to learn from a potential girlfriend that he was gay could affect Simon's perception of himself, could do all sorts of psychological damage. And end any chance of his ever wanting to see Jo Collins again. Jo wondered ruefully if that last consideration weighed the heaviest with her. She didn't know, but at least she had fairly decided, in the few seconds of hiding her face from Simon with her glass of wine, that it would be best for him if she kept quiet. It didn't look as if her father was going to tell the police, which meant Simon wouldn't hear about it from *them*.

But why hadn't she thought ...?

What's the matter?'

'Nothing. Goose over my grave.' She had shuddered at her naivety in not thinking, until that moment, that he might already know.

But not so naive. If he knew, it would have come out during those angry, tearful moments they had shared the first time they sat in that corner of the Grapes. By implication, by what he didn't say, if not in so many words. But he had dismissed his father almost as if he had no part in the equation, and she was certain that for those few minutes he hadn't held anything back.

'There's nothing else, is there, Jo?' He was looking at her intently; the glass had been a flawed shield.

Jo forced herself to meet his gaze with the luminous honesty she had studied in the mirror for use on stage. 'Nothing. I wish there were. Oh, there's my car number.'

She gave it to him. 'And here's the Gibson address for you to copy. I just hope it's the sort of place one can park. And unobtrusively. It's on the District Line –'

'Yes, ma'am. Another glass of wine, ma'am?'

'No, thanks.' The certainty of a meeting in two days' time made it easier to get to her feet, although the weekend that had to come first was presenting itself in the semblance of a desert. 'I'm supposed to be spending a holiday at home and I haven't been there since a very early breakfast. I think I ought to get back in time for supper.'

It was twenty-five to seven when Bob reached the small hidden house where Vernon had lived for the past thirty-odd years, tucked into a Dorking back alley behind his small shop in the antique-trade end of the town. Vernon's unobtrusive garage was open and empty – reminding Bob on a queasy pang of his car-parking arrangements with Caroline – and he drove into it; he'd be away before Vernon was back if Jack had got it right. Jack's car was pressed in against the padlocked doors, painted white like everything else in the tiny cul-de-sac, behind which Vernon kept some of his bulkier and less valuable stock. Bob heard Jack's uneager feet several seconds before they arrived at Vernon's handsome front door.

'Well timed,' said Jack wearily. 'Glad to see you've used the garage, I opened it for you. Come into the sitting-room.'

The charming small space had its usual civilising effect. For the first time since Jo had sprung her shock Bob found himself feeling sorry for Jack, watching his unhappy face as he poured out two scotches without asking Bob if he wanted one.

'You all right?' he asked, as he took his drink from Jack's hand. A hand from which Jo's apparent revelation wasn't making him recoil. But he was discovering there was nothing in his own feeling about Jack that inclined him to believe it, and if it turned out to be true he would still be sure Jack had never looked on him as anything but a friend.

'I suppose so. Your call worried me. Why have you come?'

The direct question was an enormous help.

'Because I may have learned something today. Jack, my daughter's a fanatic in the protection of her loved ones. When Caroline died and the police came to me, came again, Jo took it on herself to find the murderer. I didn't know until today, but I might have guessed. Jack, she got a job at the Flower Bower — no, wait — and she even shadowed you to your lunch today. In all innocence.' Bob paused, watching Jack's face, and in the alarm followed by resignation, in the lack of a trace of anger, learned for sure that Jo had been right. 'She saw — a gesture — between you and the man you were lunching with that told her something Barbara and I have never known. Something that's giving me some new thoughts about Caroline's death, and that anonymous letter. Jack, do the police know?'

'God, no! No one does. Please, Bob ...' Jack's face was sickly pale again and gleaming with sweat. 'I swear it has no bearing on the murder and if it got out now, what it would do to me ... And to you!' he added eagerly. 'The one way your secret can get out is for the police to find out where I was those Tuesday nights, and then we're both in trouble. Bob, you haven't ...?'

'Of course not. Although I had a bit of a job persuading Jo to leave it to me. It's all right, she agreed. But, Jack, you've got to answer some questions from me. Nothing seems quite so agreeably cut and dried as it did yesterday. Was Caroline the exception? Did she know?'

'Yes. When it got ... When I couldn't go on pretending any more.'

'It wasn't always the case, then?'

Jack ran his finger round the inside of his collar, shifted in Vernon's golden-velvet winged armchair. 'One or two — incidents — before I was married. But I didn't want ... I fell in love with Caroline, I did that.' Jack smiled briefly and nervously at his achievement. 'It was all right for years, and then I met someone who counted. I couldn't — keep on with Caroline.'

'It must have devastated her. And I didn't notice.'

'No.' Jack got up and shambled across the room to pour himself another drink. 'But you know — knew — Caroline.'

He stumbled on the edge of a Tabriz rug; a diagonal dash of whisky stained his pale tie. He sat heavily down again. 'Appearances had to be kept up. Appearances were life. I'm certain there was no one who would have noticed any change in her. Not that there was anyone she was really close to, no real women friends. Oh, I know she and Barbara ... They weren't real friends, were they, Bob?'

'I don't think so.'

'I'd have been glad to give her a divorce by then, but she wouldn't hear of it, and it didn't make all that much difference to me.' Jack looked down at his knees. Bob thought it was the first time he had felt embarrassed. 'It just meant I had to go on being – very careful. I gave her *carte blanche* too, of course. What else could I do? When she told me you ... Well, I felt damned sorry for Barbara but sort of relieved ... God, Bob, this is awful.'

'Yes.' But Bob felt better. He had actually done Jack a good turn, and if Jack had done anything against him it had been by accident rather than design. 'But I've some potential good news. Jo could have discovered – Caroline's other lover.'

Jack tensed, relaxed. 'Didn't she think she'd done enough? Tell me, for God's sake.'

He told Jack about Paul Gibson, what Jo had learned in the Flower Bower. That the girl had gone to the police. 'You knew him?'

'Heavens, no. Why should I?'

'Because you and Caroline kept your business lives apart, or because you were away on your own concerns more often than every other Tuesday night?'

'Both.' Embarrassment came and went again, on a brief, rosy tide. 'Look, Bob, I just hoped Caroline was – was leading her own life as fully as she wanted. For her sake – and for mine, of course, too. As she wouldn't consider a split-up, all I could hope was that she'd content herself however and whenever she wanted. I'm sorry if you thought you were the only –'

'I should be so macho. And I love Barbara.'

'Poor Caroline,' Jack mumbled. It was Bob's turn to be

embarrassed, as he saw that Jack was crying. 'Y'know, I don't think anybody ever loved her.'

'You did, at first.'

'In love. Proud. Passport to normality. That's not love, Bob.'

'No.' It was no doubt good for Jack to cry, but it added disagreeably to the unfamiliar images of him Bob's mind was trying not to accommodate. 'But she wasn't the sort of person who would ever have known.'

'You're right!' Jack blew his nose. 'I honestly don't think she was really unhappy.'

'Probably not.' But neither of them would ever be sure. 'Look, we've got to get back to you, I'm afraid. This news about Paul Gibson makes your theory about the murder even more convincing, but at the same time your own bit of news makes your end of things — a bit less waterproof. It has to, Jack! Even if you're convinced your — friend — had nothing to do with that letter, he may have other friends —'

'No!' Jack was red again, more lingeringly, with anger.

'All right. Other would-be friends, then. If one of your earlier contacts didn't have it in for you. And Jack, I'm not just talking about the letter.'

'I know, I know. You're talking about murder. Which so far as my friend is concerned is utterly —'

Bob realised something. 'The double-glazing salesman.'

'Yes. We'd had a bit of a tiff. That was why I was in the office when you rang. I — hadn't made any arrangements that night, I was going to stay at the club.'

So that he wouldn't take his wife and her lover by surprise. Or frustrate their expectations. Bob's sense of self-disgust was suddenly so strong he had to get to his feet.

'Help yourself. My friend was ringing to make things up. If Caroline had answered he would have said he wanted to talk business.'

'I'm sorry I called him a salesman.'

'He is a salesman. Oh, God, Bob, you're not really saying you think Caroline could have been killed because of my —'

'She could have been, I think you've got to face that. But we've got another salesman to think about too, now.

Why did Paul Gibson take that snapshot down?' His mind despite himself was so crowded with unwelcome images of Jack and his vulnerability, Paul Gibson felt like a breath of fresh air.

'Because he'd killed Caroline and didn't want to be connected – '

'He wouldn't want to be connected knowing someone else had killed her. Jack, did your friend, did any of your friends, ever go to your house?'

'Never! You're thinking about the gun, aren't you? Well, I've told you – '

'All right. Just tell me something more. How many people known to you could have written that letter, Jack?'

The sweat, now, was rolling unattractively down both sides of Jack's face. Vaguely he mopped at it. 'None known to me,' he said defiantly. A vigorous blink dried his weary blue eyes. 'Don't you understand? All one can go on is promises of discretion. You could rely on them. I hoped I could.'

'I see that, yes.' Although once during his last time alone with Caroline he had been assailed by the terrible fancy that she might eventually decide to use her power to blow his life apart.

'Before Caroline died,' said Jack almost pettishly, 'it wasn't a matter of life and death. I mean – it wouldn't have meant what it would mean now if someone had tried to take advantage ...'

'Blackmail's always blackmail.'

Jack shifted restlessly in his chair. 'You've just said yourself that the appearance of this Gibson chap makes my theory even more likely. No need to look any further, surely, Bob. I mean, if the fellow sneaked the photograph down, he's the most likely one to have written the letter. And if he wrote the letter, he must have killed Caroline. I mean, that stands to reason, doesn't it? The letter was written by the murderer.'

'Or by someone who knew who the murderer was, and wanted to help him. Or by someone who wanted to get his own back. Which would be rather more likely from your side. Jack ...'

'If the letter had come from my side, it would hardly

have been about *you*,' said Jack triumphantly. 'And it's just the thing a guilty boyfriend of Caroline's would have done, knowing there was someone else who could equally well fill the bill. Don't you see? You said you did.'

'I do, of course.'

'Of course you do. Oh, God, Bob! Poor Caroline.'

'But someone your end could just have been putting you to slow torture.' Jack's renewed emotion over Caroline didn't strike Bob as deep enough to warrant any temporary leniency. 'Shooting you the first time in the kneecap rather than the heart.'

'Too far-fetched.'

Jack had blown his nose again, was regaining confidence. Which he would continue to need for Hewitt and Tabley. Bob would leave it there. 'I expect so. I must go.'

'Thought you were going to get yourself another drink.' Jack had his third one in his hand.

'No, thanks. I'll have that with Barbara. Jack, as you've just said yourself, my secret's safe only so long as yours is. For God's sake be careful over the weekend.

'That's enough, Bob. I am aware of the situation.'

'Sorry.' Whatever else they did, he and Jack couldn't afford to quarrel. It was when thieves fell out ... 'Forgive me, I haven't quite taken it in. You're still all right here?'

'Of course. Vernon's wonderful. Showering me with creature comforts. Listening if I want to talk.'

'You've been tempted to talk?'

'Strangely, yes. I haven't, of course.'

'Vernon's tempted me, too. It's the nature of the man.' He got to his feet. 'Gibson should be with the police now. Let's hope that's the end of it. What's going to happen with the Flower Bower?'

'She's left it to Mrs Oliphant, so I don't know.'

At the front door Jack put out a hand to Bob, let it fall.

'It's all right,' said Bob. 'I know you're demonstrative.'

'Thanks. For understanding so quickly that I'm the same as I was this morning.'

'Of course you are. See you Tuesday.'

Backing out of Vernon's garage Bob reflected that the

amiable fellow with the big surface emotions and the cliché-ridden chat had disappeared some time before that morning. Did he know by now the full extent of his misreading of Jack Lambert, to what lengths the toughening process of his secret life had fitted him to go?

Barbara hadn't been instinctively certain that Jack couldn't have murdered his wife.

Chapter Twelve

It was an uncomfortable weekend. Bob's unease was intensified by his awareness that the police didn't work a five-day week and that their new interest in Paul Gibson would not accord him automatic immunity from another visit.

'It's the worst of both worlds, isn't it?' Jo breathed on Saturday evening into her father's ear, casting herself down on the arm of his chair in a widespread subsidence of orange silk housecoat. 'The drawbridges are up in the usual weekend way, but there's an enemy that can creep past them. I wonder how Mummy feels.'

Barbara was in the kitchen, last seen preparing supper and snatching paragraphs of a Richmal Crompton *William* book she had open on the table.

'I don't know.'

'Don't you really?' asked Jo with interest. '*I* don't, of course, but I thought you might. Was she always so self-contained?'

'Almost. We're all right, Jo.' They were. So long as he and Jack stood firm. The word *Jack*, now, fight it as he would, conjured up the image of a sieve writhing with forms that emitted a slimy drip through every square of mesh.

'Good. Oh, Daddy, good. I thought last time I was home ... I couldn't quite decide what it was, but I felt something wasn't absolutely right.'

He welcomed the hurt because of deserving it. 'I think we started to take each other for granted. When you think of years and years of being together, it isn't surprising in any marriage. This awful business — seems to have helped us realise ...' A ghastly paradox, but it had. So long as he and Jack ...

Vernon brought Jack along that night for supper, and during Barbara's further absence in the kitchen gave them a mild pep talk over their sitting-room drinks.

'The police will get there,' he said. 'And if by any unimaginable chance they don't − well, they won't arrest an innocent man.' Bob was beside him on the sofa, and Vernon put a hand on Bob's arm.

'That's all very well,' said Jack. Bob was looking directly at him as little as possible, but he couldn't get the sweaty gleam on Jack's temples out of the corner of his eye. 'People will go on wondering.'

'People forget,' said Vernon. 'And all Bob did was what he always did on alternate Tuesday evenings. If he hadn't gone to your house as usual that night, Jack, then that might have seemed strange.'

'No one saw me leave the office,' said Jack. 'It seems unbelievable, but no one did. And no one saw Bob arrive at Green Lawns.'

'The police are probably talking to someone this very moment who saw one or other of you. And if they're not, and no one comes forward, there's a *Crime Watch* series starting soon on television, it's amazing how that programme jogs the public memory. Sorry, Bob.' Vernon had felt him jerk. 'I meant to help. But probably best not to think or talk about it any more than is absolutely necessary. Jack and I've kept off it − we've scarcely mentioned it, have we, Jack? − but I've brought it up now because I detect stretched nerves and I think you've both reached a stage of needing someone to remind you to keep your spirits up. And that innocence has nothing to fear.'

'Thanks, Vernon.' Bob tried to force his face to relax as he smiled into Vernon's calm blue eyes. Tried to force himself to stop feeling guilty. He hadn't killed Caroline, it was crazy so much as to consider it, any more than he'd taken himself to the brink of death by electric live rail. A reluctant glance at Jack showed a lessening of strain he hoped was apparent in his own face. But how much was Jack dissembling? He still didn't know; all he knew about was that leaking sieve ...

'You're right, of course. I'm going to open some good wine.'

The cats were a help, too. Every time Barbara went down to them he went with her, except early on Saturday and Sunday mornings when he had at last managed to fall asleep and she crept out in her usual mouselike way without wakening him.

Some time during Sunday afternoon the fact of the police not reappearing began to feel oppressive rather than a relief. Bob started to be uneasy about whether they had grasped the importance of the photograph filched from the Flower Bower. It was Sunday evening before he managed to get Jo on her own for long enough to talk to her properly. At six o'clock the wind and rain, which had squalled without respite through the weekend, gave way to calm and a pale, descending sun, and he suggested a walk, which he gambled successfully on Barbara refusing in the interests of dinner.

'Jo, darling, this Mr Gibson and that photograph.' He had managed to wait until they had turned off the road. 'You did say you'd persuaded the girl in the Flower Bower to go to the police?'

Her father was offering her a chance of his blessing, at least for the first part of her next enterprise, and Jo decided to take it. 'I'm sorry, Daddy, I should have said I'd *tried* to persuade her, because I don't think I succeeded. She agreed at first, but then she seemed to change her mind. So I thought I'd go myself, but I didn't want to upset you when there was no need, and that's why I sort of fudged – '

'Told me the girl was going.'

'I'm afraid so, Daddy.' She shook his arm. 'It's important, darling, and if Maureen doesn't come across I'm the only alternative. The information could hardly come from *you*, and I don't think an anonymous letter – '

'Not an anonymous letter!' He shuddered, pretended he had tripped on a tree root. His dismay at learning of the probable continuing ignorance of the police about what he had been confident they were now pursuing made him feel cold, as if he had lost a layer of clothes. 'You told me you'd shown the girl her duty, so I assumed ... You're right, Jo, the information has to come from you if the girl won't give it. I'm sorry for trying to put you off. I'm not usually the heavy father, am I?'

'This is uncharted country,' said Jo dramatically. 'You were only trying to protect me. You've never been the heavy father, and you're not going to start now. I'm sorry, Daddy. I'd far rather have your blessing, honestly, that's why I've just told you the truth. I'll call on Chief Inspector Hewitt tomorrow.' After Simon had identified Paul Gibson. Or not.

'Oh, Jo!' He was ashamed of his renewed sense of hope. 'Thank you.' Blackbirds were piping, a thrush high on a hazy green birch tree was repetitively defying the dusk, there were long views across sloping fields. The sortie over the edge of suburbia was as consoling as Jo's undertaking and his realisation that there were now two women he could trust. 'Anyway, I've just discovered I don't have any parental qualms about involving you. You're a grown woman and you've involved yourself spectacularly already. You'll have to confess to your brief stint as a Flower Bower employee, but I think Hewitt will consider that a fair exchange.'

'I didn't do anything wrong. The ad was in the window for anyone who went by.' Jo hesitated, then sped over to a hedge to examine a cluster of blossom. The other thing she was planning for Monday, she decided, she would tell him about after it had happened.

He joined her. 'I'm glad to be in your confidence.'

She turned to face him, twirling a small pink flower head between finger and thumb, feeling her guilty blush. 'Daddy. About Mr Lambert. You've really decided we should keep it to ourselves?'

'I've really decided. I'm sure it has nothing to do with the murder.' If only he was! 'And even if I thought it had ... Well, I wouldn't tell them.' Even if they arrested him? How far would his loyalty to Jack go then? He and Jack, he and Jack. Again, the thought of Paul Gibson was fresh air as well as hope.

'I approve of that, Daddy. I think it's noble, in a way.'

'Well, good. Ring me at the office with the police reactions, Jo. Easier than trying to talk at home.' He hated saying that, hated getting back to Barbara and telling her only about the local progress of spring. His capitulation to Caroline had landed him in an innocent conspiracy with his daughter as well as a guilty one with Caroline's husband. Guilty of disloyalty to his wife, wherever the ultimate murder verdict pointed.

'I'm afraid I'm going to be out all day tomorrow,' said Jo last thing that night, uncoiling her above average length from her chair and collapsing it in an orange billow on the carpet in front of her mother. 'Leaving rather early. Something I hadn't expected, Mummy, and I'm sorry. I'll make up for it –'

'That's all right, Jo, don't worry.' Barbara didn't ask Jo any details, that was always Bob's role, but tonight he didn't play it. Jo saw the uneasiness in his eyes as he wondered what else she had in mind besides talking to the detective chief inspector, and was sorry to have to keep him waiting another twenty-four hours before he found out.

She must really, though, say something now. 'A friend in Hammersmith has sent me an SOS. I hope to get away before supper, but if it's tricky I'll give you a ring.'

Bob didn't believe her, and found himself a bit shocked to see the honest gaze she fixed on her mother. And it reminded him of his own.

'A depression is spreading across the country. It will be rather cold.'

Parked early next morning near Ashurst Grove, Ravenscourt Park, Polaroid camera at the ready, Jo nodded vigorously at her radio. At the end of an hour of Mozart from her mother's tapes, and the diversion of a postman pushing something through the Gibson letter box without ringing the bell, she was already cold enough to be afraid of not being able to manipulate the camera, and did a few college hand exercises as unobtrusively as possible. Then she decided to use her joker in the cause of her circulation as well as her research, tucked the camera into the glove compartment, got out of the car and walked briskly past the row of identical compact Victorian villas, detached from each other by slivers of space revealing dustbins backed by fences and spindly trees. There was no sign of life outside number 11 or behind its windows, although the shabby estate car immediately in front of the gate looking promising, the back seat strewn with road maps. But all she could do when she reached the end of the road was march back again to her own car, knowing she had used up the one possible variation in what, until Simon arrived, could be a long monotonous morning. At least she had secured the ideal parking space, across and down the road from her quarry and just enabling her to see his front door. She had been lucky to find a parking space at all, there were no garages in Ashurst Grove and its occupants' cars stood nose to tail on both sides of the roadway.

It was past ten, and her feet were as wretched as her hands, when a man came down the short path of number 11.

He was tall and lean with dark hair, a light suit and a jaunty walk, and at first glance she thought he was young. But as he came round the back of the car she saw that his hair didn't quite hide his scalp and that his thin face was seamed with lines. She had her window down by then, and the camera supported on its edge. She froze as the man stopped and looked round, aware of herself as the only figure in the landscape. But she was on the fringe of his gaze and, apparently satisfied that he was unobserved, he unlocked the car, got in, manoeuvred skilfully, and drove quickly away, leaving her with developing film and the satisfaction of having noticed a distinct furtiveness in his survey of his surroundings.

The satisfaction was short-lived. The film had done as well as the limitations of popular instant photography allowed, which meant it stopped improving at the stage of showing an indistinct distant figure.

Jo felt the temptation to go away and come back an hour or so later, but she mightn't find so good a parking place again, and she had brought her mother's biggest flask full of coffee as well as plenty of sandwiches. By half past eleven she had eaten half of them, drunk two cups of coffee, and made an undetected sortie into the back garden of an empty house. At noon a pale sun appeared, slightly warming her spirits, and her face when she switched to the passenger seat and reopened the window. She even closed her eyes into it and prepared to doze, assuring herself she was far less likely to miss a return than a departure, with the alert of the car engine coming before the figure on the pavement and the path. And having to believe it was Paul Gibson who had departed, whether or not he was the man Simon had seen.

At half past twelve the sun disappeared and Jo ate the rest of her sandwiches, lamenting her failure to ask Simon to bring further food and drink. There was still no activity at number 11 and the space left by the estate car hadn't been filled. When she had drained the last of the coffee she switched the radio on softly and settled back into the restored sunshine.

'So this is how detectives work.' Simon was at the window, and she had given the shameful shocked squeak of the awakened sleeper.

'I have been working. Get in.' He took her place as she struggled back behind the wheel, arranging a variety of plastic bags on his lap.

'I thought I'd have lunch here. I've brought for two, and some wine in a tonic bottle. Just a mouthful for you as you're driving, but you can have a whole meat pie. No photography?'

'Oh, Simon. Yes, I've got a photograph, but it was a stupid idea, the Polaroid camera just isn't made for long-distance clarity. He went off in the estate car that was in that space. Here.'

'It certainly could be,' said Simon judicially, after studying the dim square. 'But I couldn't identify him on the strength of it.'

'Of course not. But what goes out must come in. How long can you stay?' She was eating the meat pie as if she had never seen a sandwich. And as well as the wine there was more coffee.

'I've got myself some outside visiting this afternoon, so I'm flexible.' He caught her hand for a few electric seconds on its way to her mouth. 'You're frozen, aren't you? I thought you looked cold.'

'All in a good cause. I'm such a stupid optimist I never put enough clothes on. I should have learned from the Flower Bower. I'm all right, though, the sun helped.'

'And I've pushed you out of it. But it's gone, anyway. Switch the engine on a moment for the heater.'

'Too noticeable. I'm all right.'

'Finish your lunch then and I'll warm you up.'

The prospect was so devastatingly delectable that Jo's appetite for food disappeared. 'I have finished,' she managed. 'I've been eating all morning. No, thanks, no more coffee.'

'All right, then.'

Simon drained his paper cup of wine, disposed his depleted bags about his feet, then put an arm round her, rubbing his hand up and down hers. 'Better?'

'Oh, yes.'

'You're an extraordinary girl, Jo. I've never met anyone like you.'

'Well, good.' She preferred that, infinitely, to being called attractive. (No one had ever called her pretty.) Lots of girls were attractive, but an extraordinary one had the chance of being memorable ... It was extraordinary, too, and indescribably wonderful, to be discovering that at one and the same time a man could feel both familiar and strange.

'Getting warmer?' Simon's other arm came across her and his hands clasped somewhere round her elbow.

'Yes.'

'Good. I didn't think you'd enjoyed that dance, you know.'

'I didn't think *you* had.'

'It was the parents, wasn't it, beaming their awful approval?'

'With the exception of my mother, yes.'

'I could have enjoyed it.'

'So could I.'

'Jo ...'

Recognising the crucial moment, she turned her head towards him and all other considerations ceased to exist. 'We're making ourselves conspicuous,' she murmured eventually.

'On the contrary, it's the best disguise there is. One indulgent glance, and we're a lamppost ... Jo, Jo! That's not why ... Oh, Jo ... Jo!'

They drew apart as the estate car swept past them and manoeuvred economically into the space outside number

11. A man got out and walked swiftly round to the back.

'That's him, Simon.'

'That's him, Jo! It is, there's no doubt about it. I'd forgotten how vividly I'd taken him in, that awful middle-aged youthfulness, I suppose I'd pushed it down into my subconscious. Mission accomplished! We'll wait till he's inside and then we'll go and get warm. Although I must say I – Jo!'

Two men who appeared to be taking a stroll had stopped by Paul Gibson and were all at once standing one each side of him. Two men Jo had seen before. She and Simon watched in silence as a short conversation took place and, shaking his head, Paul Gibson walked along the pavement between the two men the way they had come, past the car where the watchers sat and out of sight.

'So Maureen did her stuff after all!'

'Can you see in the mirror?'

'Yes. They're getting into a car the same side as the house. I can't see inside it, but a uniformed policeman's ushering Mr Gibson into the back. Getting in after him. The detective sergeant's getting into the driving seat. The chief inspector's ... Oh, Simon!'

'Good afternoon, Miss Collins. Mr Lambert.' Chief Inspector Hewitt smiled at them through Jo's window.

'Chief Inspector Hewitt,' croaked Jo. 'We'll go quietly.'

'That's most cooperative of you, Miss Collins. How about following us to the station so that we can all have a bit of a chat?'

'I didn't tell you everything on the telephone, Daddy,' said Jo, coming back into the sitting-room after taking her mother's drink out to the kitchen.

'You didn't?'

'No. You see, Simon – Simon Lambert – saw his mother once with a man in the London Hilton, and we thought that if it turned out to be Paul Gibson it would make what I told the police sound even more significant. So what I've been doing today is running Mr Gibson to earth. We sat in the car near his house and eventually he appeared and Simon recognised him. It's got to be a breakthrough – Daddy, are you all right? I thought you'd be as pleased as I am. And I thought when you heard me say Simon Lambert ... I know I didn't tell you the whole truth yesterday but it was only because I was afraid you'd – '

'Simon ...' The name had at last caught Bob's attention, taken his mind off the fact that on the way across the street after leaving the office he had found himself propelled towards the traffic in a crowd almost as dense as the crowd there had been that time on the underground platform, and then drawn back as a bus bore down. Was the same joker still tailing him? Or had he held back a second time from taking his life? Was he in charge of himself? He still couldn't remember anything before seeing Caroline on her sitting-room floor ... Jo's wide green eyes were looking at him with gathering anxiety. He made an effort. 'Simon Lambert? I didn't think you knew him.'

'I do. The police are bothering his father, too, so he's as keen as I am about Paul Gibson.'

'But, Jo ... His mother ...'

'I'm sorry, Daddy, I know you were fond of Mrs Lambert, but Simon already suspected she was having an affair. You look awful, are you really all right?'

'I'm all right, Jo.' And had mercifully thought of something else. 'About his father ... Does Simon know?'

'I didn't tell him.'

'No, of course not. I'm sorry, darling. How did you find Mr Gibson?'

'I got his address from the Flower Bower.'

'And when Simon recognised him you went to the police.'

'I didn't actually go to them, Daddy ...'

She moved to the arm of his chair to tell him about the police.

'Jo!'

'It was all right,' she reassured him, ruffling his hair. 'I think Chief Inspector Hewitt was amused, if anything. I hadn't been to see him, I was waiting until Simon had had a chance to identify Paul Gibson, so it was because Maureen had done her stuff after all that he was there. My challenge to her that she was afraid to go to the police must have paid off. I didn't have to tell Detective Chief Inspector Hewitt about being at the Flower Bower because his men had seen me. I suppose they'd come in as customers or been hanging about outside, I should have realised. He's quite nice really, he told me he'd suspected it was me who'd told Maureen her duty, although of course she hadn't given me any credit. Daddy? Don't look like that! I promise you I haven't done any harm –'

His mind had wandered again, and he forced it back. 'I hope and pray you've done a lot of good, darling.' If Paul Gibson had murdered Caroline and the police had let him go, he could have been behind him on the traffic island as well as the Underground platform. And in that case he wouldn't have been trying to commit suicide because he wouldn't have any terrible subconscious knowledge. And Paul Gibson had gone around with Caroline, stolen a photograph of him and her together. And been taken in by the police for questioning. Why wasn't he feeling better? 'You wouldn't know if they held Gibson?'

'I'm afraid not, Daddy. We didn't see him when we got to the station, we were taken straight off to separate little rooms. Detective Chief Inspector Hewitt suggested I didn't pursue my inquiries, of course. Do any more amateur sleuthing, he called it, but not superior at all. Simon approved of him, too.'

'You approve of Simon?'

'Oh, yes. He's – if I don't see a lot more of him I'll be devastated.'

'I wouldn't want that. Are you likely to see a lot more of him?'

'Yes.'

'In that case – in any case – you must tell your mother what's happened.' It was awful, the way his mind was running back over what Jo had told him, clearing it as fit for consumption by Barbara. 'Not the part about Jack,' he went on quickly. 'I'll tell her that eventually myself. But all what one might call your own news. And pretty soon; I don't want her to think we're in cahoots.' Having defined their current relationship, he avoided his daughter's eye.

'Of course, Daddy. I'll go and find her, tell her it was easier to confess one by one. Which it is, of course.' She kissed the top of his head. 'You should be feeling better. The police have got something significant to think about at last, they'll stop pestering innocent people.'

He hated to see her go, to be alone with his thoughts, but at least she had given him something to vie in his mind with the horrors of those moments in the rush-hour traffic. He had thought there was nothing bizarre left to happen, but before he had properly absorbed the truth about Jack's sexual propensities he must grasp that the fruit of Jack's loins was his own daughter's delight.

Chapter Thirteen

Detective Chief Inspector Hewitt would have liked to station himself at the back of the crematorium 'chapel' well in advance of Caroline Lambert's mourners, but the briskness of funeral business that Tuesday morning meant that ingoing and outgoing congregations were milling together for a few chaotic moments outside the chapel door.

At least, uninhibited by the necessity of overt deference either to the dead or to the bereaved, he felt able to undertake a quick dash through the opposing eddies, and when Bob blinked his way reluctantly into the dim, religious light the first thing he noticed was the senior of his two opponents settled in a relaxed pose in the corner of a rear pew.

It was a shock but it shouldn't have been, he had known from the moment of meeting Hewitt that he would worry at Caroline's murder like a dog at a rat. And within the hour he had known he was to be Hewitt's favourite suspect.

Bob made himself ready to mime a good morning, but Hewitt wasn't looking his way and he managed to pass him without pausing, holding Barbara's unresponsive arm and with Jo on his heels, shuffling forward as part of a small crowd until greeted by Simon Lambert and ushered into a pew three rows from the front.

From the corner of his eye, as he squeezed into the space between his wife and his daughter, Bob thought he saw Jo and Simon briefly clasp hands before Simon moved out of sight behind them. He certainly saw Jo raise hers to her lips before settling it demurely in her lap with the other. Well, he liked the idea of his daughter being romantic in an unromantic age, finding kisses and handclasps significant as once he and Barbara had done. As he still did, he realised with an inward grin. Glancing the other way, he saw that Barbara's hands, too, were neat in her lap.

Simon was back in view, escorting Jack and Vernon. Jack was rosy-faced again, too rosy, temples still agleam, looking even in his dark special-occasion suit as if too much room had been left for the accommodation of his big soft body. Vernon looked neat in grey, gently protesting and trying to retrace his steps, but eventually persuaded to sit down with Jack in the front row. His brother's keeper. Well, Vernon had been keeper to them all at some crisis or other of their lives; being with him was probably the best thing that could have happened to Jack in the immediate aftermath of his wife's murder. Not just because of Vernon's understanding, but also because they knew each other just well enough.

Apart from the odd glimpse of Simon, Bob and Barbara didn't know any members of Jack's or Caroline's families. Now he thought about it, their friendship had existed in a vacuum, unrelated to the other parts of their lives. Jack's sister was said to be an invalid and unable to travel, and although Caroline had occasionally talked about hers it had only been to complain about something she had or hadn't done, and he had never met her. She'd surely be coming to Caroline's funeral, though, even from Scotland, where he thought he remembered that she lived. And suddenly he had no doubt he was looking at her, the tall blonde woman in black with the large-meshed hat veil who could be Caroline until her profile was turned to him as she sat down next to Jack. Mouthed some words at him with detached concern in a face as elegant if not quite as beautiful as her sister's. Perhaps Jack and Caroline had lived the whole of their married life in a vacuum, and Jack had needed to get out for some air . . .

Hewitt was aware of Bob Collins the moment he set foot in the chapel, felt the already familiar unwelcome spurt of envy at sight of the tall, slim figure and handsome face topped by a natural abundance of dark, wavy hair. He had been awaiting him as the cornerstone, so to speak, of his morning's enterprise. Hewitt was a childless widower and the envy was intensified by his first view of Collins as a family man with his interestingly colourless wife and extraordinary daughter. He would have liked to add the daughter to his private mental dossier on Collins, who had said nothing about the friendship between her and the Lambert son, but having met her he had to concede the ease of believing her story that no more than two or three meetings had led up to the embrace he had interrupted the day before outside Gibson's place ...

Gibson. Irritably Hewitt pushed the new suspect to the back of his mind. Robert Collins, and probably Jack Lambert too, had failed to level with him – those instincts Jago tended to jeer at had no doubt about that – and he was going to discover what they were hiding and whether they were hiding it together.

But meanwhile Collins's daughter had brought a reminiscent smile to his lips. He had envied Collins most uncomfortably of all in the face of her indignant loyalty to him, but at the same time he had been unable to prevent himself being touched and amused by it, and by the outsize energy and ingenuity that had had her turning up significant information in the van of his own team.

Possibly significant. But the thought of her devastation if – when – he managed to nail her father did give him pause.

Nail him? He couldn't say hand on heart that he was convinced Robert Collins had killed Caroline Lambert, but he would swear he had withheld and distorted the truth.

He'd had the backmost pew to himself, but the man in the tired mac who had just burst past the dummy at the door was hurling himself in beside him, preceded by a powerful wave of tobacco. Press. Whose presence he had been surprised not to see; his practised eye had already told him there were no press men or women present in the small congregation seated in front of him.

'Morning.'

'Morning,' Hewitt said grudgingly. The fellow knew he was a policeman, each of them had recognised the other's office, but he didn't remember seeing him before. Probably Press Association; Caroline Lambert's murder was no longer news enough to merit a range of reporters from individual papers which had already slaked their curiosity on the unrevealing first leg of the inquest. The cameraman would be waiting outside, but there was always the chance of something interesting during the actual proceedings.

Collins's wife really was interesting. She looked so intelligent and was so obviously short on personal vanity, Hewitt hadn't realised at once that she was a beauty. At the last moment he had decided to go to the Collins house himself, and had known right away that unless her evidence was open to corroboration it would be impossible to divine whether or not she was speaking the truth, she was beyond his instincts. But there was no doubt she had spent that day exactly a week ago in the company of her cat lieutenant. He had wanted to ask her to show him the cats for his personal pleasure, but had decided the request was incompatible with the reason for his visit. He also preferred not to hand Jago a chance to jeer on a plate.

Why was he so sure Collins had lied?

It was experience, of course, however hard Jago tried to shake his confidence. Experience of the quality of the atmosphere hanging between him and a potential suspect, of the straightness or the twist of what reached him across desk or table. There had been times when Collins's statements had not been straight, his eyes unnaturally so. In the last decade or two Hewitt's instinct had rarely let him down. His envy of Collins's ease, Collins's unthinking acceptance that the good things in his life were his due, had nothing to do with it. And he might be wrong about that, of course; his skills didn't extend into a suspect's private life.

Lambert? Hewitt moved his head a little so that Jack Lambert's round skull, thinning dark hair following its shape, could be seen in the small space between Collins and his daughter. Fidgety, even now. Then Hewitt turned to the profile behind the veil as it came briefly into his vision, mouth moving. He had only seen Caroline Lambert blown to bits but he had seen a lot of photographs, and this was clearly the sister Lambert had told him stumblingly they scarcely ever saw. Who had undoubtedly been at home in Edinburgh the previous Tuesday.

The murdered woman's only son — only child — hadn't been undoubtedly anywhere. No one in his busy, crowded office remembered seeing him after about five o'clock last Tuesday, and he had admitted to leaving his office early to do some shopping. A girlfried had rung his flat at seven-thirty and got what she had assured Jago was the usual relaxed response, but there had been plenty of time for young Lambert to get out to his parents' house and home again.

Yet he felt Simon Lambert had answered his questions truthfully.

Jack Lambert, he had been going to think about Jack Lambert. Fretfully, as his train of thought was disturbed, Detective Chief Inspector Hewitt heaved to his feet with the rest of the congregation as a smart middle-aged woman moved to the front of the chapel and turned to face them. At least the coffin was already there, light-brown grained oak lying on light-brown grained oak just short of the waiting curtains under a formal arrangement of lilies. He wouldn't have to undergo that grunting, shuffling procession up the aisle which always seemed to unblock the drying tear ducts of about fifty per cent of a funeral congregation.

There had been the usual muted, canned organ voluntary, of course, but it had died away. At least they were to be spared the cant; Hewitt, a lapsed but loyal Calvinist, had after years of investigative funerals failed to reconcile himself to the hypocrisy of the priest-in-waiting who had never met the deceased. But what if they were being faced now by that most unacceptable character of all, the woman priest? No, it was all right, the severely smart woman in the navy-blue suit was Amelia Oliphant, manageress of Caroline Lambert's Guildford flower shop and about to be confirmed as its owner. And with movements last Tuesday evening now accounted for.

'Good morning, friends. Please sit down.' Pause. Brave smile. 'Caroline and Jack Lambert have the courage of their convictions. They believe there is more in heaven and earth than we can dream of, but they do not see it as residing in the teaching of any of the established religions.' Who had composed that, for heaven's sake? 'So dear Jack has given me this enormous privilege, to say a few words to Caroline's family and friends in celebration of her life which has been so tragically ended.'

'Dear Jack' ... Hewitt ended his speculation even as it began. Mrs Oliphant at home had presented a fiercely feminist life style, while at the same time revealing herself to be as fiercely uxurious. During their visit to her immaculate bungalow, Hewitt and Jago had received tea and biscuits at the hands of her cheerful, bustling husband, and Hewitt's instincts had joined with his and Jago's common sense to tell him things were precisely as they seemed. It had been frustrating, though, after she had told them of her promised inheritance, to learn that Mrs Oliphant had received a telephone call at the Flower Bower soon after six o'clock that Tuesday evening, having served her last customer a few moments earlier. The dual alibi was no doubt why she had made no secret of her satisfaction at inheriting Caroline Lambert's business.

'... as intelligent as she was lovely.'

The woman was going it a bit, perhaps because there really wasn't all that much to say. Now he thought about it, Hewitt couldn't remember hearing a single spontaneous expression of love or sorrow during his questioning of Caroline Lambert's family and friends and contacts. Which was sad. There had been the husband, of course, apparently dazed and disorientated, but that wasn't necessarily the same thing.

The husband. Jago had called him a jelly baby, and Hewitt knew what Jago meant without being a hundred per cent convinced Lambert was what he seemed. At first he *had* seemed a soft touch, but somehow the jelly hadn't melted, Lambert had stuck to his guns and eventually even put forward a theory about the killing which Hewitt had had to agree fitted with the reception of the anonymous letter better than anything he or any other policeman had so far been able to think up: Caroline Lambert had had a lover – Paul Gibson? – who had killed her and then done his best to shift suspicion on to Robert Collins.

Why Robert Collins, if he was innocent?

The Assistant Chief Constable had vetoed his suggestion

that official tails be put on Collins and Lambert, but Hewitt had found a couple of greenhorn detective constables willing, even eager, just to see if Collins arrived off his evening train in his usual way, and if Lambert drove straight home from Guildford. They had done, of course, but if they were hiding something, they would ...

'... end with a hymn Jack tells me Caroline would have been happy to sing, in celebration of the mystery of the world where we find ourselves: God is working his purpose out ...'

Mystery of the world where we find ourselves! Jo thought scornfully as the congregation rose again to its feet, leaflets rustling. Scornfully because the words had been obliquely ascribed to Caroline Lambert, whose vision had been limited to dinner parties, make-up, clothes and adultery. Approvingly behind the scorn, because Jo herself saw the world as wonderfully mysterious and led by a divine force which in her opinion hadn't been defined by any so-called holy books. She could hardly wait to discuss it with Simon, but of course she would have to be prepared to discover that he wasn't ready.

Simon. Precisely in front of her so that her hand was only a few inches from his magnet of a head. But despite her incredulous happiness Jo felt restless and anxious, now there was nothing more to be done for her father. Anxious to hear from Barry Fox again, confirming his suggestion that she might like to work for him in Highgate. (Simon lived in St John's Wood.) Anxious, of course, to learn that Hewitt and co. had arrested Paul Gibson, so that the police would no longer have outrageous ideas about her father and she wouldn't have to deal with sudden fears that Simon ...
She hated it when there was nothing she could do, when she just had to wait. At least, though, while she waited now she had something good, something wonderful, to remember and anticipate.

Would Paul Gibson have been in that small congregation, Hewitt wondered, studying the backs of the two girls from the Flower Bower, if he and Jago hadn't caught up with him?

Gibson had been blustery and belligerent, but Hewitt, slotting him into his Seedy Rep category, had seen the fear in his eyes. He'd have another session with him when he got back, he'd have to, and after that, if he still protested his innocence, they would have to let him go. For the time being. How long would he have to wait before he could have another session with Collins? Jago's fancy had been the Oliphant woman before her double alibi turned up. Aware of that unloaded gun, neither of them was giving much thought to the police team still systematically visiting local householders and trying to match criminal fingerprints with what they had got out of the Lambert house. He mustn't let himself start being afraid, yet, that it was going to turn into the first unsolved murder of his career, deal a blow that would devastate him both professionally and personally, leave him with a puzzle he'd never be able to solve. Not before he'd had another session with Collins . . .

The service — for want of a better word — was going to be mercifully short. At the end of the hymn an elderly man with white hair whom Hewitt hadn't encountered changed places with Mrs Oliphant and suggested a final few moments of silence. The canned music started up again before anyone began to get restless, and while the reporter beside him charged out of the chapel on the first tinny notes, Hewitt stood motionless in his corner, finding the departures more interesting than the arrivals because of the general evidence of relieved relaxation, and the congregation now facing him the length of the aisle. Maureen Jones, the terrible young woman who had told him about Gibson and the photograph, gave him a triumphantly self-satisfied smile as she passed his pew. Mrs Oliphant inclined her head, offering no indication of her reaction to his presence. He could see Robert Collins preparing his face for the encounter several steps before he drew abreast and abruptly smiled and nodded. Collins's wife studied him at leisure, without expression. The daughter grinned and hunched her shoulders and he found himself grinning back. Lambert had his arm round his sister-in-law, who Hewitt thought was quickening her pace in order to escape it. Lambert had been pale that first time, as pale as the thin Alec Guinness look-alike who was Collins's wife's brother and who was walking on his own behind them, but now his round, vaguely defined face was too red. He was wiping his moist eyes when he came level with Hewitt, but Hewitt could just see that he was painfully smiling. He and the sister-in-law and Vernon Tennant were the last out, and when they had gone the coffin began to slide away and Hewitt strolled to the door preparing to stand there and witness the handshakes.

But he had forgotten about the press of business, and was forced to give way to a waiting cortege.

'Let's hope that's seen him off,' Jack murmured to Bob. 'I'd have preferred it without him. And I'd have preferred to ask you to speak for Caroline, Bob, but in the circumstances ...'

He had introduced the Collins family to his sister-in-law, and Barbara and Jo were just out of earshot.

'Of course.' Bob tried to control his shudder. 'It was — very sincere, Jack.' He felt an idiot. And although he agreed with the sentiments that had produced Mrs Oliphant as the presiding figure, hypocritically he had missed the man and the priest. 'The best it could have been.'

'I thought so.' Jack's face was briefly satisfied as his wet eyes looked vaguely round the scattering congregation. 'Simon's talking to Jo. Looks as if he knows her.'

'They met at the club dance last summer. You remember.'

'I remember how sticky they made it for — us.' The channel down one side of Jack's nose had water in it. 'They hated every minute.'

'A least they can't have been indifferent to one another. I haven't known anything about it either,' Bob went on quickly. 'But last night Jo did just hint ...'

'I think I'd like that, Bob,' said Jack sentimentally.

'Me too.' The other channel was filling up. 'Shall we play golf on Sunday?'

'I'll ring you. Why d'you think Hewitt came to the funeral when he's got Gibson?'

'He won't let us go as easily as that.' But Bob had been asking himself the same question. 'D'you see the press? I'm sure of it. That couple at a distance, one of them with a camera.'

'At least they're at a distance.'

'Their pictures won't be. Telescopic lens. Hewitt warned me. I'd expected a swarm.'

'We're stale news now, Bob, thank God.'

'Let's hope you're right.' It was only since Caroline's death that Bob had noticed the occasional cynicism punctuating Jack's prevailingly flabby conversation. 'Hello, Vernon.'

'Good morning, Bob.' Vernon had made himself scarce the moment he and Jack had emerged into the open air. No doubt, thought Bob, so that Jack could receive the congregation's condolences undiluted. He wondered how Jack could bear to stand around listening to the embarrassed attempts at comfort from friends and colleagues. It was bad enough knowing what to say when people died naturally, or even in accidents, but when they had been murdered ... Jack, though, Bob now knew, was tough as well as sentimental.

'D'you think you're ready to go now, Jack?' asked Vernon concernedly. 'You've done wonderfully well, so brave ....'

'I'm not brave, I like people. They help. Perhaps you're right, though, Vernon, I am a bit tired.'

And alarmingly rosy after those days of pallor, and with a noticeably trembling hand as it rose to wipe an eye. Hewitt had found a good spot in the angle of a wall, unobtrusive but still near enough to the milling remains of the Lambert mourners to be able to observe some detail. Not that he had learned anything new, inside the chapel or out of it, and Jago had now emerged from the car he had brought as instructed to pick up his superior officer and was miming restlessness and impatience as he walked up and down beside it, looking with unnecessary frequency at his watch. The journalist and the photographer were still prowling the bounds of the remaining mourners, continuously recording. As he decided he had kept Jago waiting long enough, Hewitt saw the Collins trio moving away from the chapel forecourt in close array, then saw the photographer stagger and almost lose balance as the daughter passed him in a welter of flying arms and scarves. And no doubt a sudden, sharp movement of a foot ... Hewitt was smiling to himself again as he set off towards the car.

'Useful, was it? I was here at half past as instructed.'

'Of course you were, Jago. No, it wasn't useful, but I'm glad I went.'

'Confirmed your prejudices, did it?'

'Very likely. Any developments?'

'I should get in.'

Jago held the door for him, and something in his words and the pleased expression of his face gave Hewitt a stab of unease.

'What is it?' He had made himself wait until Jago was behind the wheel and had closed his own door.

'It's Gibson, sir.' It wasn't the first time Hewitt had heard insolence rather than respect in Jago's 'sir'. But he still liked working with him better than with any sergeant of recent memory. 'Those prints we got off his mug of tea. They corresponded to a set collected from upstairs in the Lambert house. Upstairs,' Jago repeated, savouring the word. 'When Gibson hasn't so much as admitted ever being downstairs. Ever being inside the house at all.'

'Where upstairs?' Hewitt managed.

'Headboard of the guest bed, low down behind the pillows. The house is clinically clean, but there was a little area there that had been missed out. Likewise in the lady's bathroom — you know she and her husband each had their own — at the top of the side panel. Robert Collins, breathe again!'

'That will do, Jago. And it doesn't mean Paul Gibson is a murderer.'

'For goodness sake, sir —'

'It obviously means he was a boyfriend, I'm not denying that, and I don't imagine he will, either, when confronted by the evidence. But it's not necessarily sinister if the instinct of self-preservation made him give total innocence a try.'

'Like with Collins?'

'Possibly.' Talking as he was managing to talk was helping Hewitt subdue his disappointment.

'Don't forget there's love in the afternoon,' said Jago cruelly. 'I mean, Gibson's a salesman, he could turn up at the Lambert's then, where Collins couldn't.'

'I haven't said I think Collins was Caroline Lambert's lover.'

'No, sir.'

'Any more than I've said he killed her. I've just said, and continue to say, that I'm convinced he's hiding something.' He was protesting too much.

'Of course, sir.'

'Has Gibson been confronted with the evidence of the prints?'

'No, sir. The ACC said that should be your job.'

'Very generous of him, Jago. Well, let's get on with it.' Feeling dull and heavy, Hewitt pulled at his seat belt.

'Of course, sir.' Jago started the engine. 'Whatever the outcome, you'll agree that at the moment Gibson is the man helping the police with their inquiries?'

'Of course. Anonymously at this stage.'

'Of course. You won't be easing Collins's anxieties by telling him the role has been temporarily filled?'

The detective chief inspector turned to his sergeant. 'You know, Jago, I believe I will. Even if we have to let Gibson go after he's confessed to an affair and denied murder. It'll make him — Collins — relax. And then perhaps ... Let's get going.' The car moved off. 'I'll have done with Gibson by the evening and then we'll call on Collins at home.'

Chapter Fourteen

Beyond the crematorium gates the trio Hewitt had envied split up.

'I expect you'd like a little quiet time on your own,' said Jo, bringing them to a halt. 'And Simon ...'

'Isn't Simon going with his father?' asked Bob.

'You can be awfully conventional, Daddy. You know perfectly well Simon and his father don't exactly seek each other out.' She saw her mother smile. 'Simon's been through the motions, of course, but his father wants to go back to the office. I hope you're not going to do that, Daddy!' she added anxiously.

Barbara's smile turned into a laugh. 'I expect he is.'

'No, I'm not. I'm taking your mother out to lunch. I was looking forward to taking you, too.'

'Oh, Daddy!'

'Don't look so stricken, I'm teasing. And Simon Lambert could probably do with the right company.'

We're behaving as if we're back to normal, thought Bob on a pang of anguish. Realising bleakly that even if Hewitt got off his back, transferred his interest to Gibson, things would never be normal while his secret festered in Barbara's ignorance, unlanceable.

'Off you go, Jo,' said Barbara. 'See you for a late supper?'

'But of course!' I'm getting actressy, thought Jo, as aware of the look of outraged innocence in her face as if she could see it. But she had exaggerated everything for as far back as she could remember, long before drama school. Perhaps that was why it was so wonderful not to be exaggerating Simon. Who now was appearing through the gates with his father, causing an awkward little stand-around while her mother and father invited Jack to join them for lunch and he painfully declined.

It was in the little things, Bob decided as he shifted from foot to foot, that Jack was indecisive. Their contact had consisted of a series of little things, which must be why he had assumed that indecision characterised Jack's whole nature. It was obviously beyond him to break up the uneasy party and Simon and Jo weren't going to do it, according their elders a particular gentleness in view of their current vulnerability. Barbara, of course, would continue to wait on events in her habitual way — cats weren't concerned with a few lost or found moments ...

'We'll see you soon then, Jack,' he managed. 'Jo says you're going back to the office.'

'Best.'

'Yes. Where's Vernon?'

'Gone tactfully off.' So that Simon and his father could have the talk they of course hadn't had. Jack glanced at his son. 'He insisted we came in separate cars.'

'Typical Vernon.' Bob noticed Jack shuffling his feet. 'Yes, ring me if you'd like some golf on Sunday, Jack. And please just come to us any time at all.'

'Of course, Jack,' said Barbara.

'Thanks.'

'Let's find your car,' Simon suggested to Bob's relief, taking his father by the arm. 'See you, Mr Collins. All right, Jo?'

'I'm glad Jack didn't quite force us to leave him,' Bob said to Barbara as he watched the disappearing backs and tried to decide whether it looked a natural and inevitable thing for Jo to be walking away beside Simon Lambert. He realised that for the first time since Caroline's death he had taken Barbara's arm without thinking about it, and was shocked at his resumption of an outer confidence which was no reflection of the incurable inner reality. 'Where should we go?'

'I've got a casserole —'

'Tonight. Samantha's there?'

'Yes.'

'All right, then. You can be spared for a couple of hours. We'll go anywhere you like apart from the Antelope. That's Jack's hunting ground.' He wished he hadn't put it like that.

'Let's go Haslemere way.'

It was five o'clock when they got home, Bob so painfully enchanted with Barbara and so disgusted with himself that he felt the tiredness of a hard day's work.

'You look all in,' said Barbara in the kitchen. 'Come down to the cats.'

Samantha was there, crooning to a small neat moggy, her voice drowned by the shrill neighbouring indignation of Jingpaws. Mick got in through the door with them, and was caught and ejected by Barbara. It all helped Bob a bit.

Halfway up the garden they met Vernon.

'I just thought I'd see how you were. I did telephone but you weren't ... I hope you were out to lunch together.'

'We were. Bob's going to make a pot of tea.'

They were sitting over it round the kitchen table, minus Samantha who had a date, when the front-door bell rang.

'I'll get it.'

In the hall he slowed down, recognising the outline of the two heads beyond the coloured oval of glass in his Victorian front door.

'Sorry to trouble you yet again, Mr Collins,' said Hewitt politely. 'But might we come in for a minute?'

'Good evening,' said Detective Sergeant Tabley. Bob thought it was the first time he had offered a greeting.

'Yes. Of course. My brother-in-law's here. We're in the kitchen.'

'We'll join you in the kitchen, Mr Collins. It isn't private.'

Bob stood aside for the policemen to precede him, not bothering to announce them.

'Plenty of chairs, as you can see,' said Barbara. Vernon made a gesture of moving up, although there was more than enough room.

'Thank you.' Hewitt and Tabley sat down side by side,

but Tabley pushed his chair so far back to accommodate the stretch of his legs that he ended up behind his chief. Barbara indicated the teapot on the Aga.

'No, thank you, we're only here for a moment. With some better news, you may say. Sergeant?'

Bob saw Tabley flash a smile at the chief inspector, and interpreted it as ironic acknowledgement of Hewitt's disinclination to pass on better news in this particular direction. 'We can't say much at the moment, you'll appreciate, Mr Collins. But we can tell you that we have a man helping us with our inquiries into the murder of Mrs Lambert. We thought you'd like to know.'

'Thank you.' Gibson. Paul Gibson. It was all so obvious. And his relief was so strong it was making him light-headed. Only it wasn't lasting, ten seconds on he was realising that no news Hewitt or anybody else might bring him could heal the real hurt. 'It was good of you to come and tell me.' And make the most of the excuse for examining him again at close quarters. Even now Bob could see in Hewitt's face that he hadn't given up.

'That's very good news.' Barbara's face had actually lit up, but she spoke faintly, and with an alarm swamping all other sensations Bob saw her go deathly pale and lean her head on her hand.

'Are you all right, Barbara?' He and Vernon spoke almost in unison.

'Yes. Fine.' Barbara raised her head and smiled without reassuring Bob. 'Relief – can do strange things.'

So perhaps she had been really afraid for him.

Of him?

He wouldn't, he couldn't, believe that. She had made him so certain she had never for a moment suspected he could have killed Caroline.

Hewitt was getting to his feet. 'We'll be on our way, then.'

'We'll tell you more, of course,' said Tabley, 'if and when we can.'

'Rest assured we won't let you learn anything from the media. Goodbye, Mrs Collins, Mr Tennant. Are you sure you're all right, Mrs Collins?'

'Yes. Really. Thank you for coming, Chief Inspector.'

Bob led the way out to the hall, where Detective Sergeant Tabley assured him a second time that they'd be in touch again if and when they could. When he got back Barbara hadn't moved and Vernon was on his feet.

'I think I'll go now, Bob, Barbara seems all in.'

He heard himself urging Vernon to stay for supper.

'No, no.' Vernon led him back into the hall. 'Not tonight.' He opened the front door, then turned and put his hand on Bob's shoulder. 'It looks as thought your ordeal is coming to an end, Bob. Justice is always ultimately done.'

'I wish I could believe you.' He was more and more aware that the police news hadn't touched the real problem. 'Thank you for all your support.'

'I'll see you both again soon. Look after Barbara.'

'I'm going to do that now. Goodbye, Vernon.'

Over three recurrences of the pattern of the hall carpet Bob discovered how he was going to do it. What all at once he had to do, more compellingly than he had ever had to do anything in his life before.

He flung himself back into the kitchen.

'Barbara. Darling. I have to tell you something.' She still hadn't moved, but she raised her head to the excitement in his voice. And he felt excited. He might be about to wreck the rest of his life, but at least the wound would be clean and all at once there was no alternative.

'Can you let it wait, Bob? I feel a bit faint.'

'No, I can't let it wait. But we'll go into the sitting-room and you'll lie on the sofa while I talk. Come on.'

Her slight weight was so heavy against him as he helped her up the alarm came back. 'Have you had this before?'

'Sometimes. You know I tend to be anaemic. That's all it is. And the relief.'

'You look anything but relieved. Come on, darling.'

By the time they reached the hall she was walking unassisted, but she sagged into his arms by the sofa and let him lift her legs. He covered them with the rug from the back of her chair, sat down on the floor within touching distance. Then decided to move parallel with her head, so that he couldn't look at her while he spoke.

'Comfortable?'

'Yes.'

'Barbara. Don't say anything until I've finished unless you absolutely have to. Just listen. And just remember that I love you.' No reaction, unless he really had heard a sigh. 'Barbara, when I went to Jack and Caroline one Tuesday. About a year ago. Jack wasn't there. Caroline just said when I arrived that he had to be away. That seemed strange. Old Jack such an open book.' He could only manage it in staccato jerks. But he was managing it. 'Another strange thing was that Caroline was different. Sort of untidy. No, not untidy, well, not on the surface, but inside ...' He had to stop and cough at his dry throat. Apprehension was catching up with the excitement. 'After dinner she told me Jack was having an affair. She cried. I – I comforted her as I'd have comforted Jack. Nothing more. It – didn't occur to me. Then. Barbara, she kissed me. She made a business of drawing back, apologising, and I didn't realise right away that she'd meant to do it. Meant to start an affair with me. Which she did. Barbara.'

He had to clasp his hands to keep them away from her, stop them seeking the reaction which wasn't coming in response to his words. 'I – I was dazzled. I was the rabbit in front of the stoat.' But Caroline couldn't have done it on her own. 'I'm sorry, that sounds like an excuse, and there isn't one. I could have left then, and come home. She told me to, if I wasn't prepared ...' That was the worst thing he had to tell, and he had told it. At least, now, he would never be reluctant to meet his wife's eyes. If she was prepared to meet his. Turning his head at last he saw her pale cold profile and looked in anguish away, down to the motionless mound of her feet.

'So. It began that night. And – went on the other Tuesdays I was there. We never met anywhere else, or at Green Lawns at any other time. I didn't see Jack at home again, only at the club.' Jack's love life seemed so unimportant, he'd decide another time whether or not to tell her what he knew about it. 'For a time. For a few months. I was – I suppose I was in love with Caroline. Novelty, perhaps. It's the only time I've ever been unfaithful to you.' One of the hands clasped across her chest loosened, re-engaged itself with the other. Savagely he held on to his. 'By the time she died. Months before she died. I wanted out. The last time I was there before she died I realised while I was — with her — how much I love you. Barbara ...'

'The last time you were there before she died.'

No expression in the voice, the face still in remote profile. But the hands relaxing.

'Yes. I suppose that's why ... You didn't think I was serious — how could you? — but that's why I've had such awful moments of wondering if it was me who killed her. I wanted so desperately to break away from her. Barbara, I still can't remember going into the room, first seeing her ...'

'You couldn't kill anyone.'

'Oh, darling. Oh, Barbara, it seems such a feeble thing to say, special pleading, but it's just a statement of fact. Having an affair with Caroline taught me how much I love you. How precious ...' Another savage effort, as he managed not to cry. 'I don't mind anything, now that you know.'

'Neither do I.'

'What?' He tried to withstand the stab of joy. He had to be failing to understand what she had said.

'Neither do I, now that you've told me. Let me get up. I've something to tell *you*.'

'Barbara ...' He put his arm under her shoulders and helped her round, disentangled the rug from her legs as they dropped in front of him. Even dared lay his head against her knees.

'Let me get up,' she said again, but after a few seconds. He scrambled to his feet and took her hands.

'Sit down, Bob.' Gently she disengaged them, walked over to her desk. Obeying her, struggling against the precarious sense of joy, he watched her open the desk, take something out of one of the tiny internal drawers, walk at the same steady pace over to the cassette player on the shelf beside the fireplace, insert the tape.

'Barbara ...'

She put a finger to her lips. The unaccustomed compassion of her face reanimated his apprehension and his excitement. She sat down opposite him as the tape began.

Hello, darling, it's me.

It was a few seconds before he recognised a recording of one of his Tuesday night calls from Green Lawns.

'Barbara ...'

'When it's finished.'

... do hope the fact that you're not there to answer the phone doesn't mean a cat's ill. That was the moment he had realised he had no idea what she did on Tuesday nights. Which was the last time he had stayed at Green Lawns.

... my dear husband has gone to do something nasty in the woodshed! Caroline's voice, strong and aggressively alive, brought his heart up into his throat. Barbara's hands twisted in her lap.

Look, Barbara, if there's anything wrong, for heaven's sake ring us when you get in, you're not usually with the cats at this time. Then if we don't hear we won't worry. Good night, darling, see you usual time tomorrow.

Thank goodness that was the end of it, and Barbara would switch off and start explaining —

You resent Barbara monopolising the answerphone, don't you?

He didn't understand right away. Like an idiot he thought, Oh yes, of course, it didn't end there after all. That was what he went on thinking while he heard himself defending the answerphone arrangement, he actually felt pleased to hear himself so fair.

D'you still love Jack, Caroline?

But he hadn't said that on the answerphone ...

I worry about you.

'Oh, God! Oh, God, Barbara.'

'Hush. You told me.'

You mustn't worry, Bob. Yes, I do love Jack. Don't make me angry by reminding me.

Perhaps he'll come to his senses. You've never told me anything about him, about — this other woman. It is just one?

It was laughter, now, that he was having to choke down. Shrieking, hysterical laughter.

Just one could be worse than several, if you think about it.

It could be more serious, I suppose. But several ... That would mean he wasn't the man we've always thought him.
Carolin'e defensive public laugh. *No man's the man you've always thought him when he gets the middle-aged itch.*
I don't believe in it.
You're not suffering from it, then?
You know I'm not. I love you, Caroline.

'Barbara, for God's sake. Please. Barbara, that was the moment, the exact moment, when I knew I loved *you*. Yes, I went to bed again with Caroline. It obviously didn't suddenly become impossible, and I was in her hands. Hers and Jack's. There was no way I could stop it.'

'You could have told me.' She leaned out and switched off the machine.

'Oh, darling, thank you. Yes, I could have told you, I should have told you, had faith ... But when I realised what I'd been risking – I didn't dare. I have to ask your forgiveness for that, as well.'

'I forgive you. It's a while since I fed your faith.'

'Or I yours. Yet you ... Knowing – that – you must have suspected me. Of murder, I mean. You must.'

'Never for a moment. Not just because I suspected you of loving her.'

He hurled himself across the gap between them and fell on his knees, burrowing his head into her lap. 'You've been thinking I loved Caroline.'

'In certain moods. Since hearing you say it.'

'Oh, darling.' Her fingers were in his hair. He was imagining her coming up from the cats, sitting down alone to find out if anyone had rung while she had been down the garden ... 'You didn't let me know. You managed not to let me know.'

'Domino had died. Dear old Domino, I blessed him for that.'

'What were you going to do?'

'Kill Caroline?'

'Barbara! Anyway, you were with Samantha.'

'Ah, yes. I have an alibi.'

He was aghast at himself. 'Oh, darling, I wouldn't have suspected you if you hadn't!' Did he really have her faith?

'Samantha and I are very close.'

'Don't be absurd.' She had said that to him when he suggested he might be the murderer.

'It had to be said some time.'

He had said something like that to her. 'So it's said and done. What were you going to do?'

'I don't know. I really don't know. I only know I didn't tell you what I'd heard because I wanted you to have the chance of telling me yourself. You did.'

He held one knee, then the other. There was something else he had to find out.

'How did the tape – end?'

'On your suggestion that you both forget me and concentrate on yourselves. Then ... A few sounds. I didn't record them.'

'Oh, darling.' As he leaned up to her she leaned down to him, let him take her face in his hands. 'I put the portable phone down on that little table beside the sofa.' He dropped his head back on to her knee. 'I thought I switched it off. Barbara ...'

'Saying let's forget me was the worst thing you said. Caroline doesn't come out of it so well.'

'So well? How can you be generous?'

'I'm being fair.'

'And in bed ... Knowing –'

'I told you, I didn't want you to know I knew. And the body has its reflexes. Affection is the thing that suffers. Isn't it?'

'Yes.'

'Sit up, I want to look at you.' Obediently he raised his head, stared into her steady eyes. 'It may seem strange, Bob, but the worst thing has been your deceiving me. And doing it so well. So impeccably.'

'Oh, God, Barbara –'

She gripped his hands. 'I knew if you told me it might be as the prelude to leaving me, but I still wanted you to. I couldn't bear that you were able to look me in the eye –'

'Don't! I couldn't bear it either. If I was clever it was desperation. What the affair with Caroline did was show me I couldn't live without you. Then just now I realised that if

I didn't tell you I wasn't really living with you anyway. I've been a fool as well as a knave.'

She was laughing. Barbara was laughing. 'Not a knave, Bob. I'm sorry I haven't been able to be more openly sympathetic with you over Hewitt. Have you told him? Is that why – '

'No! After I'd – found Caroline – I had a reflex rush of self-preservation and laid a third place at the table.' Mentioning the nightie on the guest-room bed would be self-indulgence. 'After the good luck of getting hold of Jack. He saw the dining table and played along. I had no conscience about that, Hewitt was investigating a murder. Which I hadn't committed. Had I?' Bob heard his voice suddenly loud and frightened. He was on his feet, gripping the mantelpiece. 'Had I, Barbara? Had I? Oh, darling, on the station platform ... then in the road ...'

'Bob, for God's sake.'

He came back to her and told her. 'I couldn't remember going into Caroline's sitting-room, first seeing her. I still can't. Barbara, did I twice almost kill myself?'

'Of course you didn't.' Her voice was reassuring but it was feeble, her face had drained again.

'You're not well. Oh, darling.'

'I'm all right. Just a bit dizzy. You didn't tell Hewitt that, either?'

'No. He'd have thought I was mad. Whoever – it was – must have reckoned on that.' His hesitation was brief. 'Darling, there's something else. The last thing. The thing to explain Hewitt. Although even before ... Barbara, someone sent Hewitt an anonymous letter. *Ask Robert Collins about his relations with Caroline Lambert.*' He didn't have to search for the exact words. 'Even then I managed to lie.' His eyes slid away from hers, but he brought them back. 'I reminded him the nation knew I'd found Caroline's body. But he must have sensed the extra something in my shock. Not that the letter had to make me seem guilty so far as Hewitt was concerned. Of – adultery – any more than of murder. It could just have been insurance taken out by a killer who knew I was a regular visitor to the Lamberts. Jack went on lying, too ... It doesn't make things any worse, really, darling, it was just a starter for the tube platform and the traffic island – '

'Which could be a starter for ... ' Her voice died away and she sank back in her chair.

'You've got to go and lie down, Barbara. I'll bring you up some supper. Do the cats.'

'No!' Something he didn't understand had flashed across her face. 'We'll do things together as usual. I'm all right now, it was just the shock.'

'The final shock.'

'I hope so. Look, Bob, I really am all right. See.' Gently she pushed him away, got to her feet. 'A whisky will help.'

'I think there was another reason I didn't tell Hewitt,' he said as he poured them drinks. 'I couldn't have let him into a secret I was keeping from *you*.'

'Thank you. You think he's still interested in you, though, don't you?'

'Oh, yes. It's Tabley who's pleased about Gibson. Did Gibson push me, Barbara?'

She sat down again. A few drops of whisky sparkled on the velvet arm of her chair. 'Someone did. I don't want to sound melodramatic, Bob, but I think you're going to have to be careful.'

Chapter Fifteen

Bob's new happiness urged him to be carefree, it shrivelled all remaining worries in its radiant light. But Barbara in the very early morning, when they were awake from their short sleep, repeated her warning to be vigilant, and cheerfully he promised her to try.

On the Underground platform he waited well away from the edge. On the escalator he held firmly to the rail. In the street ... What could he do to protect himself in the street? Barbara had also said that for a determined criminal there were many ways ... She had trailed there into silence, eyes staring wide into his in the dawn light, after stumbling over the word *criminal*, which she had started as *assassin*.

'What would be the point of killing me, darling? The point is to rattle me, make me look furtively over my shoulder so that Hewitt and co. find my behaviour suspicious. Anyway, Gibson's probably still helping the police with their inquiries.'

'Maybe, but I have instincts. Promise me.'

So he had promised. And he supposed she was right. Even if the intention was to do no more than make him nervous, someone had already gone dangerously beyond the bounds of normal behaviour. Which would make it easier to go further still. Despite the attempt at logic with which he had tried to counter Barbara's fears, Bob knew that for the mind that had engineered his involuntary movements on station platform and traffic island, there existed an inducement to kill: suicide could spell guilt.

At least, now, he had ceased to suspect himself. Barbara

had seen to that during the intervals of conversation and companionship which had punctuated the long night, and he had not taken a great deal of convincing; if he had shared his fears earlier he would already have shed them.

'You seem better this morning, Mr Collins.'

Even Gail had commented on the exuberance he was finding so hard to restrain.

'The police have someone helping them with their inquiries.'

He used the excuse to his partner as well, to a couple of old clients, and to the barman at the White Lion. He remembered to place himself with his back against a wall or counter where this was possible. Confine himself to the office loo.

When he came out of Dorking Station at a quarter to seven Barbara was standing beside her car.

'Still in one piece, darling.' He had seen her tense body relax.

'Oh, Bob.'

It was wonderful to be able to look at her with eyes fronting a clear channel from his soul. Kiss her without feeling guilty. 'Nothing in the day beyond routine.' He closed the door on the passenger side. 'You?'

'Nothing, really.' She started the engine. 'Jingpaws has been tetchy. We've a beautiful newcomer for what I hope is the first of a regular series of visits. Samantha made me laugh at lunchtime. It appears this new boyfriend . . .'

But she wasn't hiding her nervousness. 'You really are worried, aren't you, Barbara?'

'I can't forget the attacks on you and the anonymous letter. Not normal.'

'It's just that you haven't had time to get used to them. And they weren't exactly attacks.'

'Let's not go round the circle again.' She took her hand off the wheel to touch his face. 'Let's just be careful and not talk about it.'

'You're right as usual.' But he had to search for another subject. 'Jo was in good form last night.' She had come in joyful and sensed their joy. It had been an evening as wonderful as the night, in a different way. 'What's she doing today?'

'Looking starry-eyed. She spent the morning with me so I had the chance to reassure myself that her feet haven't entirely left the ground. She was seeing a girl friend this afternoon and going on to dinner with Simon. He seems all right?'

'The little I've seen of him. Barbara. We don't want Jo ever to know about my affair with Caroline.' He was almost pleased to say it, because of being able to.

'Of course not. She'd take it as understandable human frailty in any other man, but not in you. Particularly as she considered Caroline beneath notice.'

There was an ironic smile on Barbara's profiled mouth, which warmed as she briefly glanced at him. His cup running over. 'Seen Vernon today?'

'No. I tried to get hold of him this morning, but he'd gone to a house sale somewhere on the coast. I left a message for him to come for supper. All right?'

'Of course. Barbara. Did you ever say anything to Vernon?'

'No.'

'I thought you might have done. Wouldn't it have helped?'

'Nothing would have helped.' Unprecedentedly she caught the kerb as she swung round a corner. 'I'm sorry, Bob, I'm just answering your question. Don't ask any more. You don't need to, and we've agreed not to talk about it.'

'I know. It was just that I've had wild thoughts myself about confiding in Vernon, he being that sort of person. End of subject. Do you remember how marvellous silence used to be?'

'I remember.'

They were silent for the rest of the way home, and it would have been marvellous again if he hadn't been worried by the waxen look of her.

'Won't you lie down?' he asked, as she walked laggingly into the house.

'I'm all right, Bob.'

'I didn't give you enough sleep last night.' It would be some time before he would be able to resist testing for her restored smile.

'All I wanted,' she said, turning to him with a look which was as good.

His joy surged. 'We'll go to bed early again tonight. If Vernon comes he won't stay late.'

They had the cat necessities gathered when the telephone rang. Vernon told Bob he was just back from Southsea and had found Barbara's message relayed from his shop staff.

'Good of you both to ask me, Bob. I was going to ring anyway and suggest popping in, I've a nice piece of smoked salmon I picked up at the coast this afternoon. I wasn't thinking of supper, but if you're both really sure you feel like a visitor ...'

'You're not a visitor, Vernon. Come straight over.' Grinning at Barbara, he rang off and broke the news of a three-course dinner.'

'I'll put it on pieces of that delicious brown bread.'

Hands full, on the way down the garden they rubbed shoulders. Mick's attention was distracted by some new kittens in the pen, and it was Charlie who had to be gently footed away from the door.

'Have a look at Arabella,' said Barbara as she shut them in. 'Next door to Jingpaws. He isn't impressing her.'

Arabella was a myriad muted tones of tortoiseshell, with delicate small head and tiny, expressive front paws. Jingpaws glared and growled through her emotional introduction to Bob. Flattening her head in response to Bob's hand beneath her chin, she narrowed her green eyes at the dividing mesh.

'Poor Jingpaws,' said Barbara, joining them. 'He's tormented with jealousy.'

'I'll go and have a word with him.' Bob paused in the doorway, looking back. 'She's enchanting, isn't she?'

'Yes. I'm so glad we can look forward — Bob, get down!'

Afterwards he thought he remembered it going darker, but now there was just Barbara's face a sudden mask of terror, Barbara's hands on his shoulders whirling him round and forcing him to the floor. Then a blood-curdling, high-pitched, long-drawn-out scream, which was still sounding when the echoes of the explosion had died away.

'Barbara! What was it? I can't move.'
'Neither can I.'

Her voice was a whisper. She was lying on top of him, her hair silky on his face. They were taking up most of the space on the floor of Arabella's quarters.

'If you'll just let me get out from under. The Ascot must have blown up. Jingpaws didn't like it, did he?' He still didn't understand.

'I'm afraid I can't move, Bob.' Barbara's voice was just a sigh but her mouth wasn't far from his ear. When she lay on him in bed she was never so heavy. He pressed his hands into her back to get purchase for sliding out, and she gave a terrible choked cry.

'Darling!' His hands were wet. 'Perhaps it's a water main.'

'It was a gunshot, Bob.' He could feel her fluttering breath. 'It hit me in the back. I'm afraid I can't move my legs, so if you can sort of ease your way out ...'

'You saved my life.' It must be his subconscious speaking, he hadn't taken it in. 'You saw the gun and you got in front of me. Oh, Barbara, darling ...'

'I think after all — I'll have to ask you to stay still, Bob.'

Which meant he mustn't even shout out his fury. 'Of course, darling.' There didn't seem to be much blood, but she was wearing a jacket. Please God it had helped. 'I'll be your couch until Vernon comes. I won't move.' Just lie still and will his own shameful uninjured strength up into her. Dear God, he had pressed his hands into her shattered back. Couldn't move her legs ... 'Does it hurt to move your legs, darling?'

'No. It's just that I can't, they won't take any notice of me. It isn't hurting very much, Bob, at all.'

'Vernon will be here any minute, I told him to come straight over. We'll just keep still together until he arrives. Can you feel my hands?'

'Not now. Can you hear me?'
'Yes. But don't talk if —'
'So long as you can hear me. I don't seem —'
'I wasn't worth it, Barbara.'

'You can't judge.' The words blew softly out on one effort of breath, stirring her hair into a caress.

'You were afraid of this.'

'Yes.'

'What did you see? Oh, darling, I didn't mean ... Don't try to —'

'A man in a hood. On the slope. Must have come — over the wall. Suddenly reared up. Blocked the light. Gun through that open top window. Jingpaws screaming must have — made him pull the trigger.'

And perhaps kill after all. 'Oh, God, Barbara.'

'Otherwise when I ... he'd have gone away. Come another time. When you were available.' Barbara coughed, a terrible jangled noise she could have brought on by actually trying to laugh. But he had always known she was brave. If now he felt wet on the side of his face ...

'Oh, God.' The side of his face that mattered was still mercifully dry, but the other side was suddenly warm, something soft was pushing against it. 'Arabella's joined us, darling.'

'Arabella ...'

The purring swelled, louder than Barbara's whisper. 'She's against my face, she must be squeezed in between our shoulders. I can't push her out. Can you feel her?' Please God Barbara could feel her.

'I can feel her. I can feel your mouth.' Through her hair he was just able to kiss the tip of her ear. 'It's my legs ...'

'Barbara?' Her voice had trailed away, he had the terrible impression her body was even heavier. 'Darling, hold on. Barbara, my dearest love, you'll be all right.'

'Yes ...'

His body ought to be uncomfortable, but all it was registering was Barbara's weight and the rest of him was concentrating mind, willing her not to be mortally wounded. She lay the length of him, at least he was a makeshift stretcher until Vernon came. Perhaps he should press his hands more firmly into the wet, risk that terrible choking protest in the hope of performing the office of tourniquet —

'No! No!'

He hadn't done anything, he hadn't taken the enormous decision, why was she crying out?

'Barbara! Oh, my darling girl!'

It wasn't Barbara, it was Vernon, falsetto with shock. The blood must be showing. Or something in the way Barbara was lying ... There was a cold patch on his cheek where the cat had been. He could hear it scrambling back on to its shelf.

Vernon's face was visible, glaring disembodied and distorted into his eyes.

'Thank God, Vernon. Barbara's been shot. Through the open vent. It was for me, but she saw and moved in front of me. Oh, God, Vernon, I'd give my life for her, too.' He could hardly bear to look at the rage and hate in Vernon's face, no one should be looking at Vernon's private loathing of the world which could let this thing happen to his sister. But he couldn't turn away. 'Please go for help. We must stay exactly as we are until it comes.'

'Of course, Bob. You're all right, then?' Vernon's face was back to normal, but he hadn't imagined how it had been.

'Yes, to my shame. Please go. At least she's not on the floor.'

'Don't worry, Vernon ...'

Bob felt the effort of Barbara's raised voice, heard Vernon moan, then his gulping breath as he staggered to his feet, the crash of the outside door. Then the immediate return to lock the door, pull the key free. Then nothing but Arabella's rich removed purring and the occasional simmering growl from Jingpaws.

'Shall I talk, darling?'

'If you don't mind ... perhaps ... not getting an answer. Yes. Talk.'

'I love you, Barbara. It's so simple.'

'I love you ... Bob ...' The whisper was weakening, perhaps the reassurance to Vernon had been too much. Perhaps ...

'Just hold on, darling.' One of his hands now was very wet. But at least her breathing was still quiet and regular. 'Look, you save your strength, let me do the talking.' He thought of Jo as a child, the bedtime stories. 'You remember that scene from *My Little Chickadee*? Don't answer, don't answer, it wasn't a question. Mae West has married W.C. Fields, knowing the priest's a layman in disguise. Pure greed, she's seen wads of money in his half-open bag. Monopoly money, but she doesn't know that then. Of course she's keeping him at bay in the bedroom, but having a bit of a job. When she's got him into the bathroom she opens the room door on to the corridor, where a pretty little nanny goat is handily walking by. She brings it in and tucks it into her side of the bed. Before she leaves the room she says, "Let him do the talking ..."'

'Funny, Bob ...'

'Hush, darling.' But he had learned she was still with him. 'Then d'you remember that little man in Tati's *Traffic* who keeps wandering across the screen carrying his best jacket on a hanger? Eventually the moment comes for putting it on and sitting wearing it on the stand at the motor show surrounded by cardboard silver birches and soothing music but without Tati's precious exhibit, the car for total living, the reason for all the razz matazz, which arrives when the show's over ...'

He was still maniacally rabbiting when the ambulance men arrived, and Barbara was still able to say 'Thanks' or 'Funny'. When they had lifted her away from him he went on lying there turning cold, weeping until shame overcame both his physical stiffness and the awful void where his brain should have been, and he staggered to his feet before anyone came back to help him up.

Absent-mindedly patting the calm but vigilant Arabella, smiling at the raging Jingpaws, he helped himself along by wire mesh to the door. Vernon was waiting to lock it, and Detective Sergeant Tabley was there to take the key from Vernon's hand. Bob could hardly stand, but when he saw the stretcher half-way up the garden he started to sprint after it.

Barbara's face was shrunk to bone, but when it saw him it tried to smile before turning towards Vernon, panting up on the other side.

'Vernon.'

The thinnest of whispers, but he had heard and bent towards her. 'What, Barbara?'

'Vernon ...'

When they reached the ambulance and the stretcher was still for a moment she said his name again.

'What is it, Barbara?'

'Vernon. I want ...' Her head went sideways.

'She's fainted,' said one of the men. 'It's a miracle she's kept with us as long as she has.'

'I talked to her.'

'Best thing. You coming with us, sir?'

'Of course. Vernon?'

'No, no. I'll come along later. Having rung first.' Even now the sense of fitness, the bowing to the belief that the brother was not as the husband. 'Where ...?'

'Leatherhead, sir. On our way, Tom.'

Very carefully, after a nod from the man sitting beside him, Bob picked up Barbara's hand and held it for the short length of the journey. There was no response.

He sat motionless in his room, his elbows on his stained table top, his head in his hands. A small skinny man with sparse brown hair, wearing a jacket too large for him nicked from a charity shop. Artie Haynes, petty criminal, with one conviction for GBH. Briefly and incredibly a successful assassin. Now a failed one.

Back to normal. He hadn't even been able to make a living as a thief, he'd had to get a job meat portering. But despite the look of him he had the strength for it, and there were good pickings. Not just the meat.

Artie looked at the watch nicked from a newcomer to his local Friday market. Mrs Middleton would be there any time from now on for her evening briefing, and he'd have to tell her what had happened. That instead of killing the man he had winged the woman. Quite a difference, even Artie's optimistic imagination told him that. Mrs Middleton wouldn't be pleased. He didn't know anything about her connection with the woman he had killed for her, or the man he had harassed and then failed to kill, but whatever it was, she wouldn't be pleased. Artie thought for a moment of pretending it had all gone according to plan, but that would only be to postpone the moment of truth.

She had left it to his discretion, but she had stressed it had to be done where there were no members of the public around to see or to get involved. That was why he had sniffed about the house and discovered the jungle of a garden to the place backing on to it, and that there was a slope immediately below the boundary wall which came to an end against the glass and mesh of some sort of cat house. That there was an open vent. And no mesh between it and a body standing in one of the central doorways ...

He had thought he was lucky, this had been only his second time of waiting, but that cat ... Rearing up like the Loch Ness monster and screaming like a tortured child. Mrs Middleton would have to understand about that cat. He'd have held off, of course, when the woman got in front of the man – if the cat hadn't pressed his finger down on the trigger for all the world as if it had been up on the slope with him. The woman had fallen on top of his target, into the cage, and his chance had gone. He had been tempted to shoot the cat, but there was mesh in the way and anyway it wasn't sitting up any more and it could be that Mrs Middleton liked the beasts ...

Mrs Middleton. She'd still be kind and gentle, he couldn't imagine her any other way. More in sorrow than in anger. (He had heard that somewhere.) He felt awful, really, that he had let her down. And yes, in spite of her gentleness he felt afraid. The woman might die and the man was alive and the police wouldn't be letting him continue to present himself as a target ...

Mrs Middleton. That cold January evening in the Royal Oak when she first spoke to him and asked him if he fancied a drink seemed a long way off. A nice, gentle, early middle-aged woman with a kind of saddish face. Not bad-looking but not glamorous, and so nice and refined no one would ever take her speaking to them the way it wasn't meant ... It wasn't just the drinks she bought, he liked talking to her, the way she listened so sympathetic, she had known his life history before you could say February. Even the bad bits. Not as bad as murder then, of course. Not even as bad as pushing a man at the tube line, towards a bus ... He even quite liked listening to the things she told him. About her son and daughter, both abroad, about her daily routine at home. He didn't know where home was, she had never told him that, never told him anything that could pin her down; when she left the Royal Oak she vanished into thin air. He wished now he hadn't told her where he lived, either, hadn't been so dizzy with the size of the sum she offered him for the first killing that he had broken his rule never to reveal his address and given in to her suggestion that they should go back to his place to plan it. He'd have done better, too, not to let on about the GBH that time she bought him one drink too many. But it had been a relief somehow to talk, he had never been able to talk to his wife when she was with him, or that slag of a daughter of his, or the women he occasionally chatted up for other reasons ...

Artie glanced again at the watch, wiping a water drop from the sharp red tip of his nose with the back of his hand. He hoped she'd be early tonight, get it over with.

The first time she asked him to do something for her he had thought she probably wanted a leg of lamb on the cheap. Then when he said, 'All right,' wary like, she had asked him straight out if he'd shoot someone. Shoot a woman. He had thought he was asleep and dreaming, looking into her kind, gentle face. He asked her to say it again, and when she had he wanted to get away, he had been on his feet when she mentioned the money ...

He had bought a car with the first half of it, the second-hand jalopy parked now on the waste ground opposite the house where his room was. He'd have liked to buy a new car – with the whole sum he could have afforded it – but people would've wondered where the money had come from.

She had given him the first half of the money for the second killing, and now she'd want it back. He could shoot her, the gun was on the table, but he didn't think he'd be able to, not Mrs Middleton, not someone he actually knew (although until she mentioned the money he hadn't thought he'd be able to shoot a stranger). Anyway, she wouldn't come to his room just like that, she'd have covered her back.

Perhaps she wouldn't be all that angry, perhaps she'd sit down at the table again and get him to cut out more letters from those newspapers she had given him the money to buy, stick them to another sheet off the writing-pad he had bought too on her instructions and with her cash. The last time she visited his room she had taken the pad away with the envelopes ...

The money was well hidden, he could tell her he had spent it and —

A tap at the door.

His heart suddenly in his throat, Artie got up and went across to it.

'Who is it?' There were one or two people he'd prefer not to open to.

'It's Mrs Middleton, Artie.'

Reluctantly, his movements as effortful as they were in his dreams, Artie took the chain off and opened his door.

'Come in, Mrs Middleton, dear.' He didn't even know her first name.

'Thank you, Artie.'

'Sit down, won't you?'

'Not just now.' She smiled at him as she walked into the room. 'You messed it up, Artie. You shot the man's wife.' At least he wasn't going to have to tell her. He collapsed back into his chair and she went and stood on the other side of the table, her gloved hands gripping the rail of the other chair. Mrs Middleton was ever so ladylike, she always wore gloves. 'Why?'

She was walking about the room now. Making it feel very small.

'She saw me and got in front of him.'

'So why did you fire?'

'The cat. There was a cat. Screaming like a baby. Made me jump. Made the gun fire itself, like. I was all set, you see. I'm sorry, Mrs Middleton.'

'So am I, Artie.'

She passed behind him, which was unnerving; he was glad when she was out in front of him again. He didn't seem able to swivel round, keep her in sight.

'The woman. Did she die?'

'Not yet.'

'She will? Jesus —'

'I don't know. I didn't want you to shoot the woman, Artie.'

'I know. I know, Mrs Middleton. God's truth, I'm sorry. Give me another chance! I'll see there's no one else around.'

'I think we'll leave it at that, Artie.' Mrs Middleton had paused in front of the empty grate, was looking at her neat grey hair and unobtrusively made-up face in the speckled mirror over the mantelpiece.

'The money. You'll want —'

'We won't worry about the money at the moment, Artie.' He had known her voice would still be gentle, that she wouldn't rant and rave. But he hadn't known how much that would frighten him, that he'd rather she went off her head.

'Did you unload the gun, Artie?' Mrs Middleton had turned away from the mirror, crossed back to the table.

'I ain't touched it since I brought it home, I wanted to throw it away. Honest —'

'I'm glad you didn't unload it. Have a look at this.' She was taking an envelope out of her handbag, putting it in front of him. A stamped envelope, addressed to Detective Chief Inspector Hewitt in those pasted-on letters.

He was clumsy opening it, creasing the paper as he pulled the contents out.

For a moment he couldn't believe what he was reading. Then he looked up at her in panic. 'Mrs Middleton, you wouldn't!'

'I would, Artie. I'm going to.' She had picked up the gun. 'Put the letter back in the envelope and seal it. Then push it over to me.'

The envelope fell on the floor. Mrs Middleton kept the gun on him while she bent to pick it up, while she put it back in her handbag.

'I won't be here,' Artie muttered defiantly, 'when the police come.'

'I think you will, Artie.'

Mrs Middleton walked towards him, her right arm extended. She stopped walking when she was near enough to put the gun barrel up against the bridge of his nose.

'Don't tease me, Mrs Middleton, dear,' said Artie, flinching, in the second before she shot his face away.

Chapter Sixteen

The operation on Barbara's back took a long time. Bob watched a cloudy dawn come up and let innumerable cups of tea go cold with Vernon, Jo and Simon before he was allowed to see her.

He had got hold of Jo at Simon's flat via the London telephone directory, and she and Simon had been at the hospital in three quarters of an hour. Vernon had rung a couple of hours or so after the vigil began, and Bob had told him to come and join them, be sleepless among the people who shared his fears rather than alone at home. And in a position to hear any news the moment it was available.

Detective Sergeant Tabley was there too, uninvited. Slumped on a bench in a public place near the small private room with semi-easy chairs which had been given over to Barbara's family, appearing to be dozing as Bob approached him on his many nerve-driven walkabouts, but always nodding and curtly smiling as Bob passed by. Bob had tried to divert his agony into indignation at the possibility that Tabley was going to be the first person to be allowed to see Barbara, but the sister who came regularly to tell them that no news was good news assured him that the privilege would be his.

It was seven o'clock by the time it was granted. A watery sun had broken through, and the sister came in again and told them that the operation had been a success and Barbara was conscious.

'Her legs?' said Bob. He had got to his feet, and had to go and lean against the wall.

'The bullet just missed the spine. There's damage to nerves, of course, but there doesn't seem to have been any destruction. Time will tell.'

Jo gave a sob, left Simon's arms and came and put hers round her father.

'She'll have to learn to walk again,' said the sister. 'I expect she will. You can see her now, Mr Collins. For a very few moments. Then perhaps your daughter.'

'Uncle Vernon before me,' said Jo, looking at him.

'You're a good girl, Jo.' Feeling rich again, Bob kissed his daughter and followed the sister out to the corridor. He had known Tabley would still be waiting, his long legs stretched out, but it was good to see it.

'Glad to hear it's gone well, Mr Collins.' Tabley smiled. 'Perhaps I can have a word with you when you've seen your wife.'

'He'll be out in a moment,' said the sister.

There was flesh on Barbara's face again, but it still looked too small. To Bob's unspeakable relief the hand he took hold of returned a feeble pressure. The tube from an inverted bottle appeared to be going into the back of the other one.

'Oh darling!'

'I'm all right, Bob.' Her voice was feeble too but she was trying to smile. 'All this is just routine. We've always been so healthy, we don't know ...'

'Can you move your legs?'

'I shouldn't think so, just yet. I'm not trying.'

'Of course not, I'm a fool. Don't try to talk, either.'

They sat then in silence, looking at one another, until the sister came and told him it was long enough.

'Vernon wants to see you for a moment. Sister says he may.'

'Vernon. I'd like to see Veron. Is Jo there?'

'Of course.'

'That will do for now, Mr Collins. You can come back later.'

'When you've slept, Bob,' said Barbara.

Tabley got to his feet as Bob reached him. 'Perhaps I can come into your room for a moment, sir?'

'You want another statement, I suppose?' It was all the

same to him, now that he knew Barbara wasn't going to die.

'If you don't mind, sir, and I want to talk to you about your safety,' Tabley murmured as he followed Bob into the sanctum. Jo's head shot up in alarm from Simon's shoulder, and Bob smiled a reassurance as he led Tabley to the window.

'Sit down. My safety?'

'Yes, sir.' Tabley's legs slid under the central-heating radiator as he curled into a chair. 'You and your wife could still be in danger from whoever shot Mrs Collins. We're arranging protection, but in the meantime it would help us if you stayed here at the hospital. You'll have the use of this room, and a bed will be provided for you if we haven't got our act together by this evening. I expect anyway you'd prefer to be near your wife – '

'Yes. Of course.' And Bob expected it was all going against DCI Hewitt's grain, that Tabley's chief was probably wondering if Collins might have manoeuvred his wife into a prearranged vulnerable position ... 'My daughter, sergeant!'

'Your daughter can stay here, too, if you and she think it's a good idea, sir, although we've no reason to fear – '

'There's no reason for any of it, is there? God, what a mess! But of course I'll be happier if she stays here. I'll tell her that, and see ... I'll need to ring my office, cancel a couple of appointments.'

'No problem, I'm sure, sir.' Tabley uncoiled. 'There's a constable around somewhere. I'll bring him in if I may and we'll take your statement first. Then we'll have a word with your brother-in-law.'

'You're not going to disturb my wife, are you?' asked Bob, when he had told Tabley and the detective constable the little he knew.

'Only if sister says we may. Meanwhile we'll wait nearby.' Tabley got to his feet, faintly smiling. 'A watchdog as well as an interrogator, Mr Collins.'

'I know.' Knew at last for sure that Tabley didn't share his superior officer's obsession. 'Thank you, Sergeant.'

Vernon came back in as Tabley and the constable were crossing to the door. He was crying.

'What is it?' Bob raced past the policemen.

'She's all right. She's all right, Bob ...' Vernon put his hands on Bob's shoulders, and when he bent his head his tears were wet on Bob's cheek.

'Yes. Go home now and rest.'

'I will.' Vernon straightened up, looked sadly into his eyes. 'Forgive me, Bob, it's the reaction ...'

'I know. Thanks for everything during a difficult time. The sergeant would like a word with you before you go.'

'Just a short statement, sir, about your finding Mr and Mrs Collins.'

'Of course, Sergeant.'

'We're staying here, Vernon. Until the police have arranged protection.'

'Until what, Daddy?' asked Jo, as Vernon, Tabley and the constable went over to the window.

'Until the police have arranged some kind of bodyguard. You see ...' There was no comfortable way he could put it, but Simon's presence meant he could eventually leave her and go and telephone home to make sure Samantha was there and explain why he and Barbara weren't. It was reassuring to learn that she hadn't found anything different apart from Barbara's cattery key on the hall carpet, which between them they realised the pathologists must have posted through the front-door letter box. The cats had been properly locked in and didn't appear unduly neurotic, but she'd make a special fuss of them. No, he hadn't frightened her and she'd sleep in the house until they came home, but if it was all right she'd ask her boyfriend to come and keep her company – it was the Easter vac. And she'd go straight down and close the vent. Anyway, it was a chilly morning ...

Next Bob asked Gail to make immediate arrangements for bullet-proof glass to be fitted to the cat house. After his call to the office he went back to the sanctum, and to sleep.

'You'll have read the statements, I expect,' said Tabley as he answered his chief's summons next morning. 'Not much hard evidence, but quite a human story. Collins and daughter actually want to stay at the hospital, which is handy, so no need just yet for –'

'Have a look at this, Jago. And keep your jacket on.'

He recognised the flimsy paper, the dark blocks showing through, before he had it from his chief's hand.

Artie Haynes killed Caroline Lambert and shot Barbara Collins you will find him any time at ...

Registering E1 of the address, Tabley looked up.

'Any time ... You're arranging back-up?'

'It's arranged. And I've got the authority for our own guns. Let's go.'

Half an hour or so later they bumped their way on to the waste land opposite the dilapidated end-of-terrace house the anonymous letter had indicated. 'Not so good for the tyres,' Hewitt observed as they got out of the car and strolled across the road.

The other cars had parked out of sight and the men were approaching under cover. Hewitt and Tabley paused at the grimy door, their right hands adjusting.

'On you go, Jago.'

The door gave to Tabley's push. So did the first one they tried on the ground floor, to reveal a disintegrating mattress and a dead pigeon. The second they broke down on to similar uninhabited decay, the noise bringing a woman holding a baby to the third. When she had seen their IDs she directed them to the top of the second flight of stairs.

They broke that door down, too. Hewitt had to run past the table to the nasty little kitchen in order to be sick into the sink.

'Don't disturb the evidence sir!' Tabley called after him.

The setting-up of a protective police presence being costly in terms of both money and manpower, it was indicated that Forensics should give priority to investigating the reliability of the second anonymous letter. If they established that Haynes had stuck the truth on to his bit of paper, the police presence wouldn't be called for. Keeping things going was a day's work for Hewitt.

'Collins doesn't warrant care and protection,' he said as Tabley joined him in the office twenty-four hours on. 'The bullet recovered from his wife's back was fired from the gun on Haynes's floor.' He had to paused while he dealt with the additional flow of saliva. 'The writing-pad and newspaper on the table provided the material for the letter. For the earlier letter, too. There's even a footprint on the slope behind the Collins cat house which fits one of the shoes Haynes was wearing, and the mud on it.'

'Careless. Could indicated a state of mind for taking his own —'

'Or overconfidence. Someone else with the responsibility. How did you get on yesterday, Jago? Have you managed to find any connection?'

'With Gibson? Not so far.' He was deliberately misunderstanding his chief, but it was Gibson Hewitt ought to be thinking about. 'I've broken the news to Collins and Lambert, who each gave an impression of truthfulness when saying they'd never heard of an Arthur Herbert Haynes. The woman on the ground floor at Haynes's place seems to have been as helpful as she could have been, told me where Haynes worked and that he spent an hour or so most evenings at the Royal Oak round the corner. His employers hadn't much to say about him, I'm afraid. They were aware of a few what they called discrepancies, but he was a good strong worker, the size of him notwithstanding, and they'd overlooked them to date. None of his work mates saw him out of school, general impression is that he was a loner. One interesting thing, though.'

'Yes?'

'The woman downstairs used to pop into the Royal Oak herself sometimes, that's how she knew Haynes used it, she always saw him there. Six, seven o'clock. For a couple of months after Christmas she almost always saw him talking to a woman.'

'So?'

'The same woman. Not young, not glamorous. Beautifully spoken is how the woman put it. The bar staff said something similar. Name of Mrs Middleton. She hadn't been seen for three or four weeks, then a couple of nights ago she turned up again. So just before six I went round there myself. She didn't show.'

'Nor will she again, if I know anything,' said Hewitt wearily. 'But we'll have to go through the motions for a while of expecting her.'

'Cheer up, sir. We've found our murderer. And you might come with me one evening. They pull a good pint.'

'We've found a chap who pulled the trigger, Jago.'

'We'd do well to be glad of that, sir. Think how if Haynes hadn't turned up and –'

'Yes.' And they hadn't been able to connect Gibson or anyone else with more than adultery. Jago was right, they should thank heaven fasting that they had found a murderer.

Found another victim?

'Forensics gave me a few more ideas yesterday, Jago. On the face of it Haynes's death looks like suicide. He could easily have inflicted the wound on himself, no blood had washed off in the sink' – Hewitt outstared his sergeant's quizzical gaze – 'or was to be found anywhere but where it could have been expected to spurt in the moment of death. The letter was postmarked 8.30 the next morning, so it could have been posted just before an early-evening suicide. Or just after an early-evening murder. Haynes's fingerprints were on it and there was no trace of blood, but a murderer could have prepared it in advance and somehow got Haynes to handle it. Then left the writing-pad and newspaper he'd used where we found them on Haynes's table.'

'Ingenious. Is it instinct, sir?'

'Unless Collins and/or Lambert are lying when they say this is the first they've heard of Haynes, I can't think he could have been operating on his own. If he'd just shot Mrs Lambert we could get over the fact of the unloaded gun and believe in a burglary. But with Mrs Collins being shot too, there has to be a personal motive, and I can't believe it was Haynes's. Nor can I easily believe that the fellow whose filthy little track record is coming to light would have either the conscience or the aesthetic sense to take his own life. I think we've got to look at alibis, Jago.'

'We know about Collins's, sir. He was at the hospital with his wife.'

'Yes.'

'You're letting go of him, then? In your mind, I mean?'

'You're impertinent, Jago. However. You said something just now about assuming Collins was the target. How about if he hired Haynes, manoeuvred his wife — '

'Deciding to see two women off in as many months?'

'They could have got too much for him. There's that first letter.'

'There's that snapshot Gibson pinched. Well, there isn't of course, there's only that dreadful young woman's word, but you know what I mean. Jealousy of a real or imagined affair between Collins and Mrs Lambert could have got too much for *him*. Do you really believe Collins contracted with Haynes to murder his wife?'

'No, Jago, I don't. I was just trying it out, trying to make myself feel better about him and his family going home without police protection. Now the man who pulled the trigger's dead we can't give it to him, even if Haynes's death doesn't make him safe.'

'I'd thought of that too,' said Jago. They stared at one another.

'Face blown away,' said Hewitt at last. 'I fancy a suicide would prefer to shoot himself in the heart. While a murderer, in this instance, would do what he could to prevent Collins and Lambert saying for sure that they didn't recognise the man and that therefore it wasn't credible that he could have gone for them off his own bat. There were no photographs in that room, of course.'

'There was one at the Royal Oak. In the landlord's sitting-room. A last year's jamboree. Before the days of Mrs Middleton, you might know. It's faint and fuzzy, but I'm having it blown up.'

'Go and see Collins again, and his wife and Lambert. Take the photograph. And a Haynes CV. Even if they still say there's nothing they recognise, ask them to think very carefully about the possibility of having got on the wrong side of an odd-job man, Haynes having rung door bells after coming out of prison and before getting his meat-portering job. If the Collinses finally insist they've never come across him and you believe them, turn into a counsellor and tell 'em the score. If they're as bright as I think they are, they'll probably have worked it out for themselves, but tell them.'

'Warn them the danger's still there, then say we can't help them?'

'Something like that, I'm afraid, Jago. At least you can advise Collins to make his own arrangements. We can fix for him to stay in the hospital a few more days while he thinks about what he's going to do; his wife's condition will make that easy enough. But that's all the protection we can offer, and I don't like it any more than you do.'

'You were wrong about Collins, then, sir?'

'I never said he was a murderer, Jago. And all I'm prepared to say now is that I believe there's a murderer still at large and we ought to be doing something about it.'

Hewitt's depression signalled the possibility of lifting. Haynes was more than a career saver, he was giving them a second chance; they'd have to talk to everyone again. He got briskly to his feet. 'Another inquest to be adjourned for further police inquiries, Jago.'

Chapter Seventeen

Bob tried hard to recognise the photograph, but didn't.

'Did my wife?' Barbara's medical timetable had dictated that Tabley saw her first.

'I'm afraid not, sir. I'm afraid she hasn't been able to help us at all. Perhaps you, though ... Any recollection of having got on the wrong side of a man at the door in the past two or three years?'

'I wish I had, then I might be able to believe the real killer was dead.' He was fishing for Tabley's assurance that Haynes had committed suicide.

'I'm sorry to have to tell you that with the man who shot your wife having died, sir, we are unable to offer you police protection.'

'I wasn't expecting it.' What he had hooked was an oblique confirmation of his fears. He told Tabley about the bullet-proof glass.

'A sensible precaution, sir.' Collins was making it almost easy. 'I've brought you some brochures about specialists in personal security which Detective Chief Inspector Hewitt and I suggest you might –'

'Leave them with me, Sergeant. How long can my daughter and I stay on in the hospital?'

'You can stay until your wife is discharged, sir, we've been able to arrange that for you. And of course we're continuing with our inquiries.'

'Of course, Sergeant.'

'I'll be on my way, then.' Tabley found himself uneasy rather than relieved. 'I'm sorry your wife didn't recognise'

Haynes either, but I thought she seemed a lot better.'

'She's recovering by the hour. I hope whoever hired Haynes will allow the process to continue.' Bob paused, but Tabley didn't tell him he'd got it wrong. 'Thank you for coming, Sergeant, doing what you could.'

When Tabley had gone, Bob went back to Barbara. Vernon was with her and she was propped up against a lot of pillows and looking tired.

'Tabley was too much for you.'

'No. Did you recognise the photograph? Anything about the man?'

'No. Where's Jo?'

'With Simon in your personal sitting-room.'

'Good.' He'd have to get around to telling his wife and daughter the score. If they hadn't realised it already.

'Vernon's going to Blackpool in the morning,' said Barbara. 'To see a dealer.'

'Now I know Barbara's all right. He's got some things that sound interesting. I thought I might stay two or three days, Bob, breathe some north-shore breezes. If you're both really sure ...'

'Please go, Vernon,' said Barbara. That morning she had wiggled her toes.

'Yes, do,' said Bob. Vernon couldn't be in danger, and it would do him good.

'All right.' Vernon got to his feet. 'I'll go home now, get a few things together. Bless you, Barbara. Bob.'

Bob could hardly wait until the door had closed. 'Barbara, Haynes didn't commit suicide, and the man who killed him is still walking around. Haynes didn't set out to kill me because he personally wanted me dead, he was hired. First to kill Caroline, then me – Jack's wife, then her lover.' He seized her hands. 'Barbara, I'm frightened of Jack, I slept with his wife. When we leave here I'm going to be frightened of my own shadow. But because the man who pulled the trigger is dead the police can't offer any protection.'

'No,' said Barbara. 'Even though he was murdered.'

'I knew you understood. What are we going to do?' Suddenly he was angry, on his feet and pacing the room. 'The police are carrying on with their inquiries, Tabley tells me, but what does it amount to? Paul Gibson was helping them, but they didn't arrest him. And they're not interested in Jack. Jack, Barbara, that's the worst —'

'Bob.' Her voice was still diminished, but something in it stopped him in his tracks. 'Sit down.' She reached for his hand. 'I'm going to tell you something. I've been keeping things back, too. Not ...'

'Not things like the things I kept back.'

'I'm sorry, I did mean that, yes. Not things to do with — us. And I never actually told you a lie, I just didn't tell you the whole truth and you assumed ... D'you remember asking me if I'd ever confided in Vernon?'

'Yes. We were in the car coming home from the station.'

'Yes. I said I hadn't, which was true. But it was because I hadn't had to. Bob, when I played back your answerphone message, Vernon was with me.'

'You mean — he heard — what you heard?'

'Yes.'

'He let me in the next night. He was ... There was no difference in him.'

'Domino had died. That helped us both. I made Vernon promise to do what I was going to do myself, not let you know what I'd heard. So that you'd have the choice. To choose to tell me.'

'He did very well. As well as you did.' His mind was a long way away from his voice, running about the entrances to a maze of little dark tunnels.

'Yes. But he felt — different. He didn't believe you ever would tell me, ever want to. He believed he'd — misjudged you all these years. That you were a philanderer, not the man he thought he knew. It was the shock, Bob.'

'The shock didn't do that to you.' Panic suddenly choked him. 'Did it, darling? You said —'

'No, it didn't. But I ... Bob, when — when what was on the tape was finished Vernon didn't say anything, he just sat and stared at me. I must have looked ... Well ...' She squeezed his hand. 'Then he said that in a fair world nemesis would destroy Caroline, and you would be mistaken for nemesis and pay the price of her death. I think ... I think it was himself Vernon mistook for nemesis.'

They stared at one another. 'Go on,' he said eventually.

'Vernon never mentioned again what we'd heard, or repeated what he'd said. But when Caroline was shot I knew.'

'Barbara ... You couldn't ...'

'I knew. That was his first judgement carried out, and it made you the most obvious impersonation of nemesis, with the murder taking place just when you were due at Green Lawns. I think he'd taken a gamble that Jack was always away on those Tuesdays and that you wouldn't be able to contact him. When it didn't work out like that, he sent the anonymous letter.'

'Which didn't work either. Why didn't — why wasn't the letter sent to the press?'

'I don't know, Bob, but I think it must have been for my sake. The publicity.'

'Hewitt could have given it that.'

'There was the chance he wouldn't, that he'd simply be alerted by it to try and break your story. Well, that's what he did. And failed. When Hewitt came that night to tell us Paul Gibson was helping the police with their inquiries, it was the most wonderful news, it meant I'd been wrong and Vernon was innocent. Then I saw his face. Just for a flash, but it was enough to tell me it was Hewitt and co. who had got it wrong. Even if I'd known then about Jo's activities, about Gibson stealing that photograph, the frustration and fury for that moment in Vernon's face would have blotted them out. That was why I was falling about. Shock of relief followed by shock of going back on the treadmill — '

'Oh, darling ...'

'Let me go on. When Vernon realised you weren't going to be arrested for Caroline's murder, he had to make other arrangements. Bob, I think by this stage his plan was as inevitable as a Greek tragedy, it had to be carried through. So he got hold of Haynes again — '

'Barbara. Look. No, you must listen to me for a moment.' He put a finger to her lips. 'How could Vernon have got hold of Haynes in the first place? And if he had, how could he have run the risk of putting himself into the hands of a man like that? It would have been an open invitation to blackmail, or to far worse publicity than the anonymous letter could ever have stirred up. Oh, darling, there's a whole world between saying what Vernon said and doing – '

'I have to finish.' She made a move forward in the bed; uninjured, she would have been pacing the room. 'Bob, I don't know how closely you read your copy of the police rundown on Haynes's career?'

'I read it.'

'The GBH conviction, there's some detail about that.' It was a strain for her to reach the sheet of paper beside the bed, but somehow he was unable to help her. 'It happened four years ago, and he served eighteen months of a two-and-a-half-year sentence. You read that?'

'Obviously not with as much attention as you did. Barbara – '

'I was looking for something. I found it. The GBH conviction happened at the Kensington Antiques Fair in 1986. Haynes pulled a knife on a porter who caught him trying to lift a piece of silver.'

'Yes, I did read – '

'Or perhaps you remember Vernon telling us about it? The attempted theft wasn't from his stand, but it was from one nearby, and he saw what happened. It made a big impression on him, it was probably the closest he'd been to violent crime in the whole of his blameless life.' Her eyes were suddenly glittering, but she blinked the tears away. 'So when he needed – someone like Haynes, Vernon knew where to look. Newspaper files – '

'It's an extraordinary coincidence,' he conceded, shaken. 'But it still doesn't answer my main question, how Vernon could have run the risk of putting himself at the mercy of a man like Haynes. He'd have had him on his back for the rest of his life. The game just wouldn't have been worth – '

'There's one more thing I haven't told you, Bob. Vernon has a secret life.'

'For God's sake, Barbara! Is this something else you've worked out for yourself?'

'No, this is something Vernon told me. After I found out by accident, or I don't think he ever would have done. I went to his house one day when I was expecting Jo. I can't remember why I went but I think I had some food thing for Nellie and she was going to be out and she'd suggested I took it round. We had their key in those days, you may remember. When Nellie died I gave it back to Vernon.'

'I wondered why.'

'I'm going to tell you. Bob, I let myself in, I didn't even ring the bell first, I was so sure Nellie was out and Vernon in the shop. I went through into the kitchen to dump whatever I'd brought, and there was a woman in there. Not Nellie's regular daily, a – a young woman I'd never seen before, who said she was standing in while the daily was ill. She apologised for startling me and I said that was all right and we exchanged a few remarks about the weather or something and then – oh, Bob –' Barbara stopped and stared at him, and he saw the tic at work beside her eye.

'What is it, darling? Oh, don't –'

'I have to. I realised suddenly that it was Vernon.'

'You realised –'

'Hush! I started to say his name, I tried to believe he'd been playing a joke on me, he'd dressed up a lot as a boy and then suddenly stopped in his teens ... Bob, he knew I knew, but he went on being – this woman. He said something like, "Very well, then, madam, I'll tell Mrs Tennant you were here and make sure she sees what you've brought her," and led the way to the front door. I had to sit in the car a few minutes before I could drive off, I thought I was going to have a miscarriage. The next afternoon, when you were in London, Vernon came round – as himself – and told me he was a transvestite. Cross-dresser, he called it. He made me promise never to tell you. Well, I've kept my promise a long time.'

'Barbara, I can't ... Poor Nellie.'

'She adored him and he told me she accepted it, that it wasn't the sort of perversion – I don't think he used that word – which touched their marriage. He just liked to dress up as a woman, look at himself in the mirror, walk about the house when he was alone in it. It was as bad for him to be seen – like that – by someone he knew as it was for them. Once he started talking about it, he couldn't stop. He told me he sometimes left the house as a woman if Nellie was away or out for the day, and that he got his satisfaction just from seeing the assumption in others that he had a woman's past behind him. The life of the woman he became was always in the past, elsewhere, he never wanted to act it out by more than appearance and implication. Bob, when I got used to it I felt so sorry, although I still couldn't understand. The nearest I got to it was when Vernon told me our mother had only wanted girls and dressed him in frocks up to the time I was born. At least it didn't turn him into a homosexual.'

'No.' He thought of Jack again, and that he still hadn't told her. Tried to go on being afraid of Jack ... 'So you think —'

'I think, having run Haynes to earth via the GBH conviction, Vernon in drag went to his local.' She squeezed his hand again. 'He bought him drinks and eventually offered him money, and Haynes accepted the assignment to kill Caroline. He must have cased Green Lawns while Jack and Caroline were at work and probably loaded the gun in advance after locating it — Vernon would have known of its existence from hearing Jack's sniper story over our dinner table.'

'You've thought about it a lot.'

'I've lived it.'

'While you were living my lie. Oh, darling.' He literally bowed in front of her strength, dropping his head on to her hands. 'Before I knew you knew, I asked the wrong question about Caroline's death. I should have asked, if you hadn't been afraid it was Vernon, would you have been afraid it was me?'

'No. Never.'

'Darling ...'

She turned her hand up to his cheek, gently raised his head. 'Now let me finish. After you'd told me about Caroline I tried to get hold of Vernon, let him know that I'd been right about you and he'd been wrong. I rang the shop as soon as you left for work next morning, and they told me he'd gone to Southsea. So I left the dinner message, I knew I'd find an opportunity during the evening. Oh, Bob, if I'd managed to speak to him he'd have called the second shooting off, I wouldn't be learning to walk again and Haynes would be alive. When I was — lying with you in the cat house, I was thinking about Vernon's reaction to what his man had done. His anger.'

'I saw it in his face when he found us. It was for me as well.' The loathing he had thought at the time was Vernon's fury against fate.

'I tried to tell him as I was going in the ambulance, but I must have passed out. Oh, darling, just think! Haynes had disabled his beloved only sister, maybe paralysed her for life, perhaps she was going to die! He must have changed and gone straight to that house, found Haynes and the gun. Killed Haynes in a way that would look like suicide. It would have been a cold anger, not affecting his judgement, Vernon never lost his temper. And then the mysterious lady disappeared for the last time, and Vernon came along to the hospital.'

'Haynes might have shot *him*.'

'We didn't know Haynes. Vernon would have taken the measure of the man before finally choosing him.'

'He'd have had blood on him. If he'd washed it off, if the police had found blood where a suicide couldn't have put it, they'd be talking about another murder.'

'Those little houses Nellie left Vernon. I've never seen them, but I know they're in east London. Bob, he must have used a room in one of them to ... clean up. And to turn himself each time into the woman and out of her again. Prepare the letter. He couldn't have done that at Haynes's place because of the blood ... Oh, God, Bob!'

'Don't go on now. Wait —'

'I want to get it over. When Vernon asked Jack to stay, he thought he'd finished with Haynes and the woman. Then he realised the police weren't going to arrest you ... Next time you play golf with Jack he'll tell you Vernon's been out a lot recently.'

'Jack ...' Already changing back into his clumsy, endearing old friend.

'I think Vernon had originally envisaged Jack being punished for his infidelity by the public disgrace of having to establish an alibi with a girlfriend for the time of Caroline's murder, but you getting him home let him off the hook. So I suspect Vernon's invitation to him to stay was partly so that he could create opportunities to offset Jack's escape from judgement – comments to make him uneasy under the guise of reassurance, that kind of thing – although I'm sure Jack was very much a subsidiary issue of Vernon's mission.

'As far as the lady is concerned, the police are probably dragging the Thames – a woman is more likely to be seen as another of Haynes's victims than as his boss. And no one is going to connect her with my darling brother, braving the Blackpool breezes ...' Barbara shuddered, leaned back into her pillows and closed her wet eyes. 'I love him so much, Bob.'

'I know.' He kissed her hand. 'But darling ... we'll find it difficult when he comes home. Not just so far as you and he and I are concerned, we'll have a duty –'

'No!' Barbara jerked upright, wincing. 'It's over, Bob, he's back to himself. The first time I saw him after coming round from the operation I told him what you'd told me, and it broke the spell. Took the fire out of him and the sense of purpose.'

'He was in tears when he came back to the sanctum, said he was sorry. I didn't understand. But if he gets obsessed again –'

'He won't, Bob, I'm sure of it.'

'Hewitt'll think it strange that I'm not arranging security.'

'You'll have to tell him you're a fatalist. And you were here with me when Haynes was shot, you couldn't have done it.'

'Neither could Jack or Gibson or anyone else. Barbara, if Hewitt and co. show signs of arresting an innocent man, we'll have to tell them.'

'If that happens, yes.' She stared at him sorrowfully. 'It may be easier than you think.'

The winds were high that week in Blackpool, and a middle-aged man walking the lower promenade was swept off it into the sea. The body was recovered a few miles along the coast, and identified by the deceased's brother-in-law as being that of Vernon Tennant, antique dealer, a man well known and well loved in the trade and by his family and friends.

You have been reading a novel published by Piatkus Books. We hope you have enjoyed it and that you would like to read more of our titles. Please ask for them in your local library or bookshop.

If you would like to be put on our mailing list to receive details of new publications, please send a large stamped addressed envelope (UK only) to:

    Piatkus Books, 5 Windmill Street
           London W1P 1HF

PIATKUS

The sign of a good book